Pamela Cunningham was ⟨obscured by barcode⟩ performing in both theatr⟨…⟩ founder principal of a the⟨…⟩ decades before changing ⟨…⟩ assistant. She then studie⟨d…⟩ full-time writer. She is cu⟨rr⟩ent⟨l⟩y w⟨o⟩rk⟨i⟩ng ⟨o⟩n t⟨h⟩e s⟨e⟩qu⟨e⟩l to Gherkins and Garters. Pamela is also the author of 'The Little Book of Big Happy Endings' and 'Do You Believe in Shooting Stars?'

Author's Note

Gherkins and Garters is written in loving memory of my grandparents, Syd and Mabel, who were the inspiration for this book. In reality, they were happily married and nothing like their characters. However, they did indeed meet on holiday in the Isle of Man following the death of Mabel's parents and brother. After the holiday, like her character, Mabel accompanied Syd to his family home in Liverpool where they were married shortly afterwards. They eventually returned to Sheffield to take over Mabel's family's pickle factory; renaming it Cunningham's Pickles. The brand is still popular in Sheffield although it no longer has any connection to our family.

My thanks go to the staff at the Sheffield Archive and Central Library for their cheerful and willing help. The chapters featuring The Jessop, are fictional but based on my research of records written at a time when scant gynaecological medical assistance appears to have been available to women, particularly with regard to caesarean intervention and post-natal infection. I'm also grateful for the invaluable information given to me from a private source whose relative had been a midwife during that era. Other sources rich in local social history came from my uncle, George Cunningham and his books 'By George' and 'More George', as well as 'The Walls of Jericho' by Ted Furniss. Although I've used the real place names of Sheffield and surrounding areas, all characters are purely fictitious.

Many thanks go to Howard Briggs for his continued IT support in all publications and his constant encouragement.

Also proof readers Lynn Varley, Melodie Lockwood-Cole, Tom Garvey and Alison. Finally, heartfelt thanks go to my son Myles Jackson for his ongoing support and endless patience in every aspect of producing this book.

All rights reserved. This book or any portion thereof may not be reproduced or used in any manor whatsoever without the express written permission of the publisher except for the use of brief quotations in a book review.

Copyright @ 2019 Pamela Cunningham

Gherkins and Garters

Pamela Cunningham

Gherkins and Garters

Chapter One - Sheffield 1925

The man waited by the factory wall smoking a Woodbine, its red tip glowing like a beacon through the gloom. He shifted uneasily and pulled his cap lower, the Klaxon hooter had signalled an end to the nightshift and he was attracting curious stares from workers streaming through the gates. Loiterers outside the factory were a common sight, men on their uppers, hoping to pick up a day's work. Few were as dishevelled.

Bert noticed him as soon as he walked through the gates and his heart sank. Sammy the Snout had frequented his life since he was ten years old, when, fed up with his bullying, Bert had used his strong right hook to point Sammy's nose due west, earning him his nickname and an undying respect for Bert. Nowadays the term snout held a more sinister reference. Sammy had his nose in everyone's business, he was informant to some of the most notorious villains in Sheffield.

'Hello, me old mate,' Sammy said, snuffing out the Woodbine between nicotine brown finger and thumb and dropping it into his pocket for later. 'You don't look right pleased to see a pal who's come to tip you the wink.'

'You can do me a favour alright Sammy. Shove off.'

'Don't be like that. I've heard you've hit on hard times and I've come with a proposition. The Pitch and Toss ring up at Skye Edge has had its day. Nobody's got two ha'pennies to rub together never mind toss 'em. But,' he said, giving a furtive wink, 'an associate of mine wants to set up sommat that'll draw the top brass, and your right hook's champion for it. I should bleedin' know,' he said, prodding his nose gingerly as though it was newly broken.

Bert shouldered him out of his way. 'Me fighting days are over.'

Sammy ran after him. 'Awe come on, it's easy money for a bloke like you.'

'Bare knuckle fighting's illegal and it's a young man's game. One without ties. I'll not risk me family for a few quid.'

'What's up? Frightened your missis won't fancy you with a busted-up face? She's no Belle of Broomhall now.'

Bert swung round and grabbed Sammy's throat, he seemed to shrink into his jacket as Bert raised a fist. 'You speak about my Ada like that again and next time I'll splatter your nose across your face.'

Released from Bert's grip, Sammy scampered to a safe distance before shouting, 'I'm surprised your friends on them high seas aren't helping you out. I heard Mabel's husband stocks a good supply of gin, if you catch me drift. You'd best think on my offer. I reckon you'll be needing me sooner than I'll be needing you,' he jeered, striking a match on the nearest gas lamp and retrieving the half-smoked Woodbine from his pocket. Bert watched him saunter off down the street heading a trail of smoke.

Ada's back door crashed open, tipping the metal bucket and its murky contents over the freshly scrubbed floor. Startled out of her wits, she clutched her swollen belly as the babe inside kicked in retaliation. 'You daft beggar,' she said, slamming the scrubbing brush into the bucket. 'What did you have to come crashing in here like that for? You could've set me off early with a shock like that.'

'I've had a letter from Mabel. It's come all the way from America,' Ethel said, waving the envelope. 'She's a lucky beggar that one, fancy sailing from New York round the Caribbean.'

'If you say so. I've heard there's bugs in them places that bite you and make you badly, and between you and me, I still don't reckon her Sydney's all he's cracked up to be.'

With one hand on the living room table, and the other in the small of her back, Ada struggled to her feet. 'You'd best give me a hand mopping up this water. Bert's due home from his night shift and I don't want him slipping in it, I can't afford to have him laid off with a bad back.'

'You want to try that trick after the baby's born,' Ethel giggled. 'It might give you a bigger gap between that and the next.'

Right on cue a wail began overhead, and a child's voice yelled, 'Mam our Tommy's tiddled in his bed again.'

'Now look what you've done. You've woken that lot up. I'll never get Bert's breakfast cooked in time now. He says food's his only pleasure.'

'I don't know about that,' Ethel said, nodding at Ada's abdomen and earning herself a whack across the arm with a wet floor cloth. 'Here give us that,' she said, grabbing the cloth and wringing it out over the bucket, 'you go and see to your kids.'

When Ada returned to the living room with a child on each hip and two more following on behind, Ethel had mopped up the water and was pouring mugs of milky tea for the children and a stronger brew for herself and Ada.

'Don't put sugar in the kid's tea, they're sweet enough,' Ada winked at her eldest as she helped her brood up to the table.

'I wasn't going to. I could only find condensed milk,' Ethel replied, frowning as Ada settled her youngest to her breast. 'Sophie's going to get her nose pushed out when that new baby arrives,' she said, watching the child suckle hungrily.

'She'll cope. I've fed all me others past their first birthday.'

'I couldn't find any bacon or eggs,' Ethel said, 'so I mixed some condensed milk with water to make your porridge, it's in the oven. Did I do right?' She walked over to the Yorkshire range and took down a tea towel from the curtain wire stretched across the mantelpiece to open the oven door. 'Shall I make a few slices of bread and dripping to go with this porridge? I noticed there was some on the cellar head.'

'No! No thank you. I'll do it in a bit.'

'I'll make us a fresh brew then, this one'll be stewed.'

'Leave it be.' Ada placed a hand over Ethel's, there was a plea in her eyes. 'I'll add a drop of hot water to it when Bert gets in. I expect you'll be wanting to get back to see to your Daniel.'

'He had his breakfast afore I came, and I did his snap last night.' Ethel looked at her friend with concern. She saw weariness in Ada's face, and for the first-time, fear in her eyes. 'Give us Tommy's wet sheets to wash. It's a sunny day, they'll dry in no time after I've run 'em through me mangle.'

Bert walked through the back door and was instantly bombarded by three of his offspring.

'You're late,' Ada said. 'The tea's stewed and your breakfast's all but dried up.'

'Well, that's nothing for a man to worry about when he gets such a grand welcome as this,' and he lifted Georgie, his eldest child, up onto his shoulders, before kneeling so Tommy could climb onto his back. Daisy clung to her father's leg and baby Sophie wailed for release from her high chair.

'Daddy, you smell of horse muck,' Daisy said, relinquishing his leg.

'You do an' all,' Tommy agreed, jumping down from his father's back.

'That's why I'm late. Them drays dumped a right dollop outside Wards Brewery and I thought to meself, that'll fetch a bit o' summat up at the allotments. I didn't have owt to fetch it home in, so I bundled it up in me shirt. I've left it outside in the yard.'

'I was wondering why your jacket was buttoned up to your neck in this weather. Well you and your shirt will have to be washed in plain water. I've no money for soap until next payday and there's only a sliver left for the kids bath tonight. Come on, rinse yourself down and get on with eating this breakfast. I'll fetch your other shirt.'

'Mam I'm still hungry,' Tommy said, eyeing his father's porridge.

'Well you'll have to stop hungry 'til dinner time. There's a nice bit of bread and dripping with your name on it.'

'You had your breakfast, love?' Bert asked. Ada nodded and began to clear the table. She saw Tommy watching her, a puzzled frown creasing his brow, he knew she hadn't eaten.

'Right then, our Georgie,' Bert said, handing his bowl and mug to Ada. 'No school for you today, and tomorrow's the Sabbath, so no night shift for me. That means we can get off to them allotments while it's still early. I'll need your metal bucket, love,' he turned to Ada, 'and hers from next door as well.'

'Oh aye, I can just see her lending you her mop bucket to fill with manure,' she jeered.

'We won't tell her then, will we,' he winked at Georgie. 'I reckon what Mrs Jepson doesn't know won't hurt her. Go on my son, be quick before she notices it's gone.'

Georgie ran stealthily across the yard to the shared lavatory where the bucket was stored. He thought he might as well use the facilities while he was there since they were available. They often weren't. He didn't much like having to share a toilet with the family next door, but he was glad that he didn't have a privy midden like his cousins over at Pitsmoor. No matter how much his auntie Sally scrubbed the wooden seat and mopped the stone floor, it still stank. It had been a big shock for him that first time, to see the hole filled with soil and no chain to yank to flush your business away. He didn't envy the men whose job it was to dig out the waste.

His father was waiting for him in the yard. 'Help me get this horse muck shovelled into the buckets Georgie, and then go and wash your hands.' Sophie watched the proceedings from the comfort of her big pram.

'Now then our Tommy,' Bert called into the house, 'you an' all, Daisy. We need your help as well.' Ada followed them out to the yard to see what her husband was up to. First, he lifted Daisy into the pram and tucked her in behind Sophie. Then he tied the buckets to the pram handle. 'Now lads, I need you to walk either side of the girls. Hold on tight mind, in case the weight of this horse muck tips up the pram. We don't want your sisters flying through the air.'

'Here, you'd better take this, if you're all going to the allotments,' Ada said, handing him a greaseproof paper package and a bottle of cooled boiled water with a teat on for Sophie.

He tucked the bottle in the pram and then opened the package and handed back two slices of the bread and dripping. In that moment, she realised he knew she'd gone without breakfast.

'Now then love,' he said, 'you go and put your feet up for a bit, you've not long before your time. And mind you eat that bread and dripping, you're skin and bone either side of that bump. With any luck, I'll be back with something tasty for tea.' He patted his back pocket where a sturdy catapult was stored. 'You young uns might get given an apple apiece. If not, well then, we'll just have to go blackberrying. We don't want you getting scurvy.'

'What's scurvy?' Tommy asked.

'It's something pirates get. Come on me hearties, I'll tell you a story about a couple of pirates called George and Tom and their trusty crew Daisy and Sophie.' Giggling, the motley crew walked out of the yard singing, 'Yo, Ho, Ho, and a Bottle of Rum.'

Ada watched them go. She felt blessed to have four healthy children. Bert was a good man and he loved her, if perhaps a little too much at times, she thought, rubbing her belly.

Hot and thirsty, the little crew stopped to guzzle water from the Jessop drinking fountain in Endcliffe Park. Georgie lifted the metal cup dangling from its chain. 'I'll give it a good rinse out dad, you never know who's been suppin' from it.'

'You do right son,' Bert said. 'Our Daisy can share Sophie's bottle.'

Another family walked by, their children each holding a cornet. Bert smiled as he watched them struggling to keep pace with the melting ice-cream as it dribbled over their chubby little hands. Then he noticed his own children looking longingly at the cornets and his heart constricted. The other family had brought their kids to play in the park and eat ice-cream. He'd brought his own on an outing to sell horse muck with no hope of an ice-cream. Still, he contented himself, they'd played for long enough jumping backwards and forwards over the stepping stones and seemed happy with that and the swings. Georgie and Tommy had been mesmerised by the big lads splashing about in the men's swimming pond. The unexpected sunshine had tempted them in. 'I'll teach you to swim in there when you're older,' Bert said. 'The water's a bit chilly but it's grand once you get used to it.'

    With one last lingering look they set off again, keeping to the shade until they reached the foot of the allotments. 'Now then me hearties, gather round,' Bert said. 'This is where we shout out our wares. Can you all say, fresh manure, fresh manure, to grow your marrow, as big as your barrow. Take a deep breath and try it on the count of three. Ready, one, two, three. Fresh manure, fresh manure.' Daisy got a fit of the giggles, and Tommy laughed so hard he nearly wet his trousers and had to have a hasty wee in a hedge. He'd just finished when a balding head popped up from a nearby allotment. 'I say, what the deuce do you think you're playing at making all that racket? Clear off, before I report you to the authorities for profiteering and disturbing the peace.' His eyes bulged out of his puce face, glaring menacingly at the little crew, before he bent down out of sight.

    'We'll have to think of another tactic to push this lot,' Bert said to his children. 'A quieter one. Come on let's go into the woods and pick some blackberries. Then we'd best gather some firewood. It's your bath night tonight and we'll need summat to boil up the water.' He set off again whistling quietly, amused by his lads' attempts at copying him.

Walking on up the allotment path heading for the woods, they were just passing the last gate when a light, female voice, enquired, 'Was it you I heard offering manure?'

'Yes,' three small voices chorused as the gate opened and an attractive looking woman stepped through.

Georgie stared up at her looking suitably chastened, 'An angry man down at the bottom told us to be quiet or he'd send a policeman after us.'

'Oh dear, how very rude of him, we can't have that,' she smiled sweetly at the children. Bert noticed the mischievous twinkle in her eyes as she looked up at him. They were a soft grey, but the charcoal flecks at their centre darkened as she studied his face. Her smile faded and in relaxed pose her lips looked full and inviting. To his shame, Bert felt his loins tighten. With Ada being so heavy with child, it had been a while since they'd lain together as husband and wife. It was but a split second that the woman held his gaze, yet it felt as though time had stopped. Then Sophie began to howl, and the spell was broken. She looked cross, probably fed up with sitting in the pram and soaking wet as well, he thought.

'Do you think an apple or a sweet plum with the stone removed would help?'

'Yes please,' chorused the children, not wanting to pass up an opportunity to fill their stomachs.

'That's settled then, and I'll bet you could manage a glass of lemonade to go with it, couldn't you?' She disappeared into the largest garden shed Bert had ever seen. He wondered if she lived in it, although he knew there were rules against that sort of thing. She reappeared carrying a pitcher of floating lemons, her eyes were sparkling mischievously again as she took in the children's eager faces. 'I hope it's sweet enough. I like it rather on the sharp side, myself.'

'That's alright, Miss. Our mam says we're sweet enough already,' Georgie informed her. She exchanged an amused look with Bert over his head. Her gardening apron was pulled tight across her abdomen, accentuating an already ample bosom. The day was hot for the time of year and she had unfastened her shirt buttons, perhaps lower than she realised. The sight of her breasts tumbling into the open neckline as she leaned forward to pour lemonade into the glasses, did nothing to relieve the tension in Bert's loins. 'It's a warm day right enough,' he said, removing his coat and folding it over his arm attempting to conceal the now uncomfortable restraint of his trousers.

'So, how much are you selling the manure for, young man?' she asked, handing Georgie a glass of lemonade. He looked to his father for guidance. Bert pushed back his cap and rubbed his head, the sun picked out the copper glints in his ebony hair. 'I was going to say in exchange for some produce, but this lot have made a dent in your pickings already.'

'Nonsense, you're all most welcome on such a hot day. Now, if you would be kind enough boys and girls, to help me pick some fruit and vegetables, perhaps your father wouldn't mind digging up a few potatoes and pulling a few carrots. Then we can share them out when we've done.'

'Bert Brown,' he said, removing his cap and holding it in both hands.

'Charlotte,' she said, thrusting her hand out to him. He clasped it in a firm shake. Then he picked up the spade and began to dig. Georgie's stomach rumbled. Fruit was tasty, but it didn't fill your belly. He shared out the bread and dripping, greatly relieved when Charlotte declined a slice.

He was helping his father pull the carrots when he saw a fat rabbit hop through a hole in the stone wall and help itself to one of the freshly pulled carrots. He nudged his father. Bert turned his head to see if Charlotte was looking. She had her back to him picking beans from a frame. He slid the catapult from his back pocket, reached for a stone and loaded it up. The rabbit, engrossed in feeding, was unconscious in seconds. In a flash, Bert crossed the patch of earth and twisted its neck before it woke. He reached for his jacket and stuffed the rabbit down the sleeve, then he placed it in the shade. 'Good work our Georgie, keep thee eyes open for another 'un.'

Bert had bagged two more by the time the patch of potatoes had been dug over and Georgie had made a thorough job of pulling the carrots. They carried their overloaded boxes into the shed and put them on the bench beside the other pickings. Georgie's box dropped with a bang, disturbing Daisy who'd curled up on a pile of hessian sacks in the corner and fallen asleep.

'Did you enjoy your bit of a kip, Princess?' Bert asked, his heart full of love for this child as he knelt to stroke the damp curls away from her face. She was the gentlest of his brood and sometimes overlooked because of it. The boys fought for his attention and Sophie screamed loudest. Daisy, dainty and compliant, took a back seat. Hearing Sophie let out a wail, he sighed heavily and got to his feet. 'I'd better see to your sister. Here, there's a drop of lemonade left,' he said, and poured her the dregs from the pitcher.

Georgie had already lifted Sophie from her pram. 'She's soaking wet dad, and she stinks something rotten.'

'Aye, she'll need changing right enough,' chipped in Tommy. 'Mrs Jepson says nippers get a sore arse as red as a baboon's, if you leave 'em sitting in their muck.'

'Yours'll be the same colour, our Tommy, if you don't mind your language in front of a lady,' Georgie said, scuffing his brother on the back of his head.

Bert noticed Charlotte bite her lip to stifle a giggle. Then he said, 'We've a problem alright. I don't reckon your mam was expecting us to stop out this long, she hasn't given us owt to change her into.'

'I think I might be able to help.' They followed Charlotte into the shed and watched as she cleared a wooden table of cups and glasses, before spreading sheets of clean brown paper over it. Then she opened a drawer under the bench and removed a carefully folded pile of snow-white napkins. 'I keep these for hand towels,' she said. Bert caught a glimpse of a shadow cross her face as she turned away to pour water into a bowl and take cotton wool from a medicine box screwed to the shed wall.

'Do you actually know how to change a napkin, Mr. Brown?' she said, placing the items on the table.

'Bert. Me name's Bert, and I can't say as I've ever changed one before, but I reckon I could give it a bash.'

'Give us 'em 'ere,' said Georgie, snatching a napkin off the top of the pile. 'I'll do it. Me mam showed me how,' and he proceeded to set about it, with the expertise of a mother of ten. Charlotte packed a box with fruit and vegetables so that the little crew would be ready to set off home as soon as Sophie was clean.

The pram was loaded with children and produce and Bert was preparing to push off, when Charlotte rested her hand on his arm. 'It's turning chilly,' she said, wrapping a shawl around Daisy's shoulders. 'The walk will keep you strong young men warm enough,' she smiled at the boys. 'Oh, and these will bring out the flavour of those rabbits,' she smiled mischievously at Bert, handing him a bunch of herbs.

He stared at her open mouthed. 'Thank you, you've been more than generous.'

'Thank *you*.' She emphasised the word holding his gaze, he found it impossible to look away.

'Come now,' she said to the children, breaking the spell. 'Your mother will be wondering where you've got to.'

They left in a gaggle of goodbyes and thanks. Charlotte stood staring down the allotment path long after the little motley crew had gone from view and their hearty chorus of, 'Yo, Ho, Ho, and a Bottle of Rum' had been replaced by birdsong.

A delicious smell of mutton stew greeted them as they carried the firewood and boxes of fruit and vegetables into the house. Ada was busy setting places at the table, pans of water were simmering on the fire hob and the house sparkled from intense cleaning.

'You've not had much rest then,' Bert said frowning. 'And what's happened to get all this?' He jerked his head towards the smell of stew emanating from the oven in the Yorkshire range.

'Ethel's happened, that's what. And her sisters.' Ada lifted her chin defiantly. 'She didn't involve the neighbours, so your pride won't be dented.'

He felt a flash of annoyance, but he held his peace and asked her to open the door to the cellar. He put the boxes of vegetables on the cold slab on the cellar head, feeling guilty that it wasn't stacked with meat and dairy, its intended purpose. Still, he'd got the rabbits, and he'd heard there were folks who never ate meat and survived well enough on just vegetables.

Georgie carried Sophie into the house chattering excitedly about the kind lady and the vegetables they'd helped her pick. 'She gave us lemonade to drink, it was made from real lemons, fancy that, mam. And you'll never guess, she even had a drawer full of clean napkins, so we could change our Sophie's stinky bum.'

'That's enough of talk like that, Georgie. Put Sophie in her high chair. Go and wash your hands, all of you, while I dish up this stew. The hot water's ready for your bath, after.' She took a flannel from the curtain wire above the fire and dipped it in a pan of water cooling in the hearth, then she wiped Sophie's hands and face before serving up. The children, tired and hungry, wolfed down the stew. Ada smiled watching them, her expression content at least for now. 'There's a bit of mutton left in the pot. If I add the vegetables you've brought, it'll stretch for another meal tomorrow.'

There's a whole box of cooking apples. I'll see if Smith's on the corner will trade 'em for soap, and maybe chuck in some milk and a quarter of dripping,' Bert said, wiping his plate clean with a piece of dry crust to soak up the last drop of stew.

'Can we keep some for an apple pie, dad?' Georgie asked. 'Mam makes smashing pies.'

Bert looked at Ada. 'We'll see, son. She might have all on making them rabbits into pies. But right now, how's about we give the ladies some privacy and do the washing up while they have their bath.'

'Ere! I'm not a lady,' Tommy protested. 'I'll help as well.'

Bert smiled to himself as he gathered the dirty pots and took them through to the kitchen. Kids were gullible really, if you knew how to handle them. There was no need to bash 'em, he'd never held with that, you just needed the right words. 'I'll see the lads are bathed, Ada, after we've finished in here. Right then lads, let's get a move on, it's been a long day.'

The girls were in and out of the bath in a trice. Ada rubbed Sophie's hair methodically in small circles with the towel to make it curl, she was asleep in her arms by the time she'd finished. Ada carried her up to bed before tying Daisy's hair in rags to make it curl into ringlets.

Bert emptied some of the water from the bath and topped it up with fresh warm water. 'Now then lads, in you go. Here's a flannel each, make sure you do a good job. I'll be checking behind your ears when I get back from the privy.' He collected an old newspaper from the cellar head and a box of matches to light the candle in the lavatory.

He settled himself down on the wooden seat to have a read of the news before he used the paper to wipe his backside.

He could hear his lads splashing happily when he walked into the kitchen and washed his hands at the sink.

'You took your time, dad. Me fingers are all wrinkly.'

'Can't rush nature, our Georgie. Out you come then.' He wrapped a warm towel round each boy and rubbed them vigorously in turn. 'Off you go then, up to your mam. If you're quick, you might catch the end of a lullaby.'

He stood for a moment listening to Ada's sweet voice floating down the stairs. Then smiling, he replenished the bath water. By, she'd have made a grand singer would Ada, with the right training. There'd been no money spare for singing lessons in her home, no more than there'd been in his. He was lucky if he got fed on a pay day, afore his dad came home with his wage packet. And that, he thought, going over to the cellar head and ransacking a shelf in search of a block of carbolic, is what drives me on with this union lark.

The stairs creaked as Ada made her way down, her tread sounded weary.

'Come on love,' he said, when she came into the room, 'get in the bath while it's nice and hot, you look done in.' He handed her a block of carbolic. 'Look what I've found at the back of the shelf.'

'You look tired yourself, Bert,' she said, unbuttoning her blouse. 'You've not slept in twenty-four hours, don't overdo it trying to make amends. Is the back door locked?'

'Aye and bolted. I'll wedge this chair against the door to the stairs, just in case one of them little blighters should wander down.' He turned and caught sight of Ada's plump buttocks as her skirt dropped to the floor. 'Where's your knickers, Lass?'

'Don't wear 'em indoors. I've only one decent pair and I save them for outings in case I meet with an accident.'

'Ada, I'm right sorry love. I'd no idea that bastard would drop me hours to three days to spite me for starting a union. All I'd wanted was better wages and a better standard of living for a working man. All I've managed to do is rankle me boss. If only more of the men would stand with me, it might count for summat.'

'You can't blame them, Bert. They've too many mouths to feed.'

'Aye, you're right there. Us blokes often joke that it's the only pleasure we can get for free, but it costs dear when the outcome's another mouth to feed.'

He watched her reach for a flannel before carefully lowering herself into the warm water. He'd not reckoned on the hardship his union beliefs would cause Ada, and it cut deep into his conscience. 'Give us that,' he said taking the flannel, 'I'll scrub your back.' The rhythmic strokes of the cloth were soothing and she relaxed against him. He washed her arms, her swollen breasts. She sighed as he kissed the nape of her neck and he felt the tension drain from her. Relinquishing the cloth, his hands sought the softness of her.

Wordlessly he undressed and they changed places. She soothed and caressed his aching muscles, his need obvious to them both. He reached for the towel warming by the fire and wrapped himself, before holding her as close as her swollen body would allow. She turned within the circle of his arms and the towels dropped. This is torture, he thought, as she leaned back against him. He cupped her breasts surprised anew at their increasing weight. His hand glided over her stomach and a soft moan escaped her lips, it was his undoing, 'For God's sake Ada.'

She turned and kissed him with a passion he didn't know she possessed drawing him down to nestle amongst the scattered towels. They lay caressing, exploring as though for the first time, until Ada pressed him onto his back. With the confidence of a long marriage she played him, writhing and teasing, driving him to the brink and withdrawing, until he cried out, before finally bringing him to a glittering release.

They lay entwined, the amber firelight flickering across their naked bodies. Awed by her rippling abdomen, he trailed his palm across her smooth skin. 'Everything alright in there, is it?' His lopsided grin dimpled one cheek and Ada smoothed it with her hand as though ironing it out. 'He's fine, he doesn't like excitement that's all.'

'He? You've decided it's a boy then.'

'I reckon so, by the way he kicks. Come on, best get up off these wet towels. Do you think that water's warm enough for a quick splash?'

'There's a drop left in the kettle, I'll top it up.'

As Bert drifted off to sleep, Ada's head resting on his chest, he stroked her hair and thought of the woman in the allotments. Her hair had smelled of violets, Ada's smelled of carbolic. The thought set his stomach aflame strengthening his resolve that one day working men would have a decent wage, and women like Ada could have their hair smelling of violets.

Chapter Two – Cruising – 1925

The sudden squall had passengers scurrying indoors. But Mabel found the salty breeze exhilarating. She clung to the rail, watching the white capped waves race off into the distance. Too slow to catch it, she saw her hat race after them. The strengthening wind tugged at her chignon, loosening the pins, until her glorious curls were free. Teased by the squall, they danced about her head, a riot of chestnut and copper. Sea spray splashed her face, and she tossed back her head laughing.

Hearing her name, before the wind snatched it, she turned to see Sydney staggering across the deck to reach her, one hand, held out as if to ward off the elements, the other clamping down his Fedora. His linen suit was plastered against his body, flapping behind like a sail.

'Mabel, what are you doing out here?' he said, grabbing the rail. 'Come inside at once. It isn't safe. A big storm is coming.'

She kissed him swiftly on the mouth. 'Just a little while longer, it's exhilarating. Look how fast the clouds are scudding by.' She turned to face the horizon and Sydney pressed his body against hers to brace himself. Locked together they swayed in time with the ship's motion. She could feel his strength, the hardness of him. He nudged her hair to kiss her neck, sending shivers along her spine, igniting a fire deep inside as he pressed harder, crushing her to the rail. The palm of his hand sought her belly, caressing the slight curve. 'We are to be confined to our cabin,' he breathed against her ear. 'Is it not the perfect time to create new life?' His palm travelled up over her abdomen cupping her breast, stroking a nipple already hardened by the elements. She was melting, barely able to stand. How could anyone resist Sydney at his most seductive? She almost felt sorry for those who had tried.

  Clinging together, they made the short journey across the deck. Only then did she realise the folly of being outside in such a storm. A crew member hovered anxiously beside the door waiting to secure it once they were inside. The ship rocked and rolled flinging her against the walls of the narrow corridor leading to their cabin. Inside she lay down on the bed, it seemed the safest option. The ship lurched violently, throwing Sydney on top of her. She would have laughed but the breath caught in her throat as his glittering eyes bore down on her and his mouth smothered her laughter. He had begun his magic, transporting her in a sensory explosion to some hitherto unknown place. The ship heaved and rocked, dipping and diving as they clung together, lost in their own rhythm.

Mabel woke from a deep sleep. The cabin was in darkness and she lay still, listening to the howl of the wind compete with the roar of the ocean, but the ship felt more stable. The worst of the storm had passed. Trying not to disturb Sydney, she gently shifted her leg from where it was pinned beneath him and tiptoed into the bathroom. She ran a hot bath, added a few drops of perfume, and lowered herself gratefully into the water. A little thrill bubbled up as his words echoed in her mind. 'Is it not the perfect time to create new life?' For so many years she had longed to be a mother, but Sydney had always said there was no room for a child in their kind of existence. Nor would he consider leaving her behind while he sailed the oceans. He wanted her by his side. She often wondered why, for although he denied it, there was always some starlet or chorus girl, and even a waitress or two, captivated by him. She couldn't blame them really, caught as they were like flies in a trap, helpless to untangle themselves from his silken threads of charm. He lured them all to the same fate, for it was always her arms he returned to. She had once asked him to consider taking a job in an orchestra on land. That discussion had ended very badly, and the subject of having a child hadn't been broached again, until now. She wondered what had changed his mind, and an uneasy feeling formed in the pit of her stomach. The little thrill of happiness shrivelled and died as fast as it had grown.

Reluctant to linger and give her mind chance to cloud with uncertainties, she stepped from the warm scented water and wrapped a fluffy white bath sheet around her body. She was twisting a smaller towel, turban style, around her hair as Sydney walked in.

He paused to nuzzle the nape of her neck before climbing into the bath she had just vacated. 'The hot water may not be relied upon in such a storm, therefore I must share yours,' he grinned, revealing even white teeth made more brilliant by his deep olive skin.

When he emerged, she was in the middle of styling her long hair into a complicated structure. She imagined fast modern girls like Delores, the starlet of the revue, had no such trouble styling their fashionably short hair. Mabel smiled at the memory of Sydney's horrified expression when she'd suggested getting a bob. No, he had said, he would not tolerate her cutting off her glorious chestnut curls.

She was buffing her fingernails to a mother of pearl sheen, when he took her hand and kissed it. He was dressed in his black dinner suit, ready to take up his role as band leader. He flashed her his most winning smile. 'Tonight, my darling, we dine together.'

'But what about your contract? I thought you were forbidden to publicise that you have a wife? Are you sure it will be alright for us to dine together; won't the passengers talk?'

'The contract is finishing soon, I will not be taking up the option to renew it.'

If he had noticed her shocked reaction to this news, he didn't show any sign. Instead he stooped to kiss her brow. 'Do not worry your head. And now I will leave you to finish dressing. I must check everything is well with the musicians, before we eat.'

Then he was gone, leaving her strangely bereft. She rose from the stool and walked over to the wardrobe to take out her favourite dress. An oyster silk tulle, with a smattering of diamanté stones which trailed like teardrops across one shoulder to the hem. The style was a little matronly for one so young. Her contemporaries were wearing short cylindrical styles with fringe or feathers, but Mabel, knowing her legs to be far from her best asset, chose to keep them covered. She slipped on the dress, it was instantly transformed clinging to her curvaceous figure. There was nothing matronly about the image she portrayed. The scooped neckline enhanced the milky smooth skin of her throat and breasts. She knew of young women who bound their chests to accommodate the tubular Charleston dresses. She, on the other hand had found her breasts to be something of an asset, and had caught many a husband, married to the skin and bone type flapper, taking a coveting gaze. She left her throat bare of diamonds but pinned a diamanté clasp to her hair. She had just finished securing it when there was a knock on the cabin door.

'Delivery from Mr. Sydney, Madam. Please sign here.' The steward handed her a corsage of white Gardenia. She smiled as she pinned on the heavily scented flowers, he had known she would choose to wear this dress.

It was another hour before Sydney returned. She marvelled that he managed to return looking even more perfectly groomed than when he'd left. His black hair was pomaded to a brilliant sheen and swept back from his face, not a single hair daring to misbehave.

'Thank you for waiting my darling. I hope you are not too hungry. I was delayed because the saxophonist was having difficulty with the band parts for a number which I have included for tonight.'

Mabel knew they cut a dash as a couple, she was aware of a subdued buzz as she and Sydney entered the dining salon. People were curious. Tonight, she felt beautiful. Sydney held out her chair, before the steward had chance to do so, and ordered a superior bottle of wine with dinner. She looked at him in surprise, he never drank before a show.

'Tonight, is a special occasion. Perhaps we have created something to celebrate,' he said, tilting his head with a slight lift of an eyebrow as he chinked her glass.

She blushed happily, he hadn't forgotten his earlier declaration after all. He really did want a child. The meal passed in a rosy blur and when Sydney left her to join his band on the small stage, she was content to listen to the music and watch the other couples dancing. Her happiness was complete when Sydney instructed the band to play 'Let Me Call You Sweetheart' before coming down from the stage to find her and whisk her onto the dance floor, exactly as he had when they'd first met on the Isle of Man.

He gathered her in his arms, crushing her against his chest as they waltzed around. 'This was the song the saxophonist was having difficulty with. It was important to me he got it right. Is my lateness now forgiven?'

'You know very well I had already forgiven you.'

'Mabel, my darling, you look even more beautiful than the first time we danced together.' His breath was hot against her ear, his touch searing her skin as his hand glided up to caress the nape of her neck. His lips brushed her cheek, to hover over her mouth. 'I want you Mabel,' he breathed, gathering her against his body and leaving her in no doubt. Gripping her hand, he headed straight for their cabin, leaving the band to play the last dance of the night without their leader.

Mabel woke with a start. The cabin was in darkness. She felt stiff and sore. Her head ached terribly. She had finished most of the bottle of wine herself and bereft of her senses, had followed Sydney's lead as they'd tumbled into bed. What followed had not been the usual sensory delight, the dizzying wave of passion she'd grown to expect. It had been a harsh, almost violent union and she blushed simply remembering what Sydney had done to her. She turned on the bedside lamp and reached for the jug to pour a glass of water. She was alone in the big bed. Perhaps Sydney was in the bathroom. She was too exhausted and still too intoxicated to care.

When next she woke Sydney was beside her in bed and the sun was shining brightly through the porthole. She studied him in sleep. His usually immaculate hair was flopping down over one eye, making him look ridiculously young for his thirty- two years. She reached out and traced a finger over his smooth olive cheek. He flinched but didn't wake. Her finger continued its trail along his jawline. The absence of whiskery stubble added to his youthful appearance.

    Her stomach growled, she turned to the clock, surprised to see it was almost noon. Not wishing to disturb him she slipped from the bed and into the bathroom. After a quick bath, she brushed her hair vigorously and twisted it into a simple chignon, leaving stray tendrils to curl pleasingly around her cheeks. She dressed in a pleated tunic and made her way to the luncheon salon.

Feeling in need of company and seeing Miss Chesterton beckoning from a window table, she headed in that direction. The woman was a lady's companion, and a gossip, but Mabel felt she would be happy to let her prattle on while adding the occasional nod to show interest.

    'Good afternoon my dear, how lovely of you to join me. So much nicer than dining alone.'

'Is your companion unwell?' Mabel asked, as the steward held back a chair for her to sit.

'Indeed. Mal de Mer. Although I sometimes think it is all in the mind. The ocean is as calm as a mill pond today.'

Mabel studied the menu and made her choice.

The steward was barely out of earshot before Miss Chesterton placed a hand over Mabel's and whispered, 'I couldn't help noticing that you dined with that young bandleader last night. You were looking very beautiful my dear, beautiful enough to turn any young man's head. I hope you realise it is in your best interest that I speak. You must be careful of your reputation. Shipboard alliances may seem very romantic, but they usually end in tears. Mark my words,' she tapped the side of her nose. 'I have sharp eyes.'

'Miss Chesterton, I can assure you, there is nothing untoward going on between Sydney and myself, you see he is m…

'Married. Quite my dear, that is my point entirely. He's married to the glamorous starlet in the revue. Delores, such a pretty name.'

Mabel was about to protest, explain to the bothersome woman that she'd got it all wrong, that she was Sydney's wife, not Delores. Then she realised she would learn more about Sydney's indiscretions if she kept quiet.

'He must have been feeling sorry for you,' Miss Chesterton continued, 'I mean because you're travelling all alone,' she added quickly, after seeing Mabel's eyebrows lift in surprise. 'That's why he asked you to dine with him.

I've seen him dine with lone females on previous occasions. Such a kind young gentleman. But don't read anything into it my dear.'

The steward set Mabel's luncheon down and now the sight of it made her stomach churn. She took several deep breaths before asking him to pour her a cup of tea. She didn't trust her trembling hands to lift the pot. She added two lumps of sugar.

Unaware of her distress, Miss Chesterton prattled on. Of course, they are very much in love you know, Delores and her Sydney.'

Mabel flinched at the inference, her Sydney.

'Yes, my dear, you might be forgiven for thinking that I know nothing of what goes on between a man and a woman in a marriage, what with me being a single lady, but I can assure you, that is not the case. The walls between the cabins are very thin and as my cabin adjoins theirs… Well let's say, I can confirm they are very much in love. I'm often disturbed in the early hours, but can you only imagine my surprise yesterday, when I was disturbed from my pre-dinner nap!'

Mabel stood abruptly, knocking back her chair. A steward hastily righted it.

'Oh, my dear girl,' Miss Chesterton, gasped. 'I've offended you. My sincere apologies. You mustn't mind me. Please don't go. You haven't told me all about your lovely evening with Sydney.'

'No, no don't apologise, you've been more helpful than you could imagine. I suddenly feel a little unwell, if you'll excuse me.' Mabel fled the dining salon in search of the ladies' powder room. She reached the first cubicle in time to be violently sick. All past uncertainties crowded her head. All her hopes and dreams dashed under the whip of an old spinster's malicious gossiping tongue. She splashed cold water onto her face and rinsed her mouth, thankful that she was alone.

Feeling a little more composed she went directly to the library. It was full. She had expected to find it empty and was dismayed to see the Major trying to attract her attention. She ignored him, grabbed a book from the nearest shelf and headed off to the ship's salon in search of a suitable place to sit and gather her thoughts. She found a chair obscured by a potted palm tucked away behind a marble pillar and sank gratefully into the overstuffed upholstery with the book open on her knee. It was intended as a defence should anyone approach. She was in no mood for conversation.

Settling back into the comfy chair it took some time for her heart to stop pounding and her breathing to settle. No wonder Sydney had taken so long in returning to their cabin before dinner. How dare he use their special song as an excuse for his adultery. What hurt most, was that he'd destroyed her precious memory of their first dance. Repulsed, her stomach lurched as she realised why he'd looked so perfectly groomed when he'd returned to escort her to dinner. He must have bathed and pomaded his hair before leaving Delores.

She studied her surroundings. A salon in first class was a luxurious place with walnut panelling, ornately coved ceilings and gigantic crystal chandeliers. She had attended enough civic functions with her parents for such opulence to seem commonplace. Yet as a new bride, she remembered being overawed by the magnificence. What had surprised her most, was the fact that Sydney was accommodated in such luxury when the rest of the band and performers resided in second, and in some instances, third class. It was unusual, she had subsequently discovered, for entertainment crew to be allowed into first class at all, other than for performance purposes. She had quickly learned there was nothing usual about the liberties afforded to Sydney. Almost everyone seemed to turn a blind eye to his activities. Including herself, which was irritating in the extreme. Her resolve to challenge him always crumbled. She was yet to meet anyone who could resist Sydney at his most charming.

When she had first met him, she had been bereft, heartbroken and lonely, yearning for the warmth of a caring human. Easy prey for a sophisticated man with a caring nature. And there lay the crux of the matter. Sydney did care, he cared very deeply for the one he was with and for as long as his infatuation lasted. Although, to his credit and her good fortune, he must have cared very deeply indeed, to make her his wife. Six years was a long time. On their wedding night, she had assumed he was as naive as herself. It never occurred to her to question how he knew so precisely the places where a simple caress could send such pleasure coursing through her body. His eyes had glittered at her shocked reaction to his touch, as his caresses ignited her senses.

She snapped the book shut again. She had suspected for some time that Sydney's frequent absences from their marital bed had nothing to do with extra band practice or an illicit game of cards. Now she had the proof.

'May I join you? I've ordered afternoon tea, and this seems to be the only available space.'

Mabel jumped at the sound of the voice. She didn't need to look up to know who had spoken. It was Dolores, the cause of her most recent anguish.

'By all means. I was about to leave,' she said, rising from her chair.

'Don't go,' Dolores grabbed her wrist. 'I'll order another cup.'

Aware that their interaction had caused a ripple of interest amongst those close by, Mabel sat down again.

'We can share the sandwiches, don't you think? I have to watch my figure,' Dolores explained. 'You're so lucky wearing dresses like that, all those tucks and frills hide a multitude of sins. It's such a chore keeping trim,' she drawled, smoothing down her simple tubular dress. 'I do so envy you, not being a slave to fashion. Ah, here comes the steward. An additional cup if you please.'

Mabel saw the gleam of admiration in the steward's eyes and marvelled that Dolores could somehow manage to flirt, while giving such a simple instruction.

'That won't be necessary,' Mabel said, rising to her feet before Dolores could stop her. 'I really do have to leave. Goodbye Dolores, it was pleasant talking to you.' She walked across the salon with her chin high and the words of her Governess ringing in her head. 'A lady does not show her displeasure in public.' Mabel was unsure how long she could remain a lady, and Sydney's wife.

She found Sydney in their cabin, propped up against the pillows, hands behind his head accentuating his powerful biceps. Tousled from sleep, his usually sleek hair, remained flopped over one eye, giving him that air of youth. Right on cue, a boyish grin appeared, and he said, 'Mabel, where have you been? I have missed you. Come back to bed.'

'It's the middle of the afternoon. Therefore, I've been eating lunch with Miss Chesterton, who, devoid of her companion duties and not knowing that I'm your wife, took great delight in regaling me with the details of your shenanigans, conducted in the cabin adjoining hers. After making good my escape, I was very nearly subjected to afternoon tea with your latest conquest!'

His grin slipped into a dark frown.

Here he goes, she thought, and waited to see whether his defence would be charm or anger.

'Mabel, Mabel my darling. You are my wife and I love you more than anyone in the world. Miss Chesterton is an interfering busybody. A spinster who knows nothing of life or love. She is stuck with her head in the clouds from reading too many romantic novels. Come here and sit with me.'

So, it's to be the charm, she thought. Not daring to move, knowing his touch would crumble her resolve. 'Miss Chesterton told me you and Delores were …'

'Mabel, you know how passengers are. It amuses them to link the stars of the show romantically. Delores sings love songs. I'm the band leader. She occasionally looks across to me for direction, not to make loving eyes at me!'

He left the bed and gathered her in his arms kissing the top of her head. She put her hands on his chest feeling the heat of his smooth skin, but she pushed him away. 'Miss Chesterton told me you were married to Delores.'

'She likes a good romance you know that.'

'Romance didn't come into it. She's in the next cabin to Delores. The cabin walls are very thin. Your shenanigans are waking her up in the middle of the night.' Mabel blushed indignantly, embellishing the spinster's words. 'She sees you coming and going from that cabin at all times of the day and night.'

'Of course.'

'You don't deny it?' she was stunned.

'I'm the band leader, we have to discuss band parts, I give her the music sheets for the following week's revue. You know it changes weekly. Sometimes we need to go through them more thoroughly. We can't use the public rooms, now can we?

Mabel, get this nonsense from your mind, don't let a frustrated old spinster sour what we have together.' He was stroking her back, his breath warm against her ear, making it tingle. 'What would Miss Chesterton know of making love, my sweet Mabel? The sounds she hears… Shenanigans? Is that what she says? It is probably only Delores rehearsing her dance routine. Her cabin is very small. You are a funny one, my precious girl. You need loving so much, and yet you try to throw away what we have, and all because of some foolish woman's imaginings. Come back to bed my darling, you will not doubt my love.'

Mabel stood on the first-class deck of the cruise liner, gripping the rail with one hand and holding onto her hat with the other. She could just about make out the clock tower of Liverpool's Royal Liver building, and the Liver birds at its pinnacle. The polluted fog surrounding it was dense. Even so, she was every bit as excited as when she'd first set eyes on the statue of Liberty. The tight knot in her stomach, which had accompanied her from leaving New York and throughout most of the Caribbean cruise, had finally begun to melt and let hope surface. The American starlets, who'd held her husband's attention for much of that time, had stayed in New York when the ship had returned there at the end of the cruise. Delores and the glamorous chorus girls currently residing in second class, seemed to have lost their appeal. In any case, they would be travelling on with the rest of the revue, whereas Sydney had pulled his band out when the contract was up for renewal.

    Since setting sail from New York to Liverpool, Sydney had doted on her, just as he had in the early years of their marriage. They'd barely come out of their cabin. The thought made her blush.

    He came up behind and placed a hand either side of her on the rail, cocooning her against the elements and her joy bubbled over. 'We're nearly home Syd, doesn't the Liver building look grand?'

    'It might, if it hadn't become blackened with soot since we left.' Turning away from her and leaning back against the rail he lit a cigarette. 'Come inside Mabel, it's too cold out here.'

    She turned her face to avoid inhaling the smoke. 'I'm fine as I am. I want to watch the ship sail into port.'

    'As you wish,' he said, stubbing out the barely smoked cigarette with his heel. 'I have business to attend to.' He slicked back his already immaculately groomed hair, pomaded and brushed until it lay as smooth and shiny as black silk. 'Meet me in the salon at noon, the porter will attend to our luggage.' He pressed his Fedora to a snug fit, low over his brow, but not before she had seen the glint in his eyes. She felt her bubble of happiness burst and the knot in her stomach reclaim its hold. She knew that glint well, had seen it many times in his beautiful, almond shaped brown eyes. It was a prelude to the chase, a signal that he'd set his sights on a new conquest. She had come to associate the glint with fear, fear that he was distancing her, not only from his life, but from his heart. Watching him stride off along the deck towards a door tucked away behind the funnel she saw a steward step out blocking Sydney's way and was surprised to see the man hand over a large wad of money. She quickly turned her back, focusing on the Liver building again. She knew better than to involve herself in Sydney's dealings. It didn't stop her pondering though over what shady deal he'd involved himself in this time.

  Mabel was still deep in thought about Sydney's ubiquitous dealings, and his poorly disguised infatuation with Delores and the chorus girls residing in second class, when she was startled from her reverie by a steward instructing her to go below, ready to disembark. It was the same man she had seen with Sydney. 'Excuse me,' she called him back. 'You see the door over there behind the funnel. Where does it lead to?'

  'Second class, Madam,' he replied, and her unhappiness was complete.

Fergus, Mabel's father-in-law, smothered her in one of his highland bear hugs, while his wife, Isabella, poured tea in her quiet, gentle manner. Sydney took his Eurasian good looks from his mother, though unlike hers, his olive skin had darkened ten-fold in the heat of the tropics. He had his father to thank for his stature.

Fergus released his grasp on Mabel and she watched him shake hands with his son before putting aside masculine propriety to envelop him in a tight bear hug. She saw tears glistening as he relinquished his hold to blow his nose. 'Damned soot and cinders get everywhere these days,' he mumbled.

'Well at least that rotten stench from the tanning yards is far enough away from here,' Sydney said. 'Although it followed us most of the way.'

'Aye, industry has picked up a bit round here, for now, so it has. But the air is that polluted, you can hardly breathe. There's many laid off with bad chests in the winter. Must be tough on the lads that were gassed.'

Isabella handed round cups of tea and then served the food. Fergus sat at the head of the table, looking for all the world like the Laird, even in the cramped living room. 'Come on Lassie, you know not to stand on ceremony here,' he said, handing her a plate of bread and butter. She declined, it always amused her that they ate bread with everything. She tucked into the plate of boiled ham salad and potatoes. She knew that the English dish was for her benefit, but she felt disappointed, she would have preferred Isabella's Chinese cooking. She ate slowly, content to listen to Fergus, soothed by his soft Scottish burr. 'What royalty did you have on board this trip then, Son?'

'No royalty,' Sydney laughed. 'An Earl and a couple of Barons. Several Hollywood stars, though,' and he proceeded to furnish his father with the highlights of their cruise. Mabel felt as though a knife was being plunged into her heart every time Sydney mentioned a woman's name. To her ears, it sounded as though he was ticking them off like trophies and she wondered if Fergus would be as impressed if he understood just how intimately his son knew each starlet.

'Fancy that,' Fergus was saying. 'Were they performing on board like you, or were they passengers?'

'They were passengers, but we persuaded one or two of them to sing with the band on occasion.'

'You always could charm anyone into anything, ever since you were a bairn,' Fergus laughed, slapping him on the back. Mabel looked up, perhaps he knew his son better than she thought.

She was about to help clear the table and carry the dishes through to Isabella in the kitchen, when she realised Isabella had slipped silently back into the room and was standing beside her. She was holding out an envelope. Mabel took it, frowning as she turned it over in her hands. It bore a Sheffield post mark. She slit open the envelope with a knife and withdrew an embossed letterhead. The knife clattered down as she clutched the letter to her chest. 'It's about Annie,' she gasped. 'She's dead.' Even with all eyes focused on her, Mabel couldn't conceal the smile which spread slowly to light up her face. Now she could go home.

Chapter Three – Sheffield – 1925

Mabel could smell sulphur from the works, long before the train pulled into Sheffield station. It was the smell of home. She stepped from the train in a cloud of steam and it evoked a poignant childhood memory of being held in her father's arms, clinging to his neck in terror, as the iron monster rumbled into the station. There had come a time when her father refused to take her into his arms, saying, 'You're a big girl now, there's nothing to be afraid of. You must stand on your own two feet.'

Well now she was a grown woman and certainly capable. She stamped her feet as though to prove the point and startled a pair of pigeons into flight.

There was no need to summon a porter, she had packed lightly. The autumn day was chilly, but bright, and she relished the walk to Paradise Square.

The solicitor greeted her with sombre courtesy. He did not shake her hand or hold out a chair, although he did remain standing until she was seated on the opposite side of his desk.

'Mrs. Baxter, I will come straight to the point, if I may. Your sister-in-law's untimely death left her unprepared in the making of a will. However, I can confirm that you are the sole beneficiary of her estate, due to a codicil attached to your late brother's will. It is also my duty to inform you that the family home was re-mortgaged. Unfortunately, the repayments are now in considerable arrears.'

Mabel knew Annie was a hopeless business woman and an icy grip squeezed her heart. 'What about the factory?'

'Also heavily mortgaged, and I'm sorry to say the bank are threatening to foreclose on both loans.'

She slumped back in her chair, too stunned to comprehend. Too upset that another bubble of hope had been dashed. She heard the door behind her open and she jumped as someone touched her lightly on the shoulder. A matronly woman pressed a cup and saucer into her hand. 'Drink this my dear, it will help. Hot sweet tea is the finest thing for shock.' The formidable solicitor glared at the woman, but she tilted her chin defiantly, and left.

Mabel found it difficult to concentrate on what he was saying, and she asked him to repeat it.

'My best advice is that you sell both properties immediately. In its present run-down state, the factory alone will not fetch a good price, but including the sale of the house, you would make enough to cover the arrears and have funds left over for a meagre investment.' He then made a show of glancing at his fob watch and shuffling the papers on his desk.

His pompous, condescending attitude irked Mabel. She reflected for a moment on what her father would have done in this situation. His advice had always been to sleep on important decisions. She looked across the table meeting the solicitor eye to eye. 'You have acted as my family's solicitor for decades and yet you seem to be forgetting that at the time of my brother's death and for several years before that, I was responsible for the factory's accounts.' She spoke calmly, measuring her words. 'I have, in the past, been a party to important decisions regarding the factory's development. You cannot possibly expect me to be coerced into making a decision without reviewing the facts and figures.' She nodded at the papers in his hands which her words had stilled, mid-shuffle. 'I presume those are the relevant documents in front of you.' She snatched them from under his nose and put them on her side of the desk. 'If you will now instruct me where to sign to acknowledge receipt, I won't take up any more of your valuable time. I will be in touch, should I find myself in further need of your services.' Satisfied to see a startled expression on the solicitor's face, she reached across the desk to lift the pen from its inkwell. He had discovered she was her father's daughter.

Outside in the square, her knees began to tremble. It had taken all her courage to stand up to the man. She took a few moments to steady her breathing, then squaring her shoulders, she set off with gusto up St. Paul's Parade. The Town Hall clock was striking three as she reached the Moorhead. Reluctant to spend precious money on the tram, she walked on past the stop and down the Moor, heading for Ecclesall Road. She thought about her two friends, Ethel and Ada. Her journey would take her past their homes. It had been a lucky day for her when the pair had taken her under their wings. She wondered again what her father or indeed her brother Billy would have made of the association. Factory girls were classed as being below their station. She would be forever grateful to have broken with that tradition.

By the time she reached Moorfoot, her ardour had cooled. The small suitcase, made heavier with the sheaf of documents, was tugging at her arm. Her feet seemed to have grown two sizes inside her shoes and apart from the cup of tea in the solicitor's office, she'd had nothing since leaving Liverpool. The temptation to call on Ada was too great to resist.

As she reached the corner of their road, she could see Bert, Ada's husband, walking towards her down Clarence Street. She dropped her heavy suitcase and waited for him.

'By heck, lass,' he said, as he drew near. 'You look like you've lost a shilling and found a tanner. Ada will be right glad to see you. She told me you were due back in Sheffield. Are you coming in for a cuppa? You look like you could do with one. Here, I'll take your suitcase.'

As they turned the corner a piercing scream stopped them in their tracks. Bert dropped the case and set off running to his front door, his studded boots clattering on the cobbled road. Mabel grabbed the case and followed him into the house. The younger children were wailing, and an ashen faced Georgie greeted her. Bert was taking the stairs two at a time.

'Hello Georgie,' she said, holding out her hand. 'How lovely to meet you again. I'm Mabel. Do you remember me?'

'Yes, I remember you,' he said, looking anxiously up at the ceiling. 'Me mam's right bad, she's been screaming for a long time but I daren't leave little 'uns to go and get me auntie Ethel.'

'Have you eaten, Georgie?'

'No, none of us have had owt since breakfast. I found some dripping on the cellar head, but I'm not supposed to use the knife to cut the bread. I've changed our Sophie though.'

'Splendid, Georgie. I'll just go up and see how your mam is and then I'll get you all a warm drink and make you something to eat. Can you fill the kettle with water and put it on the hob?'

'I've already done it, I heard you need lots of hot water when a babby's on its way.'

'Quite right,' she said, ruffling his hair. She turned and dashed up the stairs.

Ada's face was ashen, her hair plastered with sweat. Bert looked up as Mabel entered the room. 'Stay with her, I'm going for the doctor.'

'Bert, no!' Ada grabbed his hand. 'I've told you, get Ethel, she'll sort me out. We've no money put by for the doctor.'

'Ada, tha needs more help than Ethel can give thee. I'm fetching the bloody doctor if I have to sell every stick of furniture in this house to pay him.' He clattered down the stairs as Ada's screams vented the air. Mabel stayed with her until the contraction had passed, then she ran downstairs. 'Georgie, go and get Ethel, tell her its urgent. Here,' she said, opening her purse and pressing some coins into his hand, 'take that jug and pick up some milk on your way back, share it out between your brothers and sisters. Do you know how to fill Sophie's bottle? Or do you think she's old enough to take it from a cup now?'

He didn't stay long enough to answer her, he didn't need asking twice to get help for his mother. Mabel filled a basin with water from the kettle and took a cloth down from the wire across the mantel. Ada was in the throes of another contraction as Mabel set the basin down on the washstand in the bedroom. When it had passed, she washed Ada's face and neck, smoothing her damp hair away from her face. 'Come on, let's get you out of this nightdress, it's soaked through with sweat, you'll be more comfortable when I've cleaned you up a bit.' She pulled back the sheets and discovered what had sent Bert in frantic search of the doctor. She was used to masking horror from her days as a VAD, but this was her friend and she had to fight to remain calm as she took in the scarlet soaked sheets and nightdress. Ada was in serious trouble. Mabel watched as her body was wracked by another contraction and fresh blood trickled out as she rode the waves of pain.

'I'll let you rest until the doctor comes, your contractions are coming thick and fast, I might not have time to change your nightdress after all,' she said, settling the sheets back in place. Ada began trembling, she was going into shock. Mabel knew how to stem the flow of blood from limbs blown apart and guts partly wrenched from a stomach, but she had no idea how to stem the flow from a woman in labour. The minutes passed without a sign of Ethel or the doctor. Going to the top of the stairs she called down, 'Tommy, Tommy dear, can you hear me, your mam's alright, but I think the baby needs to be born in hospital. Can you run to Mr Beresforth's shop and ask him to phone for an ambulance to come straight away? Tommy do you know your address?'

'O' course I do. Does tha think I'm daft or summat?'

'Good chap.'

He turned and ran smack into Ethel. 'Now then young man where are you off to in such a tearing hurry?'

'Beresforth's, 'ave to ask him to send for an ambulance for me mam.'

'No lad, your mam's only having a baby she's going to be alright, come back indoors,' she said, putting an arm around his shoulders.

'No!' he squirmed free. 'Mabel sent me,' and he scampered off.

Ethel made her way upstairs. 'Well this is a fine welcome home for you, Mabel, I must say. What's all this about an ambulance being sent for? She looks content enough to me.'

Mabel pulled back the covers.

'God Almighty, you did the right thing. How long's she been like this?'

'I've no idea. Bert and I have just found her, we arrived at the same time. He's gone for the doctor, but he's taking too long.'

Ada stirred as another contraction took hold, her cries were pitiful and weaker, adding to Mabel and Ethel's concerns. 'You're doing grand, love,' Ethel said, leaning over and squeezing her hand. That doctor must have forgotten his way to your door, so Mabel's sent for an ambulance. I should think you'll make your Bert tie a bloody knot in it, after this performance.' Her banter raised a weak smile.

Mabel stroked Ada's brow with a cool flannel. 'Don't you worry yourself about paying for the doctor. I've enough put by to help you out.'

Voices downstairs announced the arrival of the doctor and the ambulance. 'There you are lass,' Ethel said. 'Helps on its way. I'll take your kids over to my house. I'll see 'em right, so there's nothing for you to worry about on that score. You just concentrate on bringing this little nipper into the world.'

Five minutes later, Ada was on her way to hospital. The doctor went with her in the ambulance. Mabel poured Bert a mug of strong sweet tea and made up some slices of bread and dripping. Then she changed the sheets and put the blood-stained ones to soak.

When she returned to the living room, he was sitting at the table with his head in his hands, the food untouched. 'I'd better be getting along,' she said. 'I'll call in tomorrow to sort those sheets out. Will you be alright?'

'Aye, I expect so,' he said, his voice tight with fear. 'Don't bother about them sheets, I'll sort 'em out and then go up to the hospital.'

'I know it will be hard, but you should try and get some sleep later, you'll be no good to Ada or your children if you're too exhausted to function.'

'Thank you for your help Mabel. I dread to think what would have happened if you hadn't turned up when you did.'

She couldn't think what to say, so she simply squeezed his shoulder and left the house. Outside on the pavement she stood for a moment breathing deeply to steady her nerves. She was exhausted. Lifting her case, she crossed the road and walked down Clarence Street to the General Post Office. It was about to close as she hurried up the steps, but she managed to send off a telegram to

Sydney. He was expecting her to return to Liverpool at the end of the week, though she knew when she left him that she had little intention of doing so. The fact that Ada and her family needed her help, simply eased her conscience. She didn't allow her mind to consider that Ada might be beyond help.

Chapter Four

Bert left the hospital, cap in hand, with all the weight of the world on his shoulders. His son had been born by caesarean section. Ada was off the critical list, but they'd told him she was still very poorly. It was credit due to the doctor who'd travelled with her in the ambulance that she was still alive when she'd arrived, but his services wouldn't come cheap. Bert hoped to God that Mabel would come true with her promise to pay the medical expenses.

He rammed his cap on and set off walking at a fast pace. He'd no idea where he was going, just that the action eased his nerves. His pride was still smarting, he couldn't believe that the bloody pompous jumped up arse of a Matron wouldn't let him have even a glimpse of his Ada and the baby.

'The next visiting hours are Sunday at two, Mr Brown. You can see your wife and son then,' she'd informed him. 'Please feel free to send eggs, fresh fruit or the likes in the meantime, should you wish to.' She had looked him up and down as she'd said it, he felt his colour and temper rise at the memory. She might just as ruddy well have come out with it and said if folks like you can afford it. The thought gave him a focus, he'd go to the allotment under the pretext of returning Charlotte's shawl. When she heard his tale, she'd be bound to give him a bag of fruit. And then he'd go to Mrs Smith's shop and try and get half a dozen eggs on tick. He'd show that miserable old cow at the hospital that his Ada was as important as any of them toffee-nosed lot who paid to have their babbies delivered in nursing homes. First, though, he'd better call in to see Ethel and his kids to tell them his news. Maybe she would keep them with her for a couple more days. He should really offer to see her right for her trouble, but he'd no idea how he was going to do that.

Bert could see Sammy loitering on the corner of his road as he made his way down Clarence Street. He was the last person he wanted to see.

'Hello me old mate,' Sammy greeted him warmly. 'How's your missis doing? News travels fast round here,' he said, lighting up a Woodbine. 'Thought you might be needing some brass to pay for your doctors' bills and I've come to tell you that my offer still stands. There's a fight arranged at Sky Edge tomorrow night at nine o'clock. You need to be there at eight-thirty sharp. I know who they're putting up against you and I'll tell thee now, you'll knock his lights out.'

'How much?' Bert said. 'I'm not doing it just for nobbings. If you pass the hat round these days it'll come back empty.'

'Ten quid. Double if you win and a pay out on your own bet.'

'Tell me how much the bookies are taking up front and I'll give you me answer.'

'Awe 'ave an heart, Bert. How the bleedin' hell are they going to take bets when nobody knows who they're betting on. But there's plenty remember you from the old days. Any mention of your name will draw the crowds.'

'Aye, it's not the old days that's worrying me, it's these days. I've not the same fire in me belly for fighting.'

'Well so long as there's still lead in your fists, you'll be reight. Are you in or what?'

'I don't see as I've a choice. Not a word to my Ada mind. And if we get raided, I'm taking all of you buggers down with me. Got it?'

'There's no chance of being raided. We've a good vantage point in seeing whose coming at Skye Edge and you know the coppers never venture there. It's too high up and bleak. That's why Pitch and Toss ring's been so profitable until lately. Any road, I reckon them coppers have a good idea what'd be waiting for 'em, so they steer clear.'

'Skye Edge's not usual place to hold a fight, is it?'

'It is now. It's anybody's guess from day to day who holds the key to the Pitch and Toss lock up.'

'Who's running the bets?'

'Same as always,'

'Bloody hell Sammy, when word gets out that he's in charge up at Skye Edge, there'll be more fighting out of the bleedin' ring than in it. What are your playing at, getting us involved in summat like this?'

'Awe, it'll be alreight. Camel Coat's set it up. You'll have seen him about. He looks a reight tater, wearing that camel coat of his. The belt hardly meets the buckle, and to crown it all, he wears a brown bowler hat. I tell thee, it looks just like a pork pie perched on top of that bladder o' lard he has for a head. He smokes them expensive fat cigars an' all, so you'll smell him afore you see him. He must be making a tidy bob or two from somewhere. I reckon we're best not knowing where. He might look a tater but not many dare cross him.'

'Bloody hell Sammy. I hope we live to collect our winnings.'

Once inside his house, Bert made himself a bite to eat. It was an odd combination of grated potato and onion, fried together like bubble and squeak, accompanied by stale bread and a scraping from the last of the dripping. He washed it down with a mug of tea. Then he went across the yard to the privy. Her next door had cut up some fresh squares of newspaper. That pleased him, he'd read all the old ones.

Mabel walked slowly down the steps from the General Post Office and crossed the road to catch the tram to Endcliffe. As she waited at the stop, she realised she couldn't face going to the empty house, just yet. So she retraced her steps and headed over to Ethel's.

Ethel and her young daughter were taking washing down from the line when she walked into their yard. 'Go on into the house, Mabel love,' Ethel greeted her. 'I'll make us a pot of tea when I've finished here. Peggy, go and get a quarter pound of boiled ham from Mrs Smith's on the corner.'

'Aye, and if it's Mr Smith that's behind the counter, tell him it's for Mabel. He might weigh it a bit on the heavy side,' Daniel said, appearing on the back step.

'Get on with you, you daft 'apeth,' Ethel laughed, brushing past him, her arms full of washing.

'Good to see you lass,' he stepped forward and took hold of Mabel's suitcase. 'By heck, what have you got in here, the crown jewels.' Mabel followed him into the warm cosy living room and was greeted by the delicious smell of mutton stew cooking in the Yorkshire range. Her stomach rumbled, reminding her she hadn't eaten since breakfast.

'Now Mabel, come and sit down, love. Take the weight off your feet. Kettle's on the boil, I'll get you a nice strong cup of tea to go with that boiled ham sandwich. It'll put you on a bit. There's stew in the oven, but we're having it late, on account of Daniel being on nights. I like to send him off with something hot in his stomach.' She folded the washing into a neat pile and put it on the dresser beside the fire. Then lifting the kettle from the fire-hob she poured scalding water into the tea pot. 'Right, I can relax a bit now I've got me washing in and we can sit and have a good old natter.'

'I'm off to fetch a Star,' Daniel announced, 'then I might call in the Lincoln for one, while I have a read of it. Give you lasses chance to natter in peace.'

'Aye, well just the one mind, you'll be drinking plenty tonight if you're smelting.'

She turned her full attention back to Mabel, 'Now then love, tell me what's up.'

Mabel took one look at her friend's kind eyes and burst into tears. It was the first time she'd cried since her brother Billy's death.

When she'd managed to compose herself, she told Ethel the news from the solicitor.

'What are you going to do then? Easiest thing would be to sell up like he says. It's not as though you and Sydney are looking to settle in Sheffield.'

Her words brought on a fresh bout of tears, and against her better judgement, Mabel found herself telling Ethel about Sydney's infidelities.

'Aye, well, I can't say I'm surprised. Ada had her suspicions from the start. That's why she went to see him after you first met him. She wanted to get a measure of the lad, find out what his intentions were.'

'And I'd never felt more embarrassed in all my life when she told me where she'd been. Still, it all worked out in the end.'

'To tell you the truth, I'm amazed it's turned out as well as it has. Holiday romances are usually best left where they are, on holiday. You two have had six good years of marriage. He's not a bad bloke deep down. He doesn't beat you or leave you short of money. Maybe he'll settle with age, them type do you know, so I'm told. Any road, one thing's for sure, you're not going back to Annie's house tonight.'

'I'll be alright, it was my family home long before Annie was married to Billy.'

'Aye, I know it was love, but it's been stood empty months while that solicitor was getting word to you, and you always said Annie never kept it well heated in the first place. You can stop here for tonight and start afresh in the morning. I'll help you anyway I can. Right now, you can help me put clean sheets on me bed. With Daniel on nights, you can kip in with me. We'll have to be quiet mind, Sophie and Daisy are asleep in the back bedroom, worn out from all that crying I shouldn't wonder, poor mites.

Georgie and Tommy have gone off somewhere with our Joe and their mates. They know when to be back if they want feeding.'

It was a raucous meal time, with lots of banter and laughter as was always the case in Ethel and Daniel's house, but with the addition of Bert and Ada's children it was organised chaos. The children were growing up fast and had inherited their father's quick wit and mother's easy-going nature. By the time Daniel left for his night shift, and she'd helped Ethel wash the pots and put the children to bed, Mabel could hardly keep her eyes open.

'You go on up love,' Ethel said. 'I'll bring you a pitcher of hot water. There's clean towels and soap on the dresser.'

'Thank you, although I don't know what sleep I'll get for worrying about Ada.'

'Worrying never helped anybody and she's in the best place she can be. Let's hope Bert comes with better news in the morning.'

After a good wash down, Mabel put on her nightgown and slipped between the cool fresh sheets, they smelled of carbolic and starch.

Ethel came into the room carrying a hot brick wrapped in rags. 'Here, put this under your feet, love. It'll warm 'em up in no time.' She lifted the pitcher and bowl of water that Mabel had used and left again. She returned shortly afterwards already washed and ready for bed. Mabel drifted off to sleep, lulled by the warmth of the hot brick, and the amber glow from the fire in the hearth.

Chapter Five

Nervous exhaustion had overtaken Bert. He'd not slept like that since his days in France, when his battalion was sent for rest and recuperation from the war-torn trenches to the villages. Where, after being deloused for scabies, they'd taken a hot, all be it communal bath, while the old women of the village washed their soldier's uniforms and burned the hidden scabies eggs by running a candle flame along the seams.

When he got downstairs, he discovered the fire in his living room grate had burned out, but he didn't plan on stopping home today. He'd ask her next door for a mug of hot water for his tea.

In the kitchen, he had a shave, as best he could in cold water, and a good scrub down to remove the stench of the factory oil from his skin. Nothing he could do about his clothes though. He'd only one other set, his wedding suit which he kept for best, and he was saving that for Sunday when he went to see Ada and the baby. Any road, he consoled himself, if Charlotte had him digging, when he went begging for fruit and veg under the pretence of returning her shawl, he didn't want to be wearing his finest.

He walked on up the path praying Charlotte would be there. He breathed a sigh of relief when he saw wispy smoke curling into the air from her allotment. She'd obviously been clearing up, preparing for the winter months. He hoped she had some crop left.

'You've been busy,' he shouted over the hedge.

'Hello there,' she said, straightening up, one hand in the small of her back. She was well wrapped up today, wearing a thick coat under her gardening apron.

She removed her gardening gloves and reached over the hedge to shake his hand. 'How nice to see you again,' she smiled, leaving Bert in no doubt that she meant it. An uneasy sensation gripped his stomach.

'I was about to stop for a cup of tea, would you care to join me?' she asked, unbolting the gate. 'I tend to keep the gate locked when I'm here alone.'

Bert wondered who she was with when she wasn't alone and suppressed a sudden and unreasonable feeling of jealousy.

'You never know who's passing. One sees some very strange folk loitering in these allotments and woods.'

Aye, and none stranger than himself, he thought, as even the sight of her in a tightly buttoned up winter coat had him feeling hot under the collar. How dare he have such feelings for a stranger, when his beloved Ada was lying just beyond death's door.

'Here, I've brought your shawl back,' he said gruffly, handing it over. 'I'd be thankful for that tea you're offering, it's a pull up the hill from town.'

Charlotte made the tea and gave him a couple of slices of date and walnut cake to go with it. 'How are the children, Mr Brown ... Bert?' she asked, indicating that he should take a seat on an upturned wooden orange box.

'Aye, they're grand, and they've a brother born this morning. His mother's in a bad way mind. It were a caesarean, lost a lot of blood before-hand, like.' Bert went quiet, why had he said mother and not Ada? He knew why, right enough. He couldn't bring himself to mention Ada's name in the presence of this woman, this perfectly respectable woman, who his treacherous body was lusting after. He ran his fingers distractedly through his hair, and then before he knew it, he'd blurted out the whole sorry tale about his union work, his short hours at the factory and how it had affected Ada and his kids.

'I expect it's because of me, and all the worry I've caused, that Ada nearly lost her life bringing that babby into the world.' To his horror, tears coursed down his cheeks. In an instant, Charlotte was on her knees in front of him, wiping his tears with her thumbs. The next moment she was in his arms and he was rocking her back and forth as though the movement would banish the guilt and torment twisting his stomach. How he came to be kissing her he would never know, but once he'd started, he couldn't stop. Her mouth responded with great hungry, greedy kisses as though sucking the life blood from him yet filling him with renewed strength and vigour. Hairpins clattered to the ground forgotten, as her hair tumbled from its twist, it was like holding strands of raven silk. His fingers found the opening of her coat and as his hand closed around her breast his mind acknowledged it was what he'd been longing to do since their first meeting that September afternoon. He groaned as she knelt up and pressed into him. Her kisses deepened until he thought his body would catch fire. Suddenly she stood up and pulled him after her into the shed. He lifted her onto the table pushing her down onto her back and pinning her arms above her head with one hand. She writhed under his grasp trying to get closer to him. The palm of his hand slid up over her calf to the smooth flesh of her inner thigh and she cried out. He could see her need, feel her readiness, but he pushed aside her petticoat to seek out the soft flesh with his lips. She thrashed her head, eyes glittering, half wild with desire when at last he fulfilled her need. Never had he felt so alive. It was like riding the crest of a wave into a glorious sunset with wave after wave of ecstasy washing over him, yet still he rode the crest until one final crescendo had him spiralling down in a glittering array. He gathered her into his arms and she clung to him, wrapping her arms and legs tightly around him. He smoothed damp tendrils away from her face and kissed her forehead, then he looked into her eyes, his own still dark with passion except for the amber flecks glowing mischievously at their centre. 'By heck lass, are all middle-class women like you?' he chuckled. 'I've not known what I've been missing.'

   Laughing delightedly, she leaned back on the table propping herself up on her elbows, her head cocked to one side so that her hair dangled over her shoulder. 'How could I possibly know the answer to that?' Her smile lit up the space as though he'd struck a match, it flared and died just as suddenly. He followed her gaze to see what had saddened her. She was looking at the pile of white napkins which she said she used as hand towels. The sight of them brought him to his senses. What had he done? What could he have been thinking? As thoughts filled his brain, his senses knew there had been no stopping it, they had been in this madness together, something bigger than them both had taken hold and he didn't think he would be able to fight it. An icy fear, mingled with guilt, twisted his bowels. Dear God in heaven, he was in enough trouble raising the brood his marriage had brought him, what would he do if Charlotte was pregnant?

He held her fiercely against his chest. 'I'm sorry, so sorry, I should have shown more restraint, controlled meself better like. What if summat should happen? I've only to look at Ada and she falls pregnant.'

A single tear slid from the corner of Charlotte's eye and trickled down her cheek. 'Have no fear on that score, Bert,' she mumbled into his chest. 'I can no longer have children.' He held her away and fresh tears trickled down her cheeks, she was still staring at the napkins. He looked at the snowy white pile, folded so neatly, so carefully, then at Charlotte. He dried her tears with kisses then folded her into his arms. 'Tell me about it.' His softly spoken words broke the dam of tears and he rocked her gently until her sobbing eased. She reached for a napkin and used it to dry her tears. 'It was seven years ago, near the end of the war,' she said. 'Everything was in chaos amongst the carnage in France. The allies were pushing through, mingling with the enemy, so that at times they were behind enemy lines without realising, until it was too late.'

'Aye, I know, I was there. I'm a dab hand at getting past barbed wire,' he whispered. 'What were you doing in France?'

'I'm a surgeon.' She didn't miss the look of astonishment on his face.

'Yes, really. We're few in numbers but there are other women surgeons. By nineteen-sixteen, I was newly qualified and newly married. My husband is, was, also a surgeon. Of course, finding a position as a female surgeon was difficult enough, but as a married one, virtually impossible. So, I used my maiden name as my professional name. After a year working at a hospital requisitioned by the Army, I knew that many limbs and lives could have been saved had surgery been performed before the injured were shipped back to England, even before they were moved from the front line. Edwin, my husband, and I talked it over at length and decided to volunteer for overseas. We were both posted to France and because I'd kept my maiden name we weren't associated, certainly not as a married couple. It wasn't easy, but made more bearable, when we managed to snatch some private moments and precious days away from the noise and filth and blood. Towards the end of the war, I fell pregnant and we were overjoyed. Of course, I had to keep it secret, and as my pregnancy didn't show, I kept working far longer than I should. Edwin was moved to set up another field hospital nearer the new front line and I stayed behind. Untold numbers of casualties were being brought in hourly, we ran out of beds. Exhausted and far advanced in my pregnancy, I should have given in sooner, but when you see row upon row of men writhing in agony...' She shrugged, spreading her hands wide and taking a few deep breaths. 'Can you imagine the feeling of desolation walking amongst them, making the decision as to who will live and who will die? In that situation, you must choose the one strong enough to withstand the surgery, never mind their injury. In the end I collapsed with fatigue, had a sort of physical breakdown. I was sent to a civilian hospital. It would have been better for me and the baby had I stayed at camp. Unfortunately, the staff in the civilian hospital thought I was a screaming lunatic. I was too ill to explain, and they didn't realise I was in the advanced stages of labour. My child, my son, was stillborn and my internal organs too badly damaged to conceive again. I suffered a complete breakdown and by the time I began the road to recovery, Edwin's unit had become embroiled in the confusion on the front lines and he and most others in his unit had been posted missing.'

Bert released his tight hold and kissed the top of her head. Then taking her hands in his, he looked into her grey eyes. 'I don't have the right words except to say I was a part of that hell, that same torment, only in a different way to you. I was one of the lucky ones, but to the end of me days, I'll carry the guilt that I lived, while me mates were blown to kingdom come all around me.'

'Then embrace what just happened between us,' she said, reaching up and stroking his cheek. 'When one has witnessed, and lived through what we have, one learns to grab each moment of joy as it comes along. I have no wish to destroy what you and Ada have. Judging from the way your children behave, I imagine you have a strong and loving bond. But, having said all that, I won't turn you away, if you come calling.' The mischievous twinkle was back in her eyes. She jumped down from the table. 'I don't know about you, but I could do with another cup of tea.'

It was late morning when Mabel woke. The pitcher of water must have been placed on the dresser sometime earlier, it was tepid. She quickly washed and dressed, shivering as she fastened the buttons on the front of her dress, the fire had burned itself out in the night.

'Morning, sleepyhead,' Ethel greeted her, as she entered the warm living room.

'I'm so sorry, I'm still on Sydney's hours, late to bed and late to rise. Where's Daniel? I didn't mean to keep him from his bed.'

'He always has his bath at Glossop Road slipper baths on a Saturday. He calls in afore he comes home when he's been on nights. He'll be starving when he gets in. There's porridge in the oven and I'll be doing some bacon and eggs, if you fancy that.'

'Porridge will be fine, thank you,' she said, knowing money was tight and the luxury of bacon was reserved for the man of the house.

'Help yourself to a cup of tea. I've not long since made it, but it should be mashed.' Ethel set about her housework, while Mabel finished her breakfast. Then she made a fresh pot of tea and sat down to join her at the table. 'Have you had any thoughts on what you might do about your situation?'

'My situation?'

'You can't pull the wool over my eyes. It isn't entirely worry over the lack of money and the factory that's furrowed that line between your eyebrows.'

Mabel flushed, and sighing placed her cup in its saucer. 'You always were an astute soul, Ethel,'

'Aye, wise beyond me years me mother always said. Come on, out with it. What's really going on in that head of yours? I can see the cogs whirring ten to the dozen.'

'I love Sydney, don't get me wrong. I've grown used to his unorthodox ways, and when he suggested we should try for a baby I was thrilled beyond belief. But I started thinking why now, what's changed his mind? Then came all the upset over his most recent infidelity, that starlet I told you about. He's usually more discreet.'

'Starlet? She sounds like a harlot to my way of thinking.'

'Precisely. Now my suspicions have become a reality I can't help thinking that with me out of the way, stuck at home with a baby, he would be free to sail off into the wide blue yonder. He could vanish from my life completely, should he choose to. Then what would happen to me? I'd have no means of support other than the money my father left to me and that won't last forever. The best I could hope for would be a room in Sydney's parents' house. No disrespect to them, they're wonderful people, but the house is cramped and what with the pollution and the stench from the tanning works, it's not an environment I would choose to bring up a child in. When the letter came telling me about Annie's death, it felt as though a decision had been made for me. I had been thrown a lifeline to make my own way, with or without Syd. Although my heart would probably break if I had to live completely without him.'

'So, what's your plan? Sounds like you could be in debt up to your eyeballs, if you're not careful. Here, pass us that teapot. I'll mash us another, it's thirsty work all this talking.'

'One thing about Syd, he's generous, I'll give him that. Mind you, he can afford to be, everyone treats him like royalty. You've no idea the endless liberties he takes, and nobody seems to have a care. We travel first class most of the time. The only drawback is that I'm not allowed to let on that I'm his wife. It's written into his contract, something about being bad for publicity if the star attraction in the band is married. Puts off the swooners I suppose.'

'Are you sure about that, love? I should want to see that contract. Sounds to me, it's more something Sydney's made up to suit himself.'

'You make me feel very gullible, but that's Sydney for you, he can charm anyone into believing anything. My point about him being generous, though, is that I haven't spent any of the money my father left me. I should have enough to pay off the arrears on the house and next month's in advance. That should buy me some time to sort something out. There'll be money left over, but I don't know if it will be enough to save the factory. I'll have to go down there, study the books and talk to people, find out just how bad things are. I've sent Sydney a telegram to say I'm stopping in Sheffield indefinitely. What with Ada and the factory.'

'Well for starters, when Daniel's had his breakfast and gone to bed, I can come up to the house with you, see what state it's in. It will need a good airing and probably a good clean after being shut up these past months.'

'What about Peggy and Joe, will you bring them with you? They can play in the park.'

'They'll be alright here. I'll leave them a sandwich for their dinner and ask her next door to keep an eye out for them. They'll be off up the road after their friends all day if I know them, and Daniel won't sleep late.'

Mabel didn't feel she could expect Ethel to walk to the house at Endcliffe, so together they made their way to the bottom of Ecclesall Road and caught the tram.

It felt strange walking through the front door of her old home knowing that Annie wasn't there waiting to pounce ready with her complaints.

She walked through the ground floor before coming to a halt in the front room. There were ashes in the grate and she wondered what had prompted Annie to light a fire. It was a luxury never extended to her after the death of her parents and brother Billy. She stood staring at the dead ashes. The hearth seemed cold and desolate. She remembered a roaring fire, her father sitting beside it, reading the evening paper and her mother sewing quietly in the opposite chair. The memory faded, and she thought how during Annie's reign as Billy's widow and mistress of the house, she had never lit a fire in the front room hearth, insisting that she and Mabel stay in the living room where the Yorkshire range provided both cooking facilities and warmth.

She looked out of the window across to the park where boys were playing football. Her heart felt heavy as she remembered seeing Edgar and Billy kicking a ball back and forth in much the same way. Both brothers gone. Dead and buried tragically young. She dragged the memory from her thoughts and pulled back her shoulders as though to strengthen her resolve.

'Come on Ethel, it's a fine day. If you don't mind, I'd like to start by airing the bedrooms and changing the bed linen.'

They worked steadily until all the sheets and lace curtains were blowing on the line, gleaming white from a good dowsing with the blue bag.

'Mabel's stomach rumbled as they came in from the garden. She looked up at the clock on the kitchen wall. 'If we make a dash for it, we can catch Two Steps, before they close. I could just fancy a nice bit of cod and chips. How about you?'

'I'll get me hat and coat.'

'No, I'll go. You get the tea mashed and cut some of that loaf we picked up this morning.'

Ethel discovered plates in a cupboard beside the fire. They were grimy. She lifted all the crockery down onto the kitchen table and used hot water from the kettle to wash it. Then she set to, wiping surfaces as she went, cleaning the table and laying two places. She was just mashing the tea when Mabel returned breathless but triumphant. 'We've got extra portions because they were closing up,' she said, placing the newspaper package in the oven.

'By heck, you were quick. I've not had chance to cut that loaf yet. If there's chips and fish left over, I'll drop them off at Ada's, her lot will make short shrift of them.'

'It was nice to stretch my legs, it gets monotonous aboard ship, walking round the decks,' she said, removing her hat and coat and hanging them on a hook behind the door. 'When we've eaten these, I'll pack as many of Annie's clothes as I can carry and come back down with you to St Silas church. I'm sure they'll know someone grateful for them. You can have first pick if you like. They're top quality. I just can't bring myself to wear anything of hers!'

'I know someone who's in great need of Annie's clothes, even down to the underwear. I should have told you sooner, I've been meaning to, but we've not had the chance out of earshot of me kids. It's Ada and Bert, they're in big trouble with money. I couldn't reckon it at first. Bert's a steady bloke and he's on the same wages as Daniel. It turns out it's on account of all this union stuff he's spouting. First opportunity and the boss's put him on a three-day week. Oh, I know firms all over the city are putting blokes on a three-day week, but so far, their firm's been seeing it's way. Bert's shot himself in the foot alright, none of the blokes will support him at his union meetings, not from that factory at any rate, for fear of the same. And they say money isn't everything,' she sighed. 'Them as believe that, should try managing with what we have to live on.'

'We're coming into winter,' Mabel said, 'Annie had plenty of white flannel and cotton nighties. They can be cut down and made into baby gowns, and petticoats for the girls, maybe a few pairs of knickers. There are several good grey wool skirts that would make trousers for the boys and maybe a couple of gym slips for Daisy. Do you think it would be alright for me to call round with them? I'll explain to Bert he's doing me a favour taking the clothes off my hands. Maybe it won't seem too much like accepting charity then.'

'Ada will be grateful, but I don't know when she'll be up to sewing clothes. Me and me sisters can give her a hand though.'

'That would be grand. I just don't know how much time I've got for sewing or I'd lend a hand as well. I need to go over the books, I'm in a bit of a financial crisis myself.'

'Sorry love, I was forgetting. We're a long way from that carefree time when we boarded the train to Liverpool on our way to the Isle of Man.'

'Not so very far away, not really, we've just gathered a lot of responsibility along the way,' Mabel said, with more confidence than she felt. She was worried about Bert and Ada. Feeding and housing a family of seven, on a works wage was difficult enough, on a three-day week it was nearly impossible. She hoped they weren't on a slippery slope to the workhouse.

'Right,' she said, after they'd eaten, 'let's make a start, there aren't many hours of daylight this time of year and there's only one gas mantle in each bedroom. We've a lot of clothes to sort through and I'd like to get my bed made up before dark. What time do you have to be back? Daniel's a good fellow, getting his own meal and seeing to his children.'

'Aye, well, we fit together right enough me and Daniel, and all he's got to do is put some stew on a plate. That's not hard, is it?'

'I know of men who won't put sugar in their own tea!'

'You're right there, him next door to me doesn't know how many sugars he takes!'

Bert whistled softly as he made his way back down the allotment path. Charlotte wouldn't give him a contact address. She told him she was at the allotment most of the time. That would have to do. His whistling stopped abruptly as he approached the plot where the grumpy sod had threatened to report him for selling manure. In the gloaming, he could just make out the shape of apples and pears dotted among the fruit trees. He stood and listened. An owl hooted in the distance, the screech of a fox nearby startled him, then all was quiet. Only the glow from the lamp in Charlotte's hut was visible and he wondered anew whether she lived there. Shaking the idea from his thoughts, he focused his brain. He circumnavigated the man's allotment searching for a weak spot, a point of entry. He found a place where fir trees shaped into a hedge had outgrown their strength, the spindly trunks had been reinforced with barbed wire. Keeping to the shadows, Bert made his way into the adjoining wood and came back with a sturdy branch. Removing his cap, shirt and jacket, he bundled them together and threw them over the hedge. Using the branch he lifted the barbed wire and wedged it up while he wriggled under, then he pulled the branch in after him in case anyone happened to be passing. Once inside he stopped and listened, all was quiet. Now he was closer, he realised that it was the fruit on the higher branches that hadn't been picked, he needed something to stand on. He found a barrel and climbed onto it, then tied his shirt sleeves to the trunk using his shirt like a net to catch the falling fruit. He studied the connecting branches to work out which ones to shake to create a domino effect. In no time at all, he had a substantial harvest of fruit and vegetables and he'd been careful to ensure that what vegetables he'd picked wouldn't be missed. Then he smoothed the ground to cover his tracks, scattering a few apples and pears beneath the trees as though they'd fallen from the branches. With his hoard bundled safely in his shirt he repeated the process with the branch and barbed wire to make his escape. He spread fallen leaves over his exit point then stealthily made his way deep into the woods to get dressed and conceal the stash about his person.

It wasn't until he was half way home that he remembered he was supposed to be fighting at Skye Edge. He looked up at the Co-op clock tower and heaved a sigh of relief. He'd have just enough time to drop off his pickings and jump on a tram. It would only take him part way, but he reckoned he could thumb a lift from a passing car if Sammy was to be believed and the big brass were attending.

Sammy's prophecy was correct. By the time Bert arrived, a circle of expensive cars had already formed, illuminating an arena. The crowd was too large for the lock-up so a makeshift boxing ring of straw bales had been erected at the centre of the circle of cars. He could see in the headlights that the bookies' pockets were bulging and most shuffled a pack of white fivers in their fists. He stripped down to his combinations exposing powerful muscles as he removed his arms from the sleeves and tied them around his waist. His rippling torso earned admiring glances from the spangled and fur clad women clinging nervously to their dinner-suited toffs. He noticed diamonds winking at the throat of one woman and bracelets worn over long gloves. He doubted they'd be there at the end of the night, not with a gang of pickpockets lurking in the shadows.

He was down to fight last, a ploy by the organisers to cash in on his reputation and keep the large crowd gathered until the bitter end. As well as making money from bets, there was a brisk trade in alcohol.

From what Bert had seen of the competitors, there'd been nobody he couldn't handle. So he pledged the full ten pounds he'd been promised for fighting, on himself to win. Now he surveyed the edges of the ring, getting a feel for the crowd. The pickpockets were still lurking but keeping to the shadows. Then his eyes settled on a figure wearing a Crombie coat with beaver lamb fur collar, and his stomach contracted. Standing beside him in a prominent position at the front of the ring, were members of one of the most feared gangs in Sheffield. He should have known they wouldn't have let something as big as this happen without their say.

Then he was called to fight and his heart skipped a beat as he entered the ring and a figure stepped from between the parked cars to stand silhouetted against the headlights. The man's head and shoulders were the size of the oxen that pulled the wagon advertising Atora beef suet. As Bert looked on, his opponent raised hands the size of plates into the air and the crowd roared. This must be how David felt when faced with Goliath, he thought. Just then, encouraged by the crowd, the man lumbered around the makeshift arena, and like David, Bert discovered the man's weak spot.

The bell rang and Bert held his ground as the Goliath like man lumbered towards him and smashed his fist towards his head. At the last second Bert dodged out of the way sending him off balance, then struck an upper cut to his bristly chin before the man knew what had hit him. As though skipping with a rope, Bert hopped from foot to foot around and behind his opponent, who swung his arms wildly, aiming for Bert's ear. But Bert ducked and the man staggered forward into Bert's fist. Blood spurted from his nose and the crowd went wild. Before he could straighten up, Bert struck three jabs in quick succession into his solar plexus and then dodged out of the way as a plate-sized fist crashed down, narrowly missing his head. Gasping for breath and half blinded by watery eyes, the man swung his fists in a wild frenzy, but Bert ducked and weaved then skipped behind and struck the side of his head. Before he had time to regain his balance, Bert had dodged round behind again and struck a blow to his jaw knocking him sideways. After struggling to regain his balance, he turned and charged at Bert, using his head like a battering ram. But Bert side stepped him and stuck out his foot sending him skidding along the gravel on his chin. Bert had had enough, he waited for him to stagger to his feet and as he raised his great fist, Bert flexed his arm as quick as a piston and smashed his fist into the giant face. For a moment the man stood rock solid, his eyes wide with shock, then suddenly like a felled tree he crashed backwards flat out along the ground. The crowd erupted cheering and whistling. Bert pushed through them and grabbing his clothes made his way over to Sammy. 'I want me money. Now!'

'Go and see him over there, he's got your takings,' he pointed to a small ferrety-looking man wearing a tweed jacket over a yellow waistcoat.

'You put on a good show tonight,' the man said, counting out a wad of notes and curling them into a roll before handing them over. 'I'll look forward to your next fight.'

'There won't be a next fight for me.'

'You don't say? I wouldn't be so sure about that, lad.'

Bert followed his gaze while struggling into his clothes and keeping a tight hold of the money roll in his fist. The man wearing the Crombie coat turned in their direction and lifted his hat. Bert's heart sank, every time he climbed out of one tight hole he went and fell into another. He wondered if that was who Sammy's associate was, not some henchmen in a camel coat, and then he suddenly knew that whoever was calling the shots, they wouldn't let him slip through their oily fingers now that he'd proved himself a money maker. What's more, he'd laid open his tactics to the opposition. Next time they'd make sure they didn't send a lumbering dozy bugger to fight him. There'd not been as much trouble as he'd expected between the gangs tonight, but he knew it couldn't last. Dear God, it was a miracle Ada had ever forgiven him for getting his wages docked and almost driving them into the workhouse. She'd never forgive him for going back into fighting, let alone getting embroiled in a gang war.

Chapter Six

Bert woke to the sound of church bells calling worshippers to prayer. The last time he'd been in church was to wed Ada. He'd lost his belief in God on the battle fields of the Somme. His brain jumped from Ada to Charlotte and his stomach gave a guilty lurch.

Getting out of bed he dressed quickly. Then took some of the fruit and vegetables he'd snaffled from the man's allotment across to Mrs Smith's corner shop. He knocked on the back door as it was Sunday.

It was Mr Smith who answered the door. 'Morning son. Come through to the living room, the kettle's on. We heard about Ada. How's she doing?'

'She's holding her own for now, but not great. They delivered the babby by caesarean. I'm going up to see her at visiting time this afternoon. Look I'll be straight with you, I only called in because I've managed to get hold of this fresh produce and wondered if I could swap it for some eggs and soap to take to the hospital for Ada.'

'Aye, son, put your box down over there, I'll have a look what you've got. Help yourself to a brew, Missis has gone to church. By heck, you've some grand stuff in here, I reckon I can do you better than six eggs and a bar of soap.'

Bert left with a dozen eggs, a pint of milk, a loaf and some dripping and a small bar of scented soap. Back home, he stripped off and had a good scrub down with carbolic. The scented soap was for Ada.

At the appointed time, Bert stood in the queue of visitors at the Jessop Hospital for Women. In his arms, he held a large brown paper bag containing half a dozen eggs, fresh fruit and vegetables and a large bunch of flowers. The scented soap nestled in his pocket. He'd taken the flowers from the cemetery. He didn't normally hold with stealing, but desperate times called for desperate measures and he'd seen enough dead men on the battle fields to know they'd no use at all for flowers. The apples and pears that he'd taken from the allotment would have rotted, most probably, if he hadn't picked them. By his reckoning, they'd have been picked by now if the miserable old bugger they belonged to had wanted them.

The Matron in charge was waiting for him as he stepped onto the ward. Her eyes widened when she saw the food parcel and flowers, but protocol prevented a comment. Bert decided that the combination of his best suit and the expensive gifts, must have impressed her, for her shoulders seemed to relax, causing her pompous bosom to sag a little. 'Mr Brown,' she said, drawing him to one side. 'I'm sorry to inform you that you will be unable to visit your wife today. She is still too poorly. She is not currently on the dangerously ill list, but the haemorrhaging has begun again. She will be taken to the operating theatre as soon as another surgeon can be located, it being a Sunday. You can of course be permitted to see your son.'

'I want to see me wife. I won't disturb her, but so long as she knows I'm 'ere it'll give her strength.'

'Mr Brown, we have our rules,'

'Bugger your rules, I've seen it in me men during t'war, a bit of comfort from a friend or loved one brings 'em on champion.'

'Mind your language, Mr Brown. I must insist you leave.'

'What about seeing me son?'

'I'm afraid you forfeited that right when you uttered foul language.' She turned on her heels and walked down the ward.

He was rooted to the spot. His legs wouldn't work. What would he do if he lost Ada? He strained his neck to look down the ward, trying to see which bed she was in, but there were visitors in the way.

'Do not turn around until I've finished speaking, Mr Brown.' The soft female voice speaking into his left shoulder startled him out of his stupor. 'Your wife is in a room along the corridor to the left of the entrance. In a few moments, slowly turn around and make your way there. Matron mustn't suspect I've spoken to you, or I'll lose my job. Give me time to get away from this ward and I'll meet you there.'

Bert was surprised to be met by a young woman wearing a smock coat over a skirt and blouse, a stethoscope dangling from her neck. He had expected to be met by a nurse.

'My name is Florence Cousins, and yes, before you ask, I was named after Miss Nightingale. I'm from a family of medics.'

That out of the way, she thrust forward her hand. 'I'm Junior House Surgeon here at the Jessop. Don't look so surprised Mr Brown, we are a growing breed.'

'I'm only shocked because you're the second female surgeon I've met in as many days.'

'Really, who was the other?'

'Charlotte, her name's Charlotte, but I don't know her surname.'

'It could be Connor. There was a Charlotte Connor who was highly acclaimed for her work on the front in France during the war, although she never received any official recognition for her skill and bravery. Did she mention where else she's worked?'

Bert wasn't listening, all his focus was on Ada, lying motionless in bed, her face whiter than the starched sheets. He lifted her hand from beneath the covers, it was ice cold. He rubbed it vigorously between his own large hands. 'Now don't you worry, Ada love. They'll have you right as rain in no time. Ethel's got our kids, so you've no worries on that score. You just concentrate on getting better. I've got you fresh eggs and a nice bit of fruit and veg to keep your strength up.' Her mouth looked dry and cracked, her lips parted and closed again as though they couldn't form the words. He pulled out a fresh clean handkerchief and dipped it in the water jug beside the bed to wet her lips. Then he kissed them softly, willing life back into her.

Florence Cousins placed a firm hand on his shoulder. 'Mr Brown, I'm sorry I daren't let you stay any longer, may I have a word before you go? I'll walk you to the door.'

This time he didn't protest. All he'd wanted was to spend a few moments with Ada, to see for himself her lovely face and hopefully give her strength to cling to life. He gently tucked her hand back under the covers and kissed her brow. 'I love thee lass, never forget it. I've never loved another the same.' Then he straightened up and made his way out.

Florence followed him and kept on walking, indicating that he should follow. She came to a stop outside, beneath the hospital windows. 'I'm trusting that what you hear from me will not be repeated under any circumstance. I'm breaking enough rules to get struck off, but I feel compelled to tell you that if Mrs Brown isn't operated on in the next few hours, her chances of survival are very slim. There's only one surgeon covering for emergencies and he's already in theatre. We've tried to contact another, but like Matron said, it's Sunday. I don't hold out much hope of him being located. You need to prepare yourself for the worst.'

'I thought you said you were a surgeon?'

'Junior House Surgeon, Mr Brown. I don't have the authority to carry out such a risky operation without supervision.'

Anger seared through him. 'They'd have made sure they located a surgeon for one o' them toffs.' Icy fingers gripped his heart, he was shivering from head to toe. Dear God, he couldn't lose Ada. His thoughts turned to Charlotte, she was a surgeon, surely, she could think of summat.

'Thanks for your help,' he said, doffing his cap. Then he was off, running at full tilt downhill to Ecclesall Road. He jumped on the back of a tram as it was pulling away, leaping off again even before it had come to a standstill, much to the conductor's chagrin. His hobnailed boots clattered against the stones as he ran up the allotment path. Charlotte must have heard the commotion for she'd flung open the gate and was waiting for him. He managed to gasp out what he'd come for before his legs gave way and he crumpled to the ground.

'Bert, I think I can help. Here drink this,' she said, handing him a glass of water before disappearing into the shed. She came out wearing her hat and coat. 'Take this letter to the Royal hospital and ask for Mr Connor, give it to him personally. Then come and meet me outside the Jessop.'

He staggered to his feet and grabbed the letter, flipped his cap over his curly hair and made to dash off. Charlotte touched his arm. 'Bert, do you want more children?'

He looked at her wide eyed for a moment. 'I love them as I've got, but it would be a relief not to have another, especially for Ada, she allus 'as a bad time of it, but this is the worst.'

Bert arrived at the Jessop just as Ada was being lifted by stretcher into a trailer ambulance attached to a large touring car. He was astounded to see at the wheel a stout middle-aged woman wearing a buff coloured driving coat and a large hat with a veil attached.

Charlotte stuck her head out of the ambulance as he came to a breathless stop, cap in hand. 'Hello, Mr Brown. You need to go in and collect your wife's belongings and the food parcel.'

He looked at the Matron standing with her arms folded across her bosom, her thin lips tightly clamped together, her beady eyes intent on overseeing Ada's transition into the ambulance.

'Never mind her belongings,' he said. 'Where's me son?'

'Already in the ambulance. Now, Mr Brown, please hurry up.'

He brushed past the matron and went inside. When he returned, the engine was already ticking over and Charlotte was waiting anxiously. 'If you could get in the back and hold Mrs Brown tightly to keep her as still as possible during the journey, we'll be on our way.'

Bert held Ada down against the stretcher, mindful of the drips simultaneously feeding liquid and blood into her. 'What's this stuff you're pumping into her?' he nodded at the clear liquid.

'It's a solution to replace what her body's lost. I've already given her an injection of 0.5mg of Ergotamine, which I'm hoping will slow the blood flow until I can operate.'

He was quiet for a while, concentrating on protecting Ada from jolts as the car swerved to avoid a series of potholes. 'Who's the woman driving?' he asked.

'Mary Jones, my housekeeper. She is also one of the best nurses I know. We worked together during the war. Her family were killed in one of the Zeppelin raids and as I'd been told my husband Edwin was missing presumed dead, we sort of stuck together. It has worked out well, as you will see.'

This trailer ambulance is a handy set up, where did you get it?'

'I have my contacts.'

The journey took them along Clarkehouse Road and down behind Endcliffe park. Bert blinked when he jumped out from the ambulance and saw the size of the houses.

'Mr Brown, do you think you could manage to carry Mrs Brown up the steps? It will be safer than trying to get the stretcher up. Mary can carry the drips. I will take your son. Give me a moment to open the door. Mr Connor should be along any time now, hopefully.'

Bert carried Ada into a room where the wooden floor was polished to a high sheen and the walls painted white. What appeared to be an operating table stood at the centre. Charlotte drew his attention to a doctor's couch pushed against one wall. Mary spread a white starched sheet over it before he put Ada down. Then she wheeled the instrument trolley over to the operating table and put a pristine cloth over it. Bert watched, mesmerised, as she took matches and spills from a desk in the corner to light the gas fire. It gave a resounding pop and spluttered into life. Then she filled the sterilizing unit with water and ignited the gas under it. Charlotte gathered her instruments together and placed them in the water.

The instruments were bubbling nicely in the scalding water and Charlotte was preparing Ada on the operating table when the front door knocker rapped loudly. 'That will be Mr Connor, let him in, will you?'

Bert opened the door on a pleasant looking man, his grey eyes the image of Charlotte's. 'Here, take this, there's a good chap,' Mr Connor said. 'I've to bring in another two yet.' Bert caught the tall cylinder as it was thrust into his arms, he staggered back slightly under the unexpected weight.

Charlotte looked up from setting out the sterilised instruments as Bert carried the cylinder into the room. 'Ada has signed the discharge papers from the hospital,' she said, 'but she hasn't signed the consent form for the operation. I'm not being modest when I say I'm a damned good surgeon with a lot of experience behind me, and Jim, my brother,' she nodded to Mr Connor, 'is the best anaesthetist I know, but Ada is dangerously ill. You need to know there's less than a fifty-fifty chance she'll survive. I need a signature, but I don't want to wake her.'

'Give us the paper,' Bert said, reaching for it. 'She's not well schooled, she were kept off a lot being the eldest of nine. Her signature's a scrawl. I'll do it on her behalf, else without you, what chance does she have?' He scrawled the signature and handed back the consent form. 'I need to tell you summat,' he whispered, holding his gaze steady. 'I love Ada more than life itself.'

Charlotte lowered her eyelids in acknowledgement, a sweet smile on her lips. When she looked up there was no malice in her grey eyes, only understanding. If Jim Connor or Mary, noticed the look that passed between them, neither made comment.

'I think it might be best if you wait outside,' Jim said, taking his arm,

'No!' Bert shrugged him off. 'I've seen enough blood and guts spilled out during the war not to be squeamish.'

'It's different when it's someone you love,' Charlotte spoke softly.

'I'm staying. Ada needs me.'

'Then you had better put on these,' Mary said, handing him a mask, cap and gown, 'and scrub your hands and arms at the sink, make sure you use the nail brush and plenty of carbolic. Rub your hands and arms with Lysol, we don't want her contracting puerperal fever.'

Chapter Seven - Liverpool 1925

Mabel's telegram was delivered to Sydney as he was about to leave his parents' house.

Unforeseen circumstances = stop = Remaining Sheffield indefinitely =stop= Please forward luggage =stop=Love Mabel = stop

The telegram boy hovered on the doorstep while Sydney read the contents.

'Will you be sending a reply, Sir?' he asked, whipping out his notepad and pencil.

'Yes. Please write down the following message. *Hurry back when you can my darling. I miss you. All my love Sydney.*'

The boy read the message back to confirm he'd written it down correctly.

'That will do very nicely thank you,' Sydney said, and pressed two half-crowns into the lad's hand to pay for the telegram and a generous tip.

'Thank you very much, Sir,' he said, doffing his cap. He glanced back in wonder as he peddled away, what was a toff doing in these parts?

Sydney set off for Lime Street station with a smug feeling of self-satisfaction. Events couldn't have gone better had he orchestrated them. Mabel was safely out of the way over in Sheffield. Dclores was touring Scotland for the winter season in a revue and then going over to the Isle of Man. She wouldn't be likely to drop in on him unannounced. He was relieved to see the back of her, for a while. She was becoming too demanding. Too assuming of her claim on him.

The train was thirty minutes late. Sydney's cool persona belied his inner turmoil as he strolled up and down the platform. If the train didn't arrive in the next ten minutes, he'd have to walk over to the General Post Office and place a telephone call to the theatre. Archie would have to take band call. He checked the time on the big clock suspended from a wrought iron bracket over the platform against his gold pocket watch. They synchronised. He'd been hoping the station clock was fast. If the get-in at the theatre didn't go smoothly, he might just make band call. Still, better to give Archie the nod, it wouldn't be the first time he'd covered for him in similar circumstances.

    Sydney flicked smuts of soot from his jacket, blowing them from his white shirt cuffs to avoid smudging them in. Thank God, he hadn't worn his linen suit. It would have been speckled by now. It had crossed his mind to wear it, because it was Lotti's favourite, but he'd decided the colour and weight of cloth was too light for the time of year in the north of England. He looked to the horizon. Clouds of steam heralded the train's imminent arrival. Excitement churned his stomach. He hadn't seen Lotti for weeks, not since her dance troupe had left the ship. The train rumbled into the station stopping in a hiss of steam. Lotti was waving frantically, half hanging out of the carriage window. A guard opened the door, and her long legs stepped one after the other onto the platform. A moment of pure lust gripped him as memories of those legs snaking around his hips rendered him motionless. Good job Mabel was out of the way for the time being. His eyes travelled up the length of Lotti's legs, over her slim hips and pert breasts to her cupid's bow lips. Platinum blonde curls framed her face. She had been brunette the last time he'd seen her.

Lotti dropped her luggage, scattering hat boxes all over the platform as she ran straight into his arms. Ignoring propriety, he kissed her deeply on the mouth. When he lifted his head, he noticed a young woman, watching from a distance, he caught a flash of her glorious auburn curls before she replaced her hat and snuffed them out. She was almost the same height as himself and her green eyes studied him curiously.

Lotti turned to see what had caught his attention. 'That's Gracie,' she said, leaving his arms to run and take Gracie's hand and drag her over to where he stood rooted to the spot. 'She's the new soubrette, and the sweetest girl I know.'

So this was the girl the agency had replaced Delores with.

'How do you do?' Gracie said, reaching out to shake his hand. Sydney took it and brought it to his lips. For the first time in his life, he was lost for words.

Lotti linked her arm through his and chattered merrily all the way to the theatre. He didn't register a word, so great was the effect Gracie was having upon him. He'd never experienced anything like it. His heart was thudding, and his brain had emptied, leaving him with the wits of a gauche youth.

'You alright Syd?' Lotti said, stopping to look up at him when they reached the stage door.

'Yes of course, I do not like being late, that is all.' He turned the handle and held open the door, Gracie walked through, and her perfume set his senses reeling as she brushed past.

'See you for tea after band call,' Lotti said, stretching up to kiss his cheek. He didn't feel a thing.

The musicians were tuning up in the orchestra pit, only Archie remained in the band room. He looked up as Sydney walked in. 'Hell's bells, man. You look like you've seen a ghost.'

'Got any whisky?'

Archie handed over a silver flask from his inside pocket and watched Sydney take two swigs one after the other. He couldn't recall a time when he'd ever seen him drink before working, let alone strong spirits.

'Are you coming?' Sydney growled, handing back the flask before he disappeared through the hatch into the orchestra pit.

The chorus girls high-kicked their way across the stage, but Sydney was too engrossed in the unfamiliar band parts to notice Lotti's long legs flashing up and down in front of him. His breathing steadied as he concentrated on each act's music, until Gracie's entrance. He'd been totally unprepared for the husky sensual tone of her voice floating across the stage and down into the orchestra pit. It was the same flowing, languid sensation he'd felt when her long limbs had sauntered towards him across the station platform, unhurried, as though time were her slave. He lifted his head to look at her, he couldn't tear his gaze away. Her red hair, caught in the spotlight, blazed under its glare, her green eyes sparkled. Then the spotlight shifted to illuminate a trumpet soloist, leaving a black stage. The contrast was spine tingling. On cue, Gracie picked up the vocals as the spotlight picked her out of the darkness. When the melody and Gracie's husky tones faded away, thunderous applause erupted from the stalls. The front of house staff, busy preparing the theatre for the evening's performance, had stopped working to listen. An unusual event, since they were used to a continuous weekly change in programme of all the top stars and therefore not easily impressed.

Sheer willpower kept Sydney on track when all he wanted to do was stop and stare at the goddess standing centre stage. Somehow, he conducted the orchestra to play her exit music and introduction for the next act.

When band call was over, he was the first to leave the orchestra pit. He left a message for Lotti with the stage door keeper on his way out, saying he'd been called away on urgent business. He couldn't face tea with her, he was sure she would bring Gracie. For the first time in his life he felt incapable of disguising his duplicity. Playing one female against another under their noses was his speciality and key to his success in seducing several of the chorus girls at any one time. His charm was such, that he had the pick of girls caught in his web of deceit. Of Gracie, he was unsure.

The opening night was a success. The rest of the week was already a sell-out. After the show, the cast gathered in the bar of the Adelphi Hotel, where Sydney had booked a suite and cut a deal with the management to get a significantly reduced rate for the rest of the cast. Lotti was to share a room with Gracie for propriety's sake but intended spending the week with Sydney. Archie found his way to the piano in the corner of the bar and instigated a sing song.

'I'm tired. I need a long soak in a hot bath,' Lotti said, yawning and stretching her arms above her head in an exaggerated gesture, announcing unintentionally to the gathering, her true meaning.

Sydney escorted her to the lift. Pressing his room key into her hand, he said, 'I'll be up in a moment, I need a word with Archie.' Then taking her into his arms he kissed her passionately, just long enough to leave her smouldering with anticipation.

'Don't be long lover boy,' she pouted, stepping into the lift. He touched his forelock as the doors closed and then turned on his heels and headed straight back to the lounge bar in search of Gracie. She was sitting on a sofa, set apart from the crowd around the piano, creating again that illusion of the world standing still at her bidding. Even the smoke from her cigarette hovered above, as though frozen in time.

'I need to eat,' he said, 'I know a club near here where they serve food late. Would you care to join me? Lotti has refused me, she prefers to take her bath.'

Gracie studied his face for several moments before stubbing out her cigarette and standing up. 'Yes, I'm hungry, I'll come with you.'

Outside the hotel, Sydney hailed a taxi to take them across town. It was a private club, accessible to a select few. The maître d' greeted them warmly. Your usual table Mr Sydney?' he said, signalling to a waiter. They were directed to a secluded booth set back from the dance floor. Sydney studied the menu. 'What would you like to eat?'

'You choose for me,' she said, sipping the champagne which the waiter had already brought to the table.

He ordered guinea fowl, followed by strawberries and cream, hoping that strawberries out of season would impress her. He hadn't failed to notice her impeccable manners, she was no working-class girl with elocution trained vowels. Gracie was perfectly at ease in this high-class establishment.

He ordered brandy with his coffee, she declined, but accepted one of his cigarettes. Flicking open his lighter he reached across the table. 'Why did you settle for soubrette? You deserve a billing. Where have you worked before?'

'Here and there,' she said, lazily exhaling a cloud of smoke.

'You're from London, yes? Have you ever worked the West End?'

'Near enough, but nowhere you would know.'

'It might surprise you to discover that I know most of the theatres and clubs in and around the city.'

She stubbed out her cigarette, keeping her eyes downcast. 'Lotti will have finished her bath by now. Don't you think we should make our way back?'

It was gone midnight when they returned to the hotel. The rest of the revue's cast had gone to bed, the lounge bar was in darkness.

'Thank you for supper,' Gracie said, ringing for the lift. 'It was very kind of you to ask me.'

He watched her get in and waited until the lift doors had closed, then he went outside for a last cigarette. Gracie was an enigma. The first woman he'd met who seemed oblivious to his charm. Her sophistication was obvious. Of course, Mabel was sophisticated, in as much as she'd had a middle-class upbringing, though hers was an unworldly sophistication. Gracie on the other hand, with her languid persona and Madonna smile, gave him the uneasy feeling that she was playing him for the fool.

Lotti was asleep when he let himself into the suite. He shaved and ran a shallow bath, adding drops of cologne before slipping into bed beside her. He moulded his body to hers, sliding his hand over her belly and cupping her breast. His need was obvious, but his excitement was for Gracie and it had caused him great discomfort throughout supper. Lotti stirred and turned within the circle of his arms. She kissed him deeply, her passion rising to match his. Pushing him onto his back, she trailed her lips across his smooth flesh, over his chest and down his torso obliterating all thoughts of Gracie.

Chapter Eight – Sheffield 1925

Charlotte sat beside the fire contentedly nursing the newest addition to the Brown family. The baby made tiny mewing sounds, nuzzling for something to latch on to. She placed the bottle teat between his rosebud lips and he sucked fiercely. 'Ada might have had trouble feeding this one anyway,' she smiled up at Bert, 'he's a chomper.'

Bert frowned, as one problem was solved another raised its head. He didn't know how he was going to afford the expense of bottle feeding. He'd probably have to go cap in hand to one of them powdered milk depots. Still, little Charlie had fought for his life in being born. The least he could do, now that he was here, was get him some decent grub.

He peered anxiously at Ada lying in the iron bedstead. 'Shouldn't she be coming round by now?'

'No, she's going to be fine, and rest is the best cure. You should know that. And you should be getting some rest yourself.'

'Aye, and so should you, you've performed a miracle here today.'

'I haven't parted with more than a pint of my blood,' Charlotte reminded him. 'Ada's lucky you're both a common blood type. I shouldn't normally have taken so much from you, but she needed it, and now your body needs to produce some more. It can only do that if you rest. Go and get your head down in one of the upstairs rooms. I'll call you when she wakes.'

Bert found a small, functionally furnished room at the back of the house. He sat on the edge of the bed to remove his boots, then he loosened his tie and fell back exhausted onto the pillow. When Charlotte had opened Ada up, there had been so much blood, he couldn't imagine how she would find what she was looking for. But with Mary's assistance she'd worked swiftly and methodically, and before long Ada was minus her uterus, the bleeding had stopped, and she'd been stitched up. Charlotte had told him she'd left Ada her ovaries, he didn't know what good they were to her now, but apparently, they were, and Ada would understand. Charlotte would explain everything to her when she came round. He tried to sleep, but he couldn't shake the images from his mind. The frosty Matron, the kind Junior House Surgeon and the miracle Charlotte had performed. He turned his face into the pillow to stifle his sobs and cried like he'd never done before. Ada was going to live, he thanked God for that, perhaps there was one after all.

'Mr Brown wake up,'

His lids felt heavy but at last his lashes fluttered and he opened his eyes.

Mary hovered anxiously beside the bed. 'I've brought you a cup of hot sweet tea and a couple of slices of toast and jam. Ada's awake and asking for you.'

He jumped up ready to go to her, but the sudden movement had his head spinning and he fell back onto the bed.

'Take it steady, it's the blood loss. Drink your tea and eat that toast. You don't want to frighten her by passing out, now do you?'

Downstairs, Bert took hold of Ada's hand and kissed it. 'By, that feels a bit warmer, lass. You were half frozen in that bloody hospital. When I saw you lying there, I thought you were done for. You would've been an' all, if it weren't for that Junior House Surgeon and especially Charlotte here.'

A tear trickled from the corner of Ada's eye as she turned her head to nod her gratitude. 'What about me kids, Bert? Are they alright?'

'Aye, they're champion. I told you, Ethel's got 'em.'

'How will we pay for it all? There's money for the doctor to find and you've stopped paying your penny in the pound contribution to the hospital.'

'I don't think it makes any difference to the hospital if one bloke can't pay his due, they're a voluntary set up. As for the doctor, Mabel's offered to pay any medical expenses. I'll work at the factory for her 'til it's paid off.'

'That might be a life sentence,' Ada managed a watery smile, 'and what do we owe Charlotte?'

'Don't worry about paying me, it was my pleasure to save a life, but if it makes you feel better, Bert could help me at the allotment,' Charlotte said, giving him a knowing look.

Anger distorted his face, how dare she be suggestive in front of Ada, even if she had just saved her life? But mixed with his anger was lust, and he turned the anger in on himself. 'Aye I'll do that, no problem. Though it'll be a bit parky this time of year.'

Charlotte laughed, acknowledging his double meaning. 'Time for another sip of water,' she said, lifting

Ada's head and holding the spout of the invalid cup to her lips. 'Only a sip, or you'll be sick and that will pull on your stitches.' Then she checked Ada's pulse before plumping the pillows and straightening the sheets. When she'd finished the simple procedures, Ada had tired, and was fast asleep again.

'What exactly is this place?' Bert asked. 'I mean you're all set up to do operations and the like. I know you told me you were a surgeon, but I expected you to work at a hospital or summat.'

'This is my home, and from my home, I help people like Ada.'

'You mean them as can't pay their way.'

'I mean women whose life is in danger because they can't afford, or can't be afforded, the treatment they need. I'm a socialist, Bert, and so was Edwin, my husband. It was our dream when we bought this house to run a discreet clinic to help women.'

She fixed his gaze. 'With your union beliefs on fair wages and working conditions for the working class, we are fighting the same cause, are we not? I can tell that you're an intelligent fair-minded man. You've already worked out that it's Ada who's taken the brunt for your actions. Therefore, you must realise that it's nearly always the women of the working-class who get the raw deal. Their bodies wrecked by multiple pregnancies, keeping the house going on a pittance and looking after their children, as well as working, taking in washing or going out cleaning. Some beaten within an inch of their life, for all their effort, when their man returns from drowning his sorrows along with his wages in a public house. I know men work hard, and that its customary even for a good man, to believe that his working day ends when he walks through the door to his house. When does a woman's day end?' Scarlet patches stained her cheeks. Her eyes, focused and determined, glittered under the bright electric light.

Aye, he thought, she has a fire in her belly, alright. The same fire as me, for social reform. She will make a powerful ally on the union front.

'You're already different from the rest, Bert,' she continued, disturbing his thoughts. 'Why did you bring your children with you that first day you came to the allotment?'

'So's Ada could have a rest.'

'That's precisely my point. In my experience, not many men would do that.'

Unsure how to react, he pressed her for a more detailed answer to his earlier question. 'Do you mean you help women here by giving them a caesarean and that?'

'Sometimes, but it's usually more of the and that.' She watched his face, waiting for her words to sink in. His eyes widened with shock as her meaning registered. She reached for his hand placing it between her own. 'Bert, I saved Ada's life tonight. Let's say, for example, her life on this occasion hadn't been in danger, but you knew another pregnancy would certainly be the death of her and yet you refused to let me sterilize her. What would you do if she became pregnant again? Would you be content to let that pregnancy go to full term and take the risk, hoping that she wouldn't die in labour? Don't you realise that it is safer and kinder for the women I treat and their families to remove all danger? And what of those mothers who do not have difficulty giving birth, but who are so malnourished through poverty, that they are unable to produce milk to feed their baby? The orphanages and workhouses are full of such casualties. We are on the same side you and I, Bert. We both want better conditions for humanity. You have no idea of the unscrupulous butchers out there, who desperate women turn too. Here, with me, they are safe in a hygienic clinical environment. I trust you will not expose me.'

He sat there rubbing his head as though the action would stimulate his brain. 'I'll not deny you've opened me eyes, and even shocked me. It's not summat I've ever given a thought to, until today. But no, I'll not expose you and I'll tell Ada to keep quiet an' all. I expect you won't want me to bring me kids here neither?'

'I think that would be best, although I feel sorry for them, I know they will be missing their mother.'

'Well it's thanks to you they still have their mam.' He put his hand over his mouth to stifle a yawn. 'What's to do now then, about Ada and the babby?'

'Ada will need to remain here for a least a week. The baby can stay here as well. Have you thought of a name for him?

'Well seeing as you saved his mam's life, I thought I'd call him Charlie. After you, like.'

She looked at the baby in his basket, a tuft of black hair was sticking up from the top of his head and a touch of wind had given him a lopsided grin. 'I think Charlie suits him perfectly,' she said. 'Now, is there anyone who can care for Ada and Charlie when they go home?'

'Well I'm on a three-day week, as you know, so maybe if we could time it so's I'm off when she first comes home, and then after that, Ethel and one of the neighbours might take it in turns. The problem is me other kids. They're too young to be on their own.'

'That's a big problem Bert, Ada won't be able to lift anything for a couple of months, especially the weight of a child. I'd offer, but I think it will cause talk amongst your neighbours.'

'Aye, you're not wrong there,' he said, stifling another yawn.

'Bert, you're all in. You need a good night's rest, get off home.'

He stood at the door, cap in hand and the food parcel tucked under his arm. 'I don't have the right words to thank you, but it was a lucky day for me family and me, the day we walked up that allotment path.'

'Here,' she said, reaching for some change from a dish on the hall stand, 'You're not fit enough to use public transport, best take a taxi. Look on it as a loan.'

All he could manage was a nod as he left the house and dropped down the steps to the road. She watched him run and catch the last tram as it pulled away from the stop. She had known he wouldn't waste precious money on the luxury of a taxi.

Bert hunched down in his seat pulling his cap low over his eyes. His head was swimming and he was short of breath. Perspiration pricked the surface of his skin, yet his back felt cold and clammy. His ears began to buzz, and darkness threatened to close in. He managed to remain conscious by one thought running through his brain. How the hell could he have rolled up in a taxi, when the whole street knew he was on short time and couldn't afford to feed his family?

He found a note on the mat when he let himself in and stooped to pick it up. The action set his head spinning again and he staggered back against the door to read it.

Same time next Saturday, you've made an admirer in high places, best for you if you show up. S

Chapter Nine

The factory appeared to be deserted. This early in the morning Mabel had expected to hear the dray horse whinnying and stamping his gigantic hooves, anxious to be getting on with his day. The stable was empty. Swept clean and stripped of its wrought iron manger and fixing rings.

She looked across to the main building, it was shrouded in silence. The windows shut tight. Icy fingers clutched her heart. In her day, the windows would have been wide open allowing the vapours of vinegar and onions to escape along with the putrid smell of piccalilli cooking. She would have heard laughter, the good-humoured banter of the workers as they chopped, pickled or boiled, onions, gherkins and cauliflower. Tom the drayman would have been whistling a merry tune as he loaded boxes crammed with jars of pickles onto the dray cart.

She crossed the yard and turned the doorknob. It twisted easily in her hand, but the door stuck. She hefted her shoulder against it, adding muscle to open the swollen door. Some things hadn't changed then.

Walking along the corridor she could hear the rhythmic sound of brush strokes growing louder with every step. At the main factory floor, she recognised the two women scrubbing out the large wooden vats and the solitary man – disassembling a gas boiler. The great wooden benches had been scrubbed white and the strength of carbolic caused her eyes to water. The three workers paused in their labours as she bid them good morning before walking up the wooden staircase to the office. The third step from the top creaked in a familiar way announcing her arrival.

'Miss Mabel!' the young woman working at the desk leaped up when she saw who was standing in the doorway.

'I'm afraid you have the advantage,' Mabel said, walking into the room.

'Gladys, Miss. Me name's Gladys. I'd just started work on the factory floor when you left. Eventually Miss Annie discovered I was good with figures and the like. It had come to her notice that I do me dad's book-keeping. He has the shop on the corner, see. Can I get you a cup of tea, Miss? You look like you could do with a strong one.'

'Gladys, I've been married for six years. Do you think you could call me Mrs Baxter? And yes please, I would love a cup of tea.'

'Yes, Miss. I mean Mrs Baxter. Do you take sugar? It might help. It must be a bit of a shock seeing the factory in this state,' she said, and scuttled off to make the tea.

Mabel removed her hat and coat and sat down in the chair which Gladys had vacated. She looked at the date in the ledger, Gladys had obviously been working on the most recent figures. She worked her way backwards, dismayed to see figures on each page documented in red ink.

Gladys returned carrying a tray. She set it down on the desk and poured them both a cup of strong, sweet tea before taking a seat on the opposite side from Mabel.

'I don't wish to speak ill of the dead, Mrs Baxter, but your sister-in-law had no head for business and no matter how good I am at book-keeping, I can't balance the books when there's more goes out than comes in.'

'I see things have been sliding for several years yet the reserve hasn't been touched.'

'Mr George had a clause written shortly after Mr Billy was wed. No one, but you, has the authority to touch the reserve. We only found out when Miss Annie tried to draw from it.'

Mabel brushed aside the wave of emotion which threatened to engulf her, love mingled with gratitude for her father's foresight. 'Just how bad are things Gladys?'

'Right bad, Mrs Baxter. The last of the stock's been sold and the suppliers won't deliver no more because we're so far in debt with each one of them. All the workers have gone except me and them three downstairs. We've had no wages for six months or more. At first, we hung on waiting for the solicitor to contact you. And then, when we never heard nothing, we decided to keep coming in until we found another job. We each have our own reasons for not wanting to be stuck at home, so we come in here every day like we always have. At least we've been getting things shipshape for your return. Do you have a plan Mrs. Baxter?'

'Not off the top of my head. I have some money saved, but I'll need to study the books. If it's as bad as you say, it could be just a drop in the ocean, even with the reserve. The solicitor painted me a very bleak picture, but he omitted to mention the reserve. I wonder why?'

'Mrs Baxter, may I have your permission to be frank, to speak out of turn, like? I feel it's important or I wouldn't be saying it. I'm not a tittle tattle, I can't abide gossips, but there's something I think you should know.'

Mabel nodded her assent,

'Well, it's like this. Things were bad enough before Miss Annie died, but if that solicitor had contacted you straight away, I know you would have turned things around. I don't understand how it could have taken him so long to have notified you, even if you were sailing the high seas. I think he delayed contacting you on purpose. I reckon he was waiting until the factory was run into the ground because he has designs on it for himself, or one of his friends. He's a member of one of them lodges. You know, where they do them funny handshakes.'

Mabel smirked. 'You mean he's a Mason. So were Mr George and Mr Billy. They do a lot of good works, Gladys, but I understand what you're saying. The solicitor didn't make much effort to find me. In the case of a death he could have contacted the ship or sent a telegram to any of the ports of call. Instead he posted a letter in a handwritten plain white envelope to my husband's family. There appeared to be no sense of urgency about it, or they would have forwarded it to me. I will look into the matter, but first I'd like to go through the books with you.'

At the end of a very long day, Mabel set off for the tram stop, too weary to walk the distance home. Her head was spinning with facts and figures. At lunchtime, she had brought in sandwiches and pork pies for everyone. It was the least she could do. Then she had gone to the bank and drawn on her untouched savings to reimburse the loyal workforce with the money they'd paid to keep the utility services connected and give them each a month's wages. Not much for six months' unpaid labour, but she hoped the gesture would buy their continued support. Each of them had been with the firm a long time and if anyone knew how to help her get the factory back on its feet, they would.

Light from the Co-op Arcade windows flooded the pavement and illuminated the baskets of flowers and streamers along the facade. The clock tower lit up in green and red, stood brilliant against the dark sky. As she paused to look at the spectacular window displays, the words co-operative kept ringing in her head. If her brain hadn't been so tired, she might have realised sooner what her subconscious was trying to tell her. It wasn't until she was sitting on the tram that inspiration struck. It hit her so forcibly she almost leaped from her seat. What if she formed a worker's co-operative? Lower wages, for a share in the profit when the factory was back on its feet. Would anyone want to take the risk? Could anyone afford to take the risk? Her only hope, in these times of growing unemployment, was if workers felt that some wages were better than none. Workers willing to take such a gamble would be more likely to pull their weight in getting the factory up and running.

She stood up to get off at the next stop, eager to share her thoughts with Ethel and Daniel, then sat down again. She had encroached enough on their family life for now. It would be best to write down her ideas first and work through the overheads. At her own stop, she left the tram with a spring in her step, her spirits lighter than they'd been in days. I didn't have a plan when Gladys asked me this morning, she thought, but I've got one now. I'm just not sure yet if that plan includes Sydney.

Chapter Ten – Liverpool 1925

Lotti dabbed the corner of her cupid's bow lips with a table napkin and put it down on the cloth, smearing both pieces of pristine linen with scarlet lipstick. The sight caused Sydney a stab of irritation. The thoughtless action would make unnecessary work for the waiter and laundry staff. He didn't quite know why it bothered him. Perhaps it was because he knew how hard his Chinese relatives worked at the laundries near his parents' home and all for a pittance of a wage. If he was honest with himself, he knew his irritation was more to do with Lotti bringing Gracie along to their lunch date. Although Gracie was no more beautiful than other women with whom he'd had affairs, she held a fascination for him that he couldn't control. She set his nerves jangling. Throughout lunch he'd suppressed an urge to reach out and touch her, to take her in his arms and kiss her plump lips until the breath left her. He watched her take out a cigarette from a silver case and he reached across to light it. She regarded him through the smoke haze with glittering emerald eyes as though she could read his thoughts, leaving him feeling vulnerable for the first time in his adult years. He caught a glimpse of her total disdain before Lotti spoke, breaking the tension.

    Unaware of his irritation Lotti gave him her most beguiling smile, fluttering the lashes of her big blue eyes. 'Can we go dancing tonight after the show, Syd? You can get us into that club of yours, can't you? You'll love it Gracie, ever so posh it is, and we always have champagne, don't we Syd?'

'You would be most welcome to join us, Gracie, but perhaps you have other plans this evening?'

'Nothing that can't be rearranged. I will look forward to it. Thank you for lunch, Sydney, it was most kind, but now I must leave you two alone.' She pushed back her chair and a waiter immediately rushed forward to hold it for her as another brought her coat. She thanked them and turned her attention back to Lotti. 'I have things to attend to. I'll see you at the theatre.'

Sydney felt the tension drain from him as he watched Gracie glide across the restaurant and smoothly navigate the revolving doors onto the street. Her choice in name had been a good one, everything about her was graceful. The magnetic attraction he felt for her was so strong, he was sure everyone around him must sense it. Lotti seemed oblivious to his enchantment, but then Gracie's magnetism held no bounds, it seemed to draw in everyone and everything around her, and he realised in that moment, that Lotti was enchanted by her too.

Lotti shimmied off to the Ladies room, to powder her nose. The sway of her hips, accentuated by the low waistline of her dress, caused a ripple of male heads turning to watch her progress.

Sydney's attention had been caught by two young chorus girls, new to the dance troupe, who were sitting at a table in the corner. He smiled, watching them deliberate over the menu, their discomfort offered him an easy route into casting a strand of enticement. One of them, a pretty brunette with a dusting of freckles on her nose, had caught his eye earlier in the week, she smiled up at him as he approached their table.

'Good afternoon,' he said, bestowing his most devastating smile upon them. 'Have you ordered yet?'

They looked up at him wide eyed, like rabbits caught in a headlight, dumbfounded to be speaking to such a revered impresario. Open mouthed, the young brunette managed to shake her head.

'In that case, I recommend the duck. Are you celebrating a special occasion?' he asked, knowing a dancer's wage wouldn't normally stretch to such an extravagant restaurant.

'Yes, it's Violet's birthday,' the brunette's companion managed to squeak. 'Her mum sent her some money, so she could enjoy herself.' Violet shot her an angry look.

'Am I allowed to ask a lady her age?'

Violet's expression immediately changed, she wrinkled her nose and giggled. 'I'm eighteen today.'

In that case, this calls for a special celebration,' he said, summoning the waiter. 'Please bring a bottle of wine to this table, something to accompany the duck.' He saw horror across the girls' faces as they looked from each other to the wine list. 'Do not worry about the expense,' he said, correctly interpreting their anxiety. 'This is my birthday present to you. Please feel free to choose what else you would like from the menu and it shall be put on my tab.' He turned to the waiter and pressed money into his hand. 'You know what to recommend.'

The girls settled back happily, overawed by his generosity, unaware that Sydney had tipped the waiter to ply them with the cheapest from both menus.

He was back in his seat by the time Lotti returned, he stood as she approached the table. She had noticed the two young dancers giggling and raising their glasses in Sydney's direction, she had no idea why, but she pointedly made a show of linking her arm through his and almost marching him through the revolving doors.

After the second house performance, Sydney escorted Lotti and Gracie to his club, it was heaving with people. The jazz band was popular and had drawn a crowd. The establishment made room for Sydney at his usual table but service was slow. By the time dinner arrived, Lotti was already half cut from drinking champagne on an empty stomach.

'Dance with me, Sydney. I want to dance.'
'I haven't finished eating, and neither have you.'
'I'm full, and in any case, I have to watch my figure,' she said, reaching over for the bottle of champagne.

Sydney moved it out of reach. 'I think you've had enough for this evening. When I have finished my meal, I will dance with you. For now, you must finish yours.' He was speaking to her as though she was a petulant child, and so, behaving like one, she turned to a man sitting at the next table. 'I say, would you care to dance with me?'

Catching Sydney's eye, he shook his head. 'Not right now, thank you, I'm eating.'

'Oh yes, so you are,' Lotti said, peering over his shoulder. 'In that case, would you mind pouring me another glass of champagne?' The man turned his back on her.

'Well if no one will dance with me, I shall dance by myself,' and she staggered on to the dance floor. A waiter escorted her back to her seat and Sydney asked him to bring her coat. By the time he'd returned, she was up dancing on her chair and Sydney had to throw her over his shoulder to get her out of the club. It took several minutes for a taxi to arrive, yet with her usual impeccable timing, Gracie appeared just as the taxi drew up alongside the kerb. 'Would you rather she slept in the spare bed in my room tonight?' she said, climbing into the taxi. 'I can keep an eye on her.'

'After tonight, I would rather she slept there for the rest of the week. This isn't the first time this has happened. In the past it was somewhat amusing, tonight she has overstepped the mark, it has lost its appeal.'

Sydney caught the taxi driver looking at them through his rear-view mirror, he knew the man would make no comment, he was used to driving drunks home from the club and knew not to speak out of turn if he wanted a fat tip.

Sydney carried Lotti discreetly up the service stairs to Gracie's room. It was a good job she was a skinny little thing, he wouldn't have made it if he'd been carrying Mabel. The thought made him want to laugh, never in a million years could he imagine Mabel in such a state. He placed Lotti on the bed, removed her shoes and stockings, then rolled her over to unfasten the back of her dress. He was slipping it from her shoulders when Gracie touched his arm. 'I can take it from here,' she said.

His smile dimpled one cheek. 'Do you think there is something I haven't seen before?'

Anger flashed momentarily in her green eyes. 'We will do this together it will be quicker.' They worked methodically. Sydney removed Lotti's clothes while Gracie searched out one of her nightdresses. The tension in the room was overwhelming, his own emotions were in turmoil, torn as he was between disgust at Lotti's drunken behaviour and lust for her naked body, so familiar and enticing. Then there was Gracie, his desire for her stretched his nerve endings to breaking point whenever she was near. Tonight, although she remained cool and aloof, a sexual energy was seeping from her. It was so powerful it was almost tangible. He slipped the nightdress over Lotti's sleeping head and smoothed it down. The gossamer thin silk was a mere token of clothing and her body was clearly defined beneath it.

Aching with desire, he took a last lingering look and turned away to find Gracie watching him, her glittering green eyes mirrored the desire in his. Reaching out he pulled her to him and kissed her, she responded, absorbing his kisses and melting against him. He held her tighter, pressing his muscular frame against her. Instantly she recoiled. 'I'm sorry, forgive me, I should never have allowed that to happen. I would like you to leave.'

'As you wish,' he said, reaching for his Fedora and smoothing back his hair before placing it low over his eyes. Without another word, he turned and left.

He needed a drink. The bar would be closed but he could tip the night porter for a bottle. As he expected, the bar was in darkness but a movement by the bay window caught his eye. Curious, he went to investigate. Curled up in a large armchair, illuminated by the light of the moon streaming in through the window, was Violet the young brunette he'd treated to a birthday lunch. Removing his hat, he perched on the arm of the chair. 'How was your birthday?' he whispered. 'Did you enjoy your lunch?'

'Oh, it was grand, thanks ever so much.'

'And was that your first taste of wine? What did you think?'

'Yes, it was, and let's say I'll be sticking to port and lemon from now on. Thanks all the same.'

'He winced at her remark, his conscience pricking slightly, he knew the waiter had served her an inferior brand of wine. He liked her spirit, her forthright way of speaking, he wondered how she had suddenly overcome the shyness she'd displayed in the restaurant. Perhaps it had been a ploy to get him to pay for lunch, perhaps she wasn't as innocent as she and her friend were making out. There was something about her though, that reminded him of Mabel. A kind of vulnerability that she would rather die than show, and yet she wore her heart on her sleeve for all to see. 'May I make so bold as to ask what you are doing sitting here in the dark and not tucked up in bed at this hour?'

'It's all Lillian's fault, she's had too much to drink, and she's sleeping that heavy, I can't wake her up to unlock the door.'

'This seems to be the theme of my evening,' he sighed, pretending it was such an inconvenience, while knowing that here was an opportunity to seduce an innocent.

'Doesn't the porter have a spare key?'

'He does, and we tried it. But she's bolted the door from the inside.'

'I see. Well then you do have a problem, but one I might quite possibly be able to resolve.'

He paused before playing his trump card, the knight in shining armour, twice in one day. 'If I may make a suggestion?' he said, his expression sincere, 'I have a suite of rooms with two bedrooms. I need only one. You are welcome to sleep in the other. Your reputation will be safe with me. If you do not wish anyone to know, it will be our secret.'

'Cor thanks, Mr Sydney, you're a real gent,' she said, jumping up from the chair and making her way to the lift. He discovered he was no longer in need of whisky.

She wandered about his hotel suite in a state of awe. It pleased him. It would enhance his air of mystique, a potent aphrodisiac.

'Strewth!' she said. 'This suite is bigger than my whole house, and there's eight of us living in it, with a shared privy across the yard.'

Her comment shocked him. Most theatricals, including himself, preferred to hide their poor background. He eyed her sagely, trying to work out what, if any, game she was playing. Then she laughed and ran lightly across the room to plant a kiss on his cheek. 'Thank you ever so much for letting me sleep here, I bet Buckingham Palace itself isn't as posh as this.' Her dark curls bounced and her eyes flashed happily, she looked so fresh, so young and innocent, he felt ashamed for questioning her scruples.

'I'll get you one of my shirts to sleep in,' he said.

She wasn't in the lounge when he returned. He found her tucked up in bed with the sheets pulled up under her chin. She looked terrified when he walked into the room. He sat down beside her on the bed. 'If there is anything you need during the night, just shout out.' Then he leaned forward to kiss her softly on the lips. Her mouth parted slightly in surprise, but her lips didn't respond. 'Sleep well, Violet. I will see you in the morning.' He left the room, closing the door behind him. He stood for a moment his hand resting on the handle, she truly was an innocent who needed nurturing carefully, but she was certainly a prize worth waiting for.

Chapter Eleven - Sheffield 1925

Mabel woke early, feeling refreshed after a peaceful night's sleep. She lit the oil lamp on the bedside cabinet and looked at the clock. It was only five-thirty, but she wanted to call on Bert before going to the factory. After a hurried breakfast, she gathered her parcels together and waited at the foot of the stone steps for a passing taxi. She was in luck. She waved frantically, relieved when it turned around at the park entrance and came back for her.

At Ada and Bert's back door she knocked tentatively, worried she might have caught him on the hop having a strip wash in the kitchen. But he was standing in the living room, snap tin under his arm, ready to leave. 'I've brought some clothes for Ada,' she said. Ethel's taken some and she's also going to make clothes for your children as well as her own from the material.' Mabel saw Bert's jaw tighten and his eyes narrow as she placed bacon, eggs and sausages on the table together with packets of tea and butter, a jar of jam and two loaves.

'I invited myself to breakfast, but I can see I've arrived too late.'

'Ethel's told you then, that I can't provide for me own family?'

'She's told me that you're on a three-day week. So's the rest of the country. Your firm's done well so far, but who knows how long they can hold out. I'm a friend Bert, all I've done is offer my friendship.'

'Aye, well, you might soon be wishing you'd held onto your brass with what's been going on at your pickle factory.'

'I'm on my way there now. I wanted to ask your advice, that's why I called in so early. But I can see it's bad timing.' She turned to leave, and he followed her out.

'I'm right sorry if I seem ungrateful. It's me conscience see. I'd no idea what trouble me union beliefs would bring down on me head. It's hit Ada right hard, but it's for families like us that I'm doing it.' He drew in a shuddering breath. 'Ada had to have another emergency operation last night. She's going on alright by all accounts, but that's what they told me last time.'

'Bert, I'm so sorry. I'm sure she's on the mend now. What about the baby. Is he faring well?'

'Aye, he's a little champion. But he'll need to be bottle fed after all the trouble Ada's had and that's another expense. Still, I can go cap in hand to the milk bank. What was it you wanted me advice on? We'll have to walk as we talk, else I'll be late for work and get me wages docked.'

'I've been up half the night working out my finances. I've sufficient funds to settle with the suppliers and get production rolling again. But after I've repaid enough of the loan to satisfy the bank, I'll have barely anything left to pay wages. I know you're fighting for a decent wage for a decent day's work and I wondered what your thoughts were on my forming a worker's co-operative?'

'I can't say as I've ever had owt to do with one. Tell us your thoughts afore I give you me opinion.'

'I don't have the money to pay a full wage for as many staff as I need. So, I'm thinking of offering a low wage but a generous share of the profits when the factory is back on its feet.'

'I think you're asking a lot love. It's a big risk, too big for some folk. An unemployed bloke with a family gets a pittance from the Relief, only food tokens enough for starvation rations and they've started sending blokes out to build new roads to Bole Hill and Lodge Moor to earn it. Poor sods could freeze to death up there come winter, and them authorities have the nerve to call it the Board of Guardians. Still, any handout's better than nowt and there's a risk that he might not get back on the Relief if he took a chance and then your scheme fell through. Not that I'm suggesting it might.'

'There are four workers who stayed on at the factory. They've been there for six months on no wages. They might be willing to take up my offer. I've paid them a month's wages out of my personal savings, but I don't have the money to pay them the full six months. What about women? They might be after some pin money and won't expect to be paid so much.'

'Now that's another of me beliefs love. There's plenty of women work as hard as men, and proved it, during the war. I don't see why they should earn less. Especially them that's been widowed because of the war. They're the bread winners now.'

'Bert, I agree with you, truly I do, but I have to get the factory up and running and then maybe I can look to your principles.'

'Start as you mean to go on lass. That's my advice. And as I'm on three days, I'll give you a hand where I can, providing Ada doesn't need me help.'

As they reached the point where their journey took them separate ways, Mabel said, 'Thanks for your advice Bert and I'd be grateful if you'd give me a hand. I'll pay you of course.'

'Aye, thanks. I'd like to say I'd do it for friendship, but tha knows I'm in no position to turn thee down. Don't forget though, that I've to work off what I owe you for the Doctor's bill. Any road, you've enough troubles of your own. Good luck to you Mabel, and I do appreciate what you're doing for me and Ada, I really do.'

Mabel's heels echoed through the quiet factory. The three workers were busy cleaning parts of the boiler that Ted, the maintenance man, had dismantled the day before.

'It was always a bit temperamental,' he explained, holding a section of the boiler aloft in a piece of soft rag. 'Should be alright after it's had a good clean.'

'Thank you, Ted. Would you mind coming up to the office, all of you. I have some news which I hope you will look on as good.'

The creaking stairs announced their arrival and an anxious looking Gladys jumped up from her chair as the four of them walked in.

'Don't look so worried, lass,' Ted gave her a gappy grin. 'Mrs Baxter here, says she has some good news for us.'

'Shall I make some tea, then?'

'I would be very grateful, Gladys,' Mabel said, 'and I'm sure everyone is ready for a break. Before I discuss the good news. I have worrying news. Ada was rushed into hospital because there were complications with the delivery of her baby. She'd lost a lot of blood and needed a caesarean. I've just seen Bert, and apparently, she's had to have another operation. The baby boy is fine and hopefully Ada's on the mend now as well.'

'What about her other kids?' Iris and Beattie said together.

'Ethel's taken them to her house. They were badly shaken up, especially Georgie. Ada had been in labour a long time by all accounts. Bert was out looking for additional work, and I think Georgie assumes the role of man of the house in his father's absence, he was afraid to leave the little ones to go and get Ethel.'

'Poor little lad, he's not much more than a baby himself,' Beattie said, lowering herself down onto a wooden chair. 'It fair takes the wind out of your sails.'

'I hope Ada goes on right enough,' Iris sighed, folding her arms across her ample bosom. 'She always has a time of it, poor lass, but going into hospital, by, she must be badly.'

'I'll get the tea,' Gladys fled from the room.

'I'll give her a hand,' Mabel said, following her out.

'Are you alright Gladys? You've gone very pale.'

'Ada was still working here when I first joined the factory, she was right kind to me, Mrs Baxter. I really hope she pulls through, but it does sound bad.' She dashed away a tear with the back of her hand as she turned to pour hot water into the teapot.

Mabel carried the tea tray through to the office, giving Gladys a few moments to compose herself. 'Come on everyone, this isn't helping Ada. All we can do for her now, is pray. Drink this tea while it's hot, and I'll tell you about my plan. If it works, it might bring some extra money into Ada's household and that's something I know will cheer her up and help her recover more quickly.'

'Aye, if she lives to know of it,' Iris muttered.

'Now then, I'll not tolerate talk like that,' Ted said, 'sup thee tea and listen to what Mrs. Baxter has to say.'

Mabel supressed a smile, Gladys must have told them that she preferred being called by her married name. Addressing the little gathering she waved half a dozen envelopes in the air. 'These contain the means to pay off our debts. If they go in this evening's post, we should receive delivery of supplies by the end of the week. Can we have the factory ship shape and up and running by then?' She looked at Ted, he touched his forelock. 'It'll be ready by this afternoon, latest, Mrs Baxter.'

'I have a proposition to put to you. I know the month's wages I gave you was inadequate for your loyalty over the past six months, but I have little money left after paying the bank, the suppliers and other debts incurred by my sister-in-law. My suggestion is that we form a worker's co-operative. I have assets enough to pay you a meagre wage for the next four months, below average I'm afraid. However, if we can turn the factory around during that time, increase sales, and make a decent profit, then I'll pay you an agreed share of the profits after overheads. It's a risk and I know I'm asking you to take a big gamble, but if we pull together, I think you'll come out on the winning side. It will mean all of us working together on the factory floor. Even you, for now Gladys. I'll have to do the books at night.'

'Don't you worry about that Mrs Baxter, you can count on me and I'll help you with the books an' all, on the nights me dad doesn't want me to do his.'

'You've no need to ask me twice,' Ted answered her enthusiastically. 'There's not a lot who would take on a bloke of my advancing years, not when there's so many young men needing work.'

'Count me in, an' all,' said Beattie.'

'And me,' Iris winked at Beattie. 'It'll keep me out of mischief.'

'This calls for a celebration,' Mabel said, opening a drawer in her late father's desk. She fiddled about at the back of it, until there was a click and a side panel swung open. She reached inside and pulled out an unopened bottle of whisky. 'I was hoping this was still in there,' she laughed, unscrewing the top and pouring a generous measure into everyone's teacup. 'Here's to our success. The people's co-operative.' Then she screwed the top back on and held the bottle aloft. 'I'm saving the rest to wet Ada's baby's head. Oh, and that reminds me, if my plan pays off, and we need an extra pair of hands, Bert has agreed to come in on a casual basis. Now I think I'd better crack on and drum up some business, and Ted, if you would be so kind as to deliver these cheques to our local suppliers and post the rest, I'd be most grateful.'

'I'll get on to it right away, Mrs Baxter,' he said through his gappy grin.

Mabel spent the morning phoning round the suppliers, existing customers and local hotels, as well as shops and restaurants trying to make new contacts.

It didn't take long for the news of her return to business to reach suppliers, so that some were expecting her call. Once they knew their outstanding invoices would be paid in full, they began delivering supplies that afternoon. The members of the newly formed co-operative immediately set the wheels in motion, and in no time at all, the sound of peeling and chopping was accompanied by the unmistakable smell of simmering piccalilli floating around the factory and out of the open window.

Next day, once the factory was working to full capacity, Mabel went up to the office and continued working her way through the order book trying to drum up business. Everyone was pleased to hear she was back and nearly all her past customers wanted to chat, it was a frustratingly slow process, but by early evening she had taken a considerable number of orders.

The sight of row upon row of jars of pickled onions, red cabbage, mixed pickles and piccalilli standing on the benches, neatly labelled and ready to go, almost reduced her to tears. 'My goodness, that's a sight to warm your heart,' she said, 'and I've enough orders placed to carry off that lot. Well done everyone.'

'The carrying off bit might be a problem. Have you thought how we're going to transport them?'

Mabel's hand flew to her mouth, 'I can't believe I didn't think of that before.'

'Aye well, there's four more of us who never thought of it either. I've me bike. I daresay we could get hold of a delivery basket on the cheap. That'd be a start for now.'

'Me dad's got a spare one at the shop,' Gladys said. 'One of his delivery boys came a cropper on his bike. He's always doing daft tricks to show off. Last week he went too far, the bike's beyond repair, so dad's given him the sack. I bet he'd let you have the basket until he can afford a new bike.'

'That would be grand if your father wouldn't mind lending it to us for a week or two if you feel up to doing the deliveries, Ted?'

'Aye, I'm not quite in me dotage yet, lass. Though I dare say I seem it to you.'

'Ted, can you drive a motor car?'

He looked taken aback for a moment, and scratched his head as though trying to remember. 'Well I drove anything on wheels during the war, it's been some time, but I expect I'd soon get the hang of it again. What have you in mind?'

'If we get repeat orders on this scale, we should soon be able to afford a little van or something to take the deliveries round.'

'Advertising, that's what we need Mrs Baxter,' Iris pointed out, 'and word of mouth is the best, that would be an easy job for me and Beattie,' she laughed, and Beattie playfully gave her a good shove.

'What about going in for pickled eggs? They go down a treat, same as pickled onions on a pub counter.'

'That might be a part of the job you'd enjoy, Ted,' Mabel laughed, 'touting for business around the public houses.'

'So long as he doesn't end up more pickled than the eggs,' Iris laughed.

It was a good feeling Mabel thought, to be down on the factory floor having a laugh with people who were once her father's employees and regarded by him as below her station, but who were now her friends and colleagues in the newly formed co-operative.

Ted had taken on the role of security and Mabel left him to lock up. She was feeling anxious about Ada and intended calling on Bert on her way home. Earlier in the day she'd telephoned the hospital and had been surprised to learn that Ada wasn't there. The person she'd spoken to wouldn't give out information since she wasn't family.

She arrived at Ada and Bert's house to find it in darkness. She looked at her watch. Bert must have left early for his night shift. Ethel might know what's going on, she thought, and set off to her house.

Ada's children greeted her excitedly as Ethel opened the door. 'Mam's had the baby and he's called Charlie, dad's gone to visit her, but we can't go 'cos kids aren't allowed at the hospital.'

Mabel looked enquiringly over their heads at Ethel.

'You'd best come in,' Ethel said wearily. 'I'll put the kettle on. Have you eaten? I daresay you'll not turn your nose up at a bit of beef stew and dumplings. I've made enough for the street, seeing as I've been feeding an army of folks.' She nodded pointedly at the children. Bert's been eating here 'an all, although he did provide the vegetables, and some apples for a pudding.'

'Where's Ada?' Mabel whispered. Then looking across at the group of hopeful young faces, she fished in her handbag and brought out some pennies. She gave one to each of the children and watched them tumble out of the door, anxious to spend their penny at Smith's corner shop. 'That's better, we can talk now. What's going on?'

'All I know is that she's at a lady surgeon's house and it's all to be kept secret.' Ethel said. 'Apparently, when Bert went to visit Ada in the hospital, she was that bad they wouldn't let him see her. Well, he got mad with the Matron's attitude and lost his temper and was ordered from the hospital without seeing the baby either. Anyway, while he was gathering his thoughts, the Junior House Surgeon took him to one side and told him on the quiet, like, that Ada was probably going to lose her life because they couldn't get hold of a surgeon, it being a Sunday. It turns out that the woman Bert's been doing some digging for at the allotments was a surgeon in the war. So, he went dashing off to find her and ask her advice. Would you credit it, she told him she has facilities at her house for doing operations, so they discharged Ada from hospital and took her there. Saved Ada's life, she did, by all accounts. Bert had to give Ada some of his own blood. Turns out they've the same type or summat. Well, I don't know what else that lady surgeon does up at her house, but it's all got to be kept quiet, that's why the kids think Ada's still in hospital. I've heard tales of a woman who helps the likes of us out of a mess, if you get me meaning, on the quiet, like, and for no payment.' Then seeing Mabel's blank expression, Ethel sighed, 'Aye well, let's hope you never need to find out. I thought it were a myth. But I'll tell you this for nowt. If half the tales I've heard about her are true, then she's a ruddy guardian angel.'

Mabel replayed the conversation with Ethel in her head on the tram home and suddenly everything fitted into place. She wondered if it was the motion of the tram that nudged her brain into action because she seemed to have her most profound thoughts on there. Perhaps it was simply the only time her brain was at rest allowing her thoughts room to surface. Her next thoughts were not so pleasant as she suddenly wondered how many of Sydney's liaisons had resulted in a trip to such a person. She hoped they had found someone like the woman who'd helped Ada. The welfare of Sydney's women should not be her concern. She certainly shouldn't feel sorry for them, but somehow, she did. Perhaps because generally they were decent, innocent sorts of girls taken in by his irresistible charm, as she herself had been. The only difference was that she had retained her innocence until after he had married her.

Chapter Twelve – Manchester 1925

On the opposite side of the Pennines, Sydney was walking away from the General Post Office, his spirits high. He'd posted a letter of love to Mabel which he'd written the previous night. He'd poured his heart and soul into it, declaring how he was missing her more than she could possibly imagine and wishing he could drop everything and go to her immediately, if only to spend just a few moments in her arms. What he'd written was true, in part. Mabel was the only woman he had ever come close to loving. Her middle-class upbringing and good education were evident in her sophisticated manner, in the way she carried herself when she walked across a room and her complete ease in any social setting. She could conduct a conversation on most topics and in several languages. All these things excited him in a way none of the flashy showgirls did or the most brazen of chambermaids. Mabel had moved in the social circles he had aspired to as a child and infiltrated as a man. Perhaps that was the attraction Gracie held for him, her manner oozed a privileged background. Violet, on the other hand, held all the innocence of the convent school educated young woman Mabel had been when he'd married her. All the loving words he'd written to Mabel were true. But while she was in another city, he was having the most marvellous time without worrying that she might discover his infidelities. It had been a close call with Delores on board ship, but he felt confident that he'd convinced Mabel his only infidelity was the imaginings of an old maid.

He had also sent a letter of love to Delores, knowing full well her contract had six months yet to run, but hoping to keep her sweet. He smiled smugly and let his thoughts turn to Violet. He'd contrived to catch her alone in the corridor after last night's show and invite her to lunch. He looked at his watch and lengthened his stride. He did not want to be late.

Lotti, once she had sobered up, had wormed her way full of apologies into his bed during the night. Today, he'd told her he had an important business meeting. Well the meeting was important to him and he treated seduction as a most serious business.

He was not feeling so smug when Violet was thirty minutes late. When she eventually arrived, he decided the wait had been worth it. She could have stepped out of a bandbox. Her hair, immaculately groomed, peeped very fetchingly from beneath an ivory coloured cloche hat trimmed with black marabou. The collar and cuffs of her matching coat were also trimmed. The hemline dipped dramatically at the back and was gathered by a clasp slung low over her hips where it bounced provocatively.

'I'm sorry to be so late, Mr Sydney, only the hairdresser took an age. I did leave myself enough time when I made the appointment, honest I did.'

'I think we can dispense with the mister when we are alone Violet,' he smiled, relaxing into his chair, impressed by the fact that she had visited a hair salon in his honour. Perhaps she was going to be easier to win over than he'd anticipated.

'Would you like to look at the menu, or shall I choose for you?'

'You choose,' she said, resting her elbows on the table and cupping her chin in her hands to gaze up at him wide-eyed.

He instructed the waiter and then turned his full attention on her. 'Are you enjoying being in the show, Violet?'

'I should say so. I love the routines and the other dancers are a grand set of girls. Of course, it was a step up the ladder for me being in one of your shows.'

He didn't question her remark, he knew it to be a fact. Many artists aspired to be in his revues. It meant he got first pick of the beautiful as well as the talented.

The meal progressed pleasantly enough. He could not fault Violet's manners, but she didn't possess the same natural ease which Gracie displayed.

'Do you like the Picture Shows, Sydney?'

'Some are amusing, but they do not draw me in like live theatre.' He looked at the rain drumming against the window. He could think of many pleasant ways to spend a rainy afternoon, but today the opportunity for such pleasures would not present itself. 'Would you like to go to the matinee performance at the Picture House, Violet?'

'I should say so. Rudolf Valentino is on.' She clapped her hands together excitedly, reminding Sydney how young she was. 'Ah, yes,' he said. 'The Son of a Sheik, it is about a man falling in love with a dancing girl, is it not? Quite apt wouldn't you say?' He was heartened to see Violet cast down her eyes and a flush stain her cheeks.

Huddled together, sheltering from the rain under the large umbrella which Sydney had procured from the restaurant, they dashed into the cinema foyer. He went off to find an usherette under the pretext of purchasing the obligatory box of chocolates, but essentially to tip her into making room for them on the back row. He could have saved his money, the cinema was full of housewives come to swoon over Valentino, the back row was deserted.

    He helped Violet off with her damp coat. Then placing his hand in the small of her back, he guided her into her seat, sliding his palm a little too low before removing it. The house lights dimmed, the screen flickered into life and the piano accompaniment reached a crescendo as the Sheik appeared in his white robes, staring out at the audience through smouldering kohl-enhanced eyes. Violet's noisy attempt at opening the chocolates had heads turning and tongues clicking. Sydney reached over to help her with the box and saw that she hadn't smoothed down her dress. The milky flesh of her inner thigh was clearly exposed and the white lacy garters holding her stockings in place seemed to add further purity to her virginal appeal, and Sydney felt his loins stir. Seemingly unaware of her exposure, or its effect on him, she crossed her legs hitching the dress higher. Then she delved into the chocolates. Selecting one, she bit it in half to look at the centre before popping it into her mouth. She selected another, and this time lifted it to Sydney's lips. He caught her wrist, holding it until the chocolate began to melt in her fingers, then he released his grasp enough to allow her to put the sweet into his mouth. Still holding her wrist, he closed his lips around the tip of her finger until the chocolate had dissolved.

Aroused by her wide-eyed expression and tremor at his touch, he worked his way along her fingertips until all the chocolate was gone. He chose a chocolate and would have placed it in her mouth, but her tongue stopped its progress and she gently sucked until half had dissolved. Moulding her lips over the ends of his fingers she snaked her tongue between them and flicked the sweet into her mouth. 'We are missing the start of the film,' she giggled, wrinkling her nose childishly.

She had caught him off guard, she was turning into as much of an enigma as Gracie. His gut feeling was that she was also playing him for a fool and that she was far more experienced than she was portraying. Then he wondered if perhaps she really was an innocent, and simply following his lead to cover her inexperience. He liked that thought better.

They had to hurry to reach the theatre before the half-hour call. 'You go in first,' he said. 'It will not do to be seen arriving together. I know our afternoon has been perfectly innocent, but quite apart from my being married to Mabel, the girls in your dressing room might give you a difficult time. You know how jealous some can be. If they feel they are missing out, they will quite possibly accuse you of giving favours to further your career. Take my advice and keep our outings to yourself.'

'Outings?' she looked up at him, her eyes round and childlike.

'Yes, of course outings. I am assuming you enjoyed your afternoon and would like to repeat the experience.'

'I should say so,' she said, and scurried through the stage door.

The Sydney Baxter Revues were as famous for their spectacular staging and costumes as they were for their talented artists. Audiences were dazzled by the glamour of glittering backdrops, sequins and lights. Sydney picked up his baton at the helm of the orchestra and watched the fire curtain rise revealing luxurious red velvet gold tasselled curtains. The house lights dimmed, and the overture began. The curtains parted and the gauze cloth appeared in all its glory. Splashed across it, written in black and silver, was Sydney's name and the title of the revue surrounded by golden musical notes. The overture ended and when the orchestra struck up again, the lighting changed, fading through the gauze to back light the stage and pick out a cloud of white ostrich feathers before the gauze was whisked unnoticed up to the flys. On cue, the white feathers parted creating a giant fan surrounding spangled-clad dancers with Gracie at their centre. In stark contrast, Gracie was wearing a black beaded gown and turban headdress with three plumes held in place by a diamante clasp. Her husky tones filled the theatre and seemed to propel the white feathers into a revolving Ferris wheel. Then the dancing girls, breaking formation, kicked their legs and manoeuvred their supple bodies, creating ever changing patterns and shapes as though pulled into motion by the giant feather fans they held in each hand.

The scene closed to thunderous applause. Sydney's trademark was to dazzle an audience from the offset. The white feather fan number was a proven showstopper.

He never tired of standing at the helm of the orchestra watching the stream of slick-moving variety acts follow on, one after the other. The comedy acts and tumblers had an audience rolling in the aisles with laughter, while the acrobats and adagio, kept them spellbound with terror. The magician left them gasping in astonishment.

Clever use of scenery and lighting changed the mood. None was so dramatic in Sydney's opinion as the midnight blue cloth studded with hundreds of lights and hung from the back bar. His personal favourite use of the cloth was to suspend a glittering crescent moon from a fly bar further downstage. Sitting on the moon, perched high above the stage and captured in spotlight, the soubrette would sing her solo seemingly surrounded by millions of stars. In this revue, to add to his fascination, the soubrette was Gracie. The long train of her silvery white gown billowed with the motion of the swinging moon, she looked like an angel of fire with her red hair blazing under the lights. Sydney was convinced her husky voice could drive any man to the devil.

After the show, unable to help himself despite her continued rebuffs, Sydney waited for Gracie in the shelter of the tobacconist's doorway, pretending to light a cigarette out of the wind. When she appeared, he stepped in line with her. 'I was about to hail a taxi to take me to my club. Would you care to join me?'

Although he'd appeared out of the darkness, she hadn't flinched. It was as if she had been expecting him. 'No,' she replied, giving him her full attention, 'thank you for asking me, but I'm not hungry.'

'Where are you going?'

She looked him up and down, and for a moment he fully expected her to ask what it had to do with him. But she simply shrugged her shoulders and said, 'Back to the hotel of course.'

'Then I will walk you there.'

'What about Lotti, shouldn't your concerns be for her?'

'She is sulking. She has gone to a club with a group from the revue since I have refused to take her after her last drunken performance.'

'In that case I'm grateful for your company,' and she linked her arm through his. He had never known her to be tactile and his arm tingled through his coat as though she was burning him.

'Will Lotti be going to your room or mine on her return from the club?'

'You had better leave your door unlocked. I told her before she left the theatre that I have an early start tomorrow and do not wish to have my sleep disturbed.' He saw a flash of emotion in her green eyes, moments before she lowered her lids. Was it simply a trick of the gaslight or did he register desire glittering there?

Gracie surprised him again by accepting his invitation to a drink in the hotel bar, and then asking for a double scotch and a cigarette. He watched in fascination as the exhaled smoke hovered in rings above her head as though obediently waiting to be dismissed.

'You must miss your wife very much,' she said, looking him directly in the eye.

She had succeeded in wrong footing him. 'Yes,' he said, and changed the subject.

The bar was closed when he walked Gracie back to her room. At the door, he took hold of her hand and brought it to his lips. He felt her tremor, saw passion flare in her eyes. Taking it as a signal, he stroked her cheek with his fingertips and cupped her chin to plant a kiss, so delicate, his lips barely brushed hers. He felt her quiver and deepened the kiss pulling her to him. Instantly she pushed him away. 'It's late,' she said, opening the door.

Sydney looked past her into the darkened room at the shape lying in one of the beds, then he clearly heard Lotti say, 'You're late, what kept you? I fell asleep waiting.' He thought she was speaking to him, and made to enter the room, but before he could get a foot through the door, Gracie slammed it in his face.

He didn't quite know what had just happened. Lighting a cigarette, he dropped down the stairs not bothering to wait for the lift. He was heading for the front door and his club when his eyes were drawn into the darkened bar by a shape huddled in a chair. As he approached, the shape took on a familiar form. 'Hello, Violet. Have you been locked out of your room again? I was just about to hail a taxi. Would you like to come with me to my club?'

'Cor, I should say so,' she replied. 'I'm not in the least bit sleepy, but I didn't know what else to do other than bed down here.'

'Then it is settled, we shall go,' he said, offering his arm.

Young and naive, Violet hung on to his every word and followed his lead when champagne was poured and the meal served. Her manners were impeccable, though they held more than a trace of a charm school. He wondered why she hadn't bothered with elocution lessons. 'Would you like to dance?' he said, taking her hand and standing up before she had time to answer. He swept her onto the floor gathering her in his arms, she moulded to him as though her curves had been designed specifically, the opposite of Gracie who recoiled whenever their bodies touched, and yet, she was the one who set his senses ablaze like no other. He dismissed the thought and concentrated on whispering sweet nothings into Violet's ear, weaving strands of charm, drawing her further into his seductive web.

Outside the club, Sydney hailed a taxi, he opened the door and made sure Violet was seated, before he said, 'There is something I have forgotten to do. I must go back inside and speak to the manager. Here is the key to my suite, I will meet you back at the hotel.' As he watched the taxi drive off, he sensed the bulk of a man step from the shadows and join him at the kerb. He didn't need to look up to guess who it was. The man's shoes alerted him and Sydney's blood ran cold. The last time he'd seen a pair of black patent and white leather brogues, was on the streets of New York. He turned and looked up into a face that was permanently drawn into a lopsided grin by a vivid scar puckering one cheek.

'How you dooin' Mr Baxter? I've come over to take in the sights for a few days and to have a quiet word in yer shell-like. You've been interfering in some very important people's business dealings on the other side of the Atlantic, contacting some of their more elite clients. They're not happy. I've come to tell you if you don't back off, you'll be doing some sightseeing of your own, down by the Mersey. Only you'll be viewing it from the bottom wearing cement boots.'

Sydney turned and tried to walk back into the club but the gangster's giant hand clapped him on the shoulder. 'You ain't that hard to find, Mr Baxter. Just in case you was thinking of dooin' a runner.' He drew a revolver from his coat pocket to validate his meaning.

Sydney's relaxed persona belied his terror. 'It is most fortunate for those important people across the Atlantic, that you have approached me at this very moment. If you come inside with me, I can introduce you to my contact. He can supply you with the finest liquor available. It is of no importance to him who buys it, so long as he is paid generously. After I have introduced you, I will adhere to your request and back off most graciously.'

'Don't try any funny business. I'll be watching you,' the gangster said, shifting the revolver in his pocket to jab the barrel point into Sydney's back.

The manager's face didn't register surprise when Sydney walked back into the club with the stranger so close at heel. Nor did he need to see the shape of the gun barrel protruding through the man's coat pocket to know America's gangsters had rumbled Sydney's alcohol smuggling ring. The man's clothes were so out of place in this Lancashire city, they screamed it louder than a Klaxon.

The manager didn't speak until he'd smoothly flicked back a velvet curtain revealing a green baize door. 'I thought you'd changed your mind when I saw you leaving the club,' he said, producing a key on a long silver chain from his trouser pocket and unlocking the door.

After they were inside the room with the door locked behind them Sydney handed over a roll of bank notes. 'Here is your money, you know the address. I trust you have everything prepared.'

'Already crated up and waiting at the docks. Only thing stopping it sailing was this.' He opened the roll of notes and spread it flat on the desk, then he licked his finger and flicked back each note with lightning speed as he counted. 'It's all here, nice doing business with you.'

Then Sydney inclined his head to the man at his back. 'We have not been officially introduced, but this gentleman has come all the way from New York and while he's here, he might be interested in doing business with you.'

'Well, why don't we do the introductions over a sample of the goods?' the manager grinned. 'Give me a moment.' He scooped up the money and disappeared through a door leading from the small office. He returned carrying a tray of glasses, a bottle of Malt Whisky and a box of cigars. 'Help yourself gentleman.'

The gangster downed his Whisky in one and reached for a cigar. Sydney picked up a pair of silver cigar cutters from the tray and made a show of demonstrating their use. The gangster simply bit off the end of his cigar and blew it out of the corner of his mouth with scant regard for its destination. While he was distracted in this crass display, the Manager slipped a powder into his glass then poured in more Whisky. As before, he downed the contents of his glass in one and by the time his cigar was alight, the gangster's lights had gone out.

'What did you give him?' Sydney stared in horror at the crumpled figure on the office floor.

'Enough dope to lay out a horse. Either way, makes no difference where he's going.'

'You imbecile! They will trace him back to me and quite probably you.'

'No they won't. We'll transport him to Liverpool and send him back across the Atlantic same route as the goods, only he'll arrive and the goods won't. If you've any sense, you'll send the liquor a different route. Then, when he turns up floating around the Statue of Liberty, the gang that sent him will think a rival gang got to him before he ever made it out of New York.'

'I'll hold back on that latest consignment,' Sydney said. 'I know a warehouse near to the docks where it can be stored until I've worked out a new route for getting it into country. But on second thoughts, is that a smart idea? If the goods suddenly stop coming into New York they'll know I've been warned off.'

'Let's hope they think a rival gang got him on his return then! Go on, your business here is done. I'll see him on his way. But remember Sydney Baxter, you owe me, and I always collect my favours.' Then he grinned. 'Same deal next month is it?'

'Don't prepare anything until I have contacted you,' Sydney called over his shoulder walking out of the room.

Back at the hotel, Sydney tipped the night porter for a bottle of champagne. He instructed him not to pop the cork just in case Violet had gone to sleep in the spare bedroom.

He found her sitting on the sofa with her legs crossed revealing an expanse of thigh and a good deal of peachy buttock. Instantly his loins tightened. He put the champagne down and wound up the gramophone before popping the cork and pouring the fizzing liquid into two glasses. She took a sip of champagne as she moved into his arms. He held her there, swaying in time to the music. She rested her head against his shoulder and her chestnut curls tickled his neck, sending shivers down his spine, he pulled her closer leaving her in no doubt as to his desire. She looked up at him, not in wide-eyed innocence, more like the cat who'd got the cream. He bent his head and devoured her lips. Her response sent fire raging through his veins, but instead of reacting, he released her. He changed the record and rewound the gramophone before topping up their glasses and taking her back into his arms. He cradled her head kissing her slowly, his long supple fingers skilfully massaging the nape of her neck, working down her spine until he found the curve of her hip. His hand rested there allowing his heat to warm her senses, before sliding across to the base of her spine. When she didn't protest, he explored lower until he had the globe of her buttock nestling in the palm of his hand. An image of her thigh and garters flooded his brain, and he pressed closer delighting in her gasp and the feel of her wriggling closer still. He didn't linger there, instead he trailed his hand up over her ribs massaging the sensitive muscles beneath her armpit. Taking the soft mound of her breast into his mouth he blew through the fabric of her dress. She gasped as the heat burned and he lifted his head to capture her mouth, stroking his thumb over her sensitised nipple before moulding her breast in the palm of his hand. He drew her down to sit on the sofa, gathering her to him as though she was the most precious being alive. Smothering her in kisses he trailed the back of his fingertips along her arm. 'It is late, we must sleep,' he breathed through his kisses.

    Violet untangled herself and stood up, pulling him with her into the bedroom. He followed obediently, allowing her to think she had reached her own conclusion. Had she glanced back, she would have seen the triumphant grin on his face.

Chapter Thirteen – Sheffield 1925

Bert hadn't known what to do with his winnings at first. He knew folk would get suspicious if he suddenly appeared flush and he was terrified Ada would eventually find out about the fights. But with debts piling up he couldn't see what else he could do but spend it. First, he paid the landlord what he owed and a couple of weeks rent in advance. Then he ordered coal to be delivered so the house was warm for Ada and Charlie to come home to. He sent the coal man round to Ethel's as well to repay her kindness and expense.

He'd gone further afield inside the Walls of Jericho to buy groceries. There, the shop keepers didn't know him by name. On a Saturday night the hawkers on Meadow Street sold their wares, anything from a mop and bucket to a freshly plucked chicken, long after the Low Drop public house and Charlie's Wall, had turned out. By midnight they were willing to sell off their fresh produce to the highest takers just to get rid of it and Bert knew he could pick up a joint of meat for a shilling with sausage and bacon for his breakfast thrown in. He'd gone there after his fight, this time with a pocket full of coins from his winnings. He wouldn't want to be seen flashing large notes about in a district where most blokes were unemployed. He didn't know what went on within this area but he knew there were villains loitering over in the east end of the City who waited for blokes turning out of the steel works on a Friday just to relieve them of their hard-earned wages. He didn't want to chance it here in a crowd neither. Besides he doubted that the hawkers would be happy parting with all their change. As he reached the corner of Hamond Street he saw a large circle of men. The familiar cries of 'A pound on heads. Five quid on tails,' belied Sammy's news that Pitch and Toss was losing its appeal. Hearing such high stakes being shouted out, it seemed there was brass coming from somewhere into this dilapidated community. The pikers on lookout duty eyed him warily as he passed by. A new face near the Pitch and Toss was a face to watch with caution.

When Ethel had tried to pay him back for the coal, he'd had a quiet word with her about where his money had come from. He'd half expected her to know already. Some of the lads from the factory had been at the fights and he thought Daniel might have got wind of it. 'I've never kept owt back from Ada before,' he'd explained, 'but she's been to hell and back lately and this would be the last straw in her eyes.' He rubbed his face vigorously with both hands as if it was itchy, then smoothed back his hair. He looked up at Ethel, half apologetic, half appealing. 'You know more than most how we're fixed. I don't see as how I've a choice.'

'Ethel patted his hand. 'The least said soonest mended. I just hope you know what you're getting yourself into.'

'Aye, so do I. Only time will tell on that one.'

Ada and baby Charlie arrived home in style. A curious crowd formed along the street and it didn't take long for a group of children to gather around the car. Ada laughed at their calls of 'Gee us a ride in thee motor, Missis.'

'I feel like Queen Mary,' Ada said, stepping out of the great touring car assisted by Bert and Mary.

'Ethel's bringing the rest of our kids back later,' Bert said. 'She thought we'd like a bit of time on us own. The kettle's boiling and she's laid out a grand spread for tea.'

Ada entered her living room in wonderment, a fire roared up the chimney and a new brightly coloured peg rug fronted the hearth. As if to confirm the illusion of grandeur a feast fit for a Queen was spread across the table. Slices of bread, both brown and white cut into triangles sat next to a giant bowl of salad and a comforting smell of baked potatoes wafted over from the Yorkshire Range. She couldn't remember the last time she'd seen a slice of tongue or boiled ham, but there they were, piled up on a plate infront of her, at least a pound of each.

'Oh Bert, what have you done,' she said, her lip quivering as she sank into the nearest chair.' Bert's heart constricted so much, he felt short of breath. He was on the verge of telling her the truth, but the well-rehearsed lie sprang to his lips. 'They're a bit pushed at the factory, they had a rush job come in and I've worked a couple of weekend shifts. I wanted to keep it a surprise. In fact, I'm on tomorrow night. But don't worry, Ethel's going to put the kids to bed. I know you're not supposed to be lifting.'

He settled Charlie in the big pram, then lifted the kettle from the fire hob keeping his eyes shielded from Ada. He hoped she hadn't seen the lie hidden in their depths. 'I'd better make you that cup of tea. I thought you'd be pleased, but this must have come as a bit of a shock, all the colour's drained from your face.'

On Saturday night, Bert left home at the usual time for working a night shift. At the door Ada handed him his snap and kissed his cheek. He reached out and crushed her to his chest kissing her passionately. 'What's that for? You soppy 'apeth,' she giggled, smoothing back her blonde curls.

'Nowt. Just letting you know I love thee.'

He was down to fight last and had a few hours to fill beforehand. Guilt, mingled with fear, gripped his stomach as he set off for Charlotte's house to wait until it was time to go up to Sky Edge.

For the first time, Charlotte had insisted on driving him to the fight ground. She said she would wear a tweed cap and jacket. At her height, with the roof pulled down on the tourer and under the cover of darkness, she could easily be mistaken for a man. Besides, with the headlights switched on to light the ring the car would merge into darkness. So for once he didn't argue. He had a bad feeling about tonight and thought maybe she had picked up on his unease. The event had trebled in size. Once word had got about, unemployed men drawn by starvation into fighting and gambling, hoping to earn a bob or two, illegal or not, had come in their droves. Now that the crowd had grown, so had the stakes. The trouble was, the smell of big money had drawn the professionals as well as the hopefuls. Now his opponents had strength and skill to match his own. So far, he'd not lost a fight. But with that reputation, came big bets. He didn't dare think of the consequences if a gang's financial empire took a dive because he'd been beaten.

Charlotte drove past a line of motor charabancs and coaches and through the milling crowd to park her large tourer car in the last slot of the arena ring, illuminating a fight in progress. Despite all her years spent patching up soldiers and taking apart women's insides, her stomach churned at the sheer brutality she was witnessing. 'Why doesn't someone call a halt. If they carry on, they'll be fighting to the death.' At last a bell rang signalling the end. 'Is this what you've set yourself up for?' she said, turning to look at Bert. He didn't return her gaze, instead he looked straight ahead. Someone close by struck a match and she could see the hard set of his jaw in silhouette. Suddenly a man's face pressed up against the car window and she jumped as a knuckle rapped sharply. Bert kept his gaze forward as he wound down the window and a cloud of cigar smoke puthered in.

'Going up in the world I see,' the face said, peering into the motor. 'I've just dropped by to tell you that you've some stiff opposition tonight. I know you'll not let me down.' Another cloud of smoke entered the car as the face withdrew into the dark.

'How did he know you were inside this car?'

'He's a villain, he makes it his business to know and Sammy keeps him up to date. It's a dangerous game I'm playing, and I don't just mean the fighting.'

It was gone midnight by the time Bert's fight was called. He stripped off in the car and threw his clothes onto the back seat, ready for a hasty get away. He'd bought himself a pair of boxing shorts and proper boots with his earnings. Now the fight meetings had upped the game, he'd have felt foolish in his combinations.

In any case, they gave his opponent something to grab hold of. They didn't follow the Queensbury rules here.

He made his way between the parked cars edging the ring and was stopped in his tracks by the sight of Sydney Baxter, Mabel's husband, talking to the camel coated villain. He shouldn't have been surprised that Sydney had found his way to the local criminal fraternity. They were standing in the shadows but his only route through was to pass by them.

The cloud of cigar smoke reached him before the voice. 'Here comes the man himself. You're already acquainted with Bert here, I understand,' he said, patting Sydney on the shoulder.

Sydney stepped forward to shrug away the hand. 'Yes, Ada once worked in my wife's factory.'

Bert bristled at the intended slight on Mabel and Ada's friendship but didn't take the bait. He knew it would be in Sydney's interest to see him rattled before his fight. Instead he made to walk on, but Camel Coat grabbed his arm. 'What's your hurry? Don't you want to know who you'll be fighting? Sydney here has sent for his own champion to come all the way from Liverpool. He'll be no easy pushover like your usual opponents. I hope you have your wits about you. I've a monkey riding on you winning.'

'Then you've more money than sense,' Bert said, looking back at Charlotte's car. He hoped she'd have the engine cranked up and ready for a quick getaway. At the edge of the ring Sammy crept out of the shadows and stood behind Bert. 'Don't look round at me,' Sammy whispered. 'Just put yer 'ands behind your back, nonchalant like.'

'What you playing at now Sammy? Haven't you got me into enough bother? Bloody Camel Coat's got five hundred quid riding on me winning.'

'Aye, I know. That's why I've come to help you. That bastard, who Sydney's put up against you, is one of a gang of dockers he's got working a fiddle for him down at Liverpool docks.'

'I didn't know Sydney was in Sheffield.'

'No? Then I bet his missis don't know neither.'

'What fiddle's he got going on at the docks?'

'I'll tell you later. Give us yer 'ands. I'm rubbing mustard over the backs. Just remember not to rub your own eyes with 'em. I've heard of this docker bloke before. Dirty fighter.'

'You mean the rest of us are playing fair?'

'Now listen to what I'm telling you. If he suggests wearing gloves to fight, refuse. His pair will be weighted, and if he hits you with one of them, you'll not wake up till Christmas.' And another thing, he'll have smeared sommat nasty on his hands just like you, so don't let his fists get near your face. I'll keep an eye on him best I can, but if he makes a play for the shadows, you can guarantee he'll come back out with a knuckle duster and lose it again just as quick before you know what's hit you. He's fit Bert, he spends his days lifting bleedin' heavy crates. He's light on his feet an' all, you'll not tire him out with any of your fancy foot work. Good luck pal.' Sammy patted him on the back and skulked off into the shadows.

With hardly time to consider what Sammy had told him, Bert found himself in the centre of the ring facing his opponent. They were equally matched in stature and age, each eyeing the other as they circled round, weighing up their first move. Bert saw that the docker held something in his clenched fists and made a mental note to dodge clear. Suddenly the docker sprang forward. In a whirling frenzy he threw a handful of dry sand at Bert's eyes following through with a succession of punches. Bert had been prepared. He ducked, and as sand flew over his back he dodged to the right. The docker punched the void. Bert leaped up into the air landing with a side punch to his opponent's head. The docker counteracted with a similar move, but Bert leaped backwards, crouched, then popped up within the circle of the docker's arms and punched him square on the nose stunning him momentarily as blood spurted in all directions. Bert took the opportunity to drive an uppercut to the man's jaw, but he mistimed his sidestep and as he turned away the docker punched his fist into Bert's right kidney. Pain shot through him taking his breath and he crumpled to the ground. He thought he'd been stabbed with a red-hot poker. The docker closed in, aiming for Bert's left kidney, but he manged to roll away and somehow find the strength to punch the docker's eye. The mustard did its job and the docker scrubbed at his eye, clearly forgetting whatever substance he'd applied to his own knuckles, it added fuel to the fire burning his eye.

  Still hunched over and breathing through his pain, Bert didn't see the docker reach back into the Shadows. But Sammy did and he whistled as loudly as he could the warning he and Bert had used as kids when they were up to no good and in danger of being caught. The warning came too late. As Bert got to his feet the docker swung a right hook at his left eye. It was like being struck by lightning as a burst of stars flooded Bert's vision and he growled with the pain. Just in time he remembered the mustard on his hands and used his forearm to shield his eye. Tears mingled with blood, streamed down his cheeks as the crowd cheered and roared all around them.

He couldn't see, but the trauma had heightened his senses. He could feel the heat of his opponent's body, smell his sweat. Instantly his mind was back in France crawling along endless tunnels in total darkness to lay mines under enemy trenches. It was there that he'd learned to judge distance by sense and feel, reaching out in the darkness to silently communicate with his cohorts. Always alert to danger from the enemy heading towards him on a similar mission.

Taking a chance that the docker held his fists aloft enjoying the crowd's cheers as the victor, Bert struck out with his right fist. Even in his current weak state his fist had the power of a piston and he drove it with all his might into the docker's relaxed, unguarded solar plexus. He crumpled and Bert drove his fist into his back aiming for his kidney then pounded his jaw with a succession of rapid blows until he heard the soft thud of a body hitting grass. A hush descended and Bert felt bile rise to his throat as in a moment of panic he thought he might have killed the bastard. He sensed someone drop down beside his opponent and it was as though the crowd was holding its breath waiting for the verdict. Then, someone raised his arm above his head and dragged him to his feet, the crowd went wild cheering and whistling, even honking their car horns. He knew he had to get away. The police might turn a blind eye to some of the goings on up here, but they couldn't ignore a racket like this at the dead of night. He staggered forward and would have fallen if Sammy hadn't caught him. Then Charlotte was beside him, he could smell violets. She placed something cool and soothing over his damaged eye. Then everything went black.

Bert regained consciousness on Charlotte's operating table squinting up at her through one partially open eye. The other was heavily padded. He had a thumping headache and a throbbing pain in his lower back.

'How are you doing, Champ?' Charlotte smiled, before stooping to kiss his lips.

'Bloody awful. How did I get here?'

'Sammy and one of Camel Coat's henchmen carried you in.'

'Aye, I expect they're protecting their interests. I've got to get out of this fighting lark.' He tried to sit up and growled as red-hot pain from his kidney shot through him.

'You're not going anywhere just yet,' she said, propping him up with extra pillows and handing him a wide neck glass bottle. 'You'll have to use that for now. It's not as though I haven't seen it all before,' she laughed, but turned away and busied herself tidying her instrument trolley and placing the used instruments into the sterilizing unit.

'That colour doesn't look too healthy,' Bert said, handing over the bottle.

'It's normal after trauma to a kidney. The time to worry is if it doesn't run clear in a day or two. Here drink this, it will ease the pain and help you sleep.' She waited for him to finish the bitter tasting liquid, then gently removed the extra pillows and helped him to lie flat again. 'Bert, you need to listen to me and don't argue. This is serious. I've had to operate on that eye. You're lucky I specialized foremost in eye surgery. You need to lie flat and keep still as much as possible, which means you can't go home for a week at least.' She waited for what she'd told him to sink in, then she said, 'You'll have to contact Ada. What will you tell her? You could always say you were injured at work and asked them to bring you here because you can't afford to go to the hospital.'

'No. It's time to tell her the truth. Will you get word to her? Maybe you could ask whoever you send to call in on Ethel first. She's knows what I've been up to with the fighting. When Ada finds out, she might need Ethel there. Her house is in the next road down from ours. She lives at the far end on the left. If they can't find her house, ask a neighbour or else send our Georgie to get her.' He sighed heavily, the sedative was taking effect slurring his speech. 'It looks like I'm back in your debt again, lass.'

'That's perfectly alright Bert. I look forward to receiving payment.' Her grey eyes twinkled mischievously, but Bert was asleep.

Charlotte knew she was only being nosey, but she couldn't resist. An hour later she was standing in her most serviceable clothes on Ethel's doorstep. 'Hello. Ethel is it? I'm Charlotte Gregory. I'm a friend of Ada and Bert. May I come in for a moment?' If Ethel was surprised to see her, she showed no sign and stepped aside to allow Charlotte into the front parlour. Ethel had known it was a stranger knocking. Nobody round here would have come to the front door. She was glad she kept the parlour for best. It was a bit chilly since she didn't light a fire except on special occasions, but there was no way she was going to take Charlotte through to the living room. Daniel had got newspapers spread out over the table busy with his Sunday morning ritual of cleaning the family's shoes. He maintained that even though they were second hand, and not always the right size, there was no excuse not to have a shine on them.

'Can I get you a cup of tea?' Ethel asked.

'No. Thank you. I only came to tell you that Bert's been hurt in a fight. He's at my house. I've had to operate on his eye and he has trauma to a kidney. He's been telling Ada the money's come from working extra shifts and she thinks he was working a shift last night. She must be wondering where he is by now. Bert wants us to tell her the truth.'

The colour drained from Ethel's face and she sank down beside Charlotte on the sofa. 'She's not going to take the news well. She only agreed to marry Bert once he'd stopped fighting, even though she was four months gone. She's stood by him over this union lark, but there's no telling what she'll do when she finds out he's been fighting behind her back.'

'Well personally, I don't think it's our place to tell her. Bert was in a lot of pain and heavily sedated when he sent me on this mission. He can't have been thinking clearly.'

'I'll get us that cup of tea anyway and you'd better come through to the living room where it's warmer. I'll get my Daniel to do his polishing outside. On second thoughts it might be better for the three of us to get us heads together over the best way to approach Ada. At least me kids are at Sunday School, so we won't have them nebbin' at what we're saying.'

On reflection, Charlotte realised she hadn't given sufficient thought to her reason for wanting to see Bert and Ada's home. She'd certainly not envisaged the extent of humiliation her presence would cause Ada. It soon became obvious by the way Ada was bobbing about clearing the table and setting out her best china, her cheeks flaming as she apologised for the mismatched cups and saucers, that she viewed Charlotte akin to royalty. Charlotte reached out and stilled Ada's busy hands. 'We've had a cup of tea already. Sit down while I make you one, you're in for a bit of a shock.'

'I'll get the tea,' Ethel said. 'I know where everything is. You tell Ada what's to do.'

'Can it wait till Bert gets home? I'm expecting him any minute.'

'It's about Bert that we've come,' Charlotte said, still holding on to Ada's hands. 'There's been an accident. He's alright,' she added quickly. 'He was brought to my house and I've operated on one of his eyes. He has bruising to his back and one of his kidneys.'

'What's happened to him?' Ada looked up at Ethel.

'That's for Bert to explain. We're not right sure.'

'When can I see him?' Ada turned back to Charlotte.

'You can come as soon as you like.'

'Drink that tea first, you look like you could do with it,' Ethel said. 'I'll stay here and wait for Georgie and Tommy to come back from Sunday School, then I'll take everyone back to my house. Unless you want me to come with you.'

'No. Thanks anyway. It's best if you see to me kids. I'll take Charlie with me though.'

Charlotte looked past the odd assortment of china cups to the darned tablecloth. Although threadbare, it was freshly starched and ironed. It epitomised the rest of the room, threadbare and sparse, but so pristinely scrubbed and polished that the ambience outshone the holes in the linoleum and darned fabric. She was beginning to understand the fierce pride burning in people like Ada and Bert, making do the best way they could, putting up a good front until life's struggle rendered them helpless. Now she also understood why Bert had risked his life for his family. She only hoped Ada would see it that way.

Bert was still asleep when Ada arrived. So she sat quietly beside his bed until he began to stir.

'You daft bugger,' she whispered. 'What were you doing to get that handsome face of yours all bashed up? It's a good job I don't just love you for your looks. And it's a bloody godsend we've friends like Ethel and Charlotte.'

'And Mabel,' he croaked, squinting at her through his one good eye. 'Pass us that glass bottle afore Charlotte gets back. Don't worry when you see the colour. I'm told it's normal after an injury to a kidney.'

Once Bert was settled comfortably again, Ada said, 'How did you come to injure your eye and your back? Did summat fly off your machine?'

'No. Ada love give us yer 'and. I've summat to tell you and you're not going to like it. But I'm tired out and sore and I'd be right glad if you'd let me finish before you lose your temper.' He saw the look of fear settle in her eyes. He hated himself for putting it there. The first time he'd noticed it was after he'd started on three days at work and the rent man had called. They'd hidden in the cellar because they'd no money to pay him. That look of fear had lifted once he'd started bringing home more money because Ada thought he was doing extra shifts.

'Listen to me love. When you were rushed into hospital having Charlie, I thought you were going to die and I'd have sold me soul to the devil to save you. I love you more than life itself. I always have. Do you remember Sammy the snout from school? Well he'd been pestering me for weeks to fight up at Sky Edge. That day I came away from the hospital I'd not a brass farthing to me name. There was no food to speak of in the house and I owed a month's rent. As I turned the corner of our street, Sammy was waiting for me. He caught me at a weak moment, I couldn't see no other way out. All I could see of our future was the inside of the workhouse. So I took up his offer. I've been fighting when I said I was working. Now I can't seem to get out of it. There's some nasty villains running the gambling because the fight meetings have grown massive. They've had me over a barrel because they threatened to tell you if I didn't keep fighting. Last night, Mabel's bloody Sydney put some Liverpool docker up against me. Sammy tried his best to tip me the wink, but the scouse bastard still managed to slip a knuckle duster over his fist. Charlotte can't say for sure yet whether me eye's done for. But I promise you this Ada, I'll see the inside of the workhouse afore I'll fight again. He closed his eyes and lay back exhausted against the pillows. Ada's chair scraped along the floor and he grabbed her wrist. 'Don't leave me,' he whispered.

She bent to kiss his lips. 'You should have told me sooner. It would have saved you a lot of trouble. I'm sorry that you've had to go through this on your own. Yes, you've put me through purgatory, these past months, but I won't be leaving you. I love you Bert, and I know for a fact that if you hadn't been fighting, we'd have been in the workhouse.' She went to lift Charlie from his pram and then settled back down with him in her arms to feed him.

Bert reached out and gently stroked Charlie's downy head. 'Now you know everything, we can use some of that money to get straight. I still need to pay off Charlotte and Mabel, but once I'm fit, if everyone's agreeable, I'll carry on working off me loan then we'll have some cash behind us. If you need owt for now, you'll find it in the cellar. There's a loose brick under the stone table with a tin of cash inside the cavity.'

'Hush, you need to rest,' Ada said.

When Charlotte returned, Bert was sleeping and Ada was softly singing a lullaby to Charlie in her sweet clear voice. Taking in the scene, Charlotte's smile was one of relief as she silently closed the door.

Chapter Fourteen– Sheffield April 1926

'Time passes that fast, I can't believe he's six months already. He looks bonnier every time I see him,' Ethel said, watching Ada feed ground rice and stewed apple to baby Charlie. He winced every time he took a mouthful of the sour concoction, but he still opened his mouth for another spoonful.

Both women held their gaze for a moment. Neither needed to say that things could have been very different, had Bert and Charlotte not intervened.

'Aye, sometimes life has a habit of throwing up a lucky break,' Ada, said. 'God knows we needed one.'

'You seem to have turned a corner all round,' Ethel said, noticing the remains of boiled eggs and soldiers. She turned away from the table to watch Daisy and Sophie sitting on the colourful rag rug contentedly playing with a tin of buttons in front of the warm hearth. Daisy was counting each button as she threaded it onto a shoelace. 'You're going to have a bright one there, Ada.'

'Yes, well, I'm doing me best. As you know I didn't have much schooling, so I've been asking Mabel for advice on the best way to go about helping me own kids. Georgie and Tommy are doing alright at school and I'm helping the girls to get a good start afore they go. There's more opportunity for lasses these days to get a good job, and things will only improve if my Bert's to be listened to. Young lasses won't just have to choose between domestic service or working behind a counter, or god forbid, doing a mucky job like the buffer girls in a little mester's cutlery shop. And Mabel's helping 'em to speak proper an' all. I hope I've brought 'em up to have nice manners already.'

Ethel nodded her head. 'There's no questioning that, folks are always saying how polite your kids are, Ada.'

They sat in companionable silence for a while, Ethel drinking tea and Ada feeding Charlie. Then Ethel said, 'Bert seems more settled now. Has he had any backlash from giving up the fighting?'

'No. A one-eyed bloke's not much good to 'em. Any road, since that new bloke's been put in charge of Sheffield's police force, they're making great strides in breaking up the gangs, so I don't think any of 'em will be knocking on our door.'

'Bert doesn't seem to be spouting as much about that union lark these days, according to my Daniel.'

'Well he's still of a mind to it, but he's keeping it quiet, he doesn't want to lose his job altogether. Now they've reduced all the men to a three-day week he's worried they might lay him off if he steps out of line. That and the fact he blames himself for me trouble birthing Charlie. Mabel's a big help of course. She paid for me doctor's bills and so Bert works for her on his days off, but she sends him home with that many jars of pickles and the likes, he's been flogging 'em to Smith's and the lads at work.'

'The factory's doing alright then, is it? Mabel's not always one to share her troubles.'

'Yes, as far as I know. She's branched out a bit, selling staple products and that, just in case there's a general strike, because when times is hard only them with a bit of brass can afford the luxury of pickles. I think she's talking of selling her pickles in other cities and abroad as well.'

'Exporting?'

'Aye, that'll be it. Only I can't quite recall what Bert said. Any road, she's making enough to have bought a little van for the deliveries and Ted's been teaching Bert to drive. He says motors are the thing of the future. Not that we'll ever afford one, mind.'

'Does Bert still work up at the allotments?'

'Aye, only Sundays in the winter, but now the nights are coming lighter, he goes up of an evening when he's not on the night shift.'

'He's not over doing it, is he? Gardening's hard graft. I know he's only working three days in the steel works, but it's heavy work and all on top of what he's doing at Mabel's factory.'

'He seems to be thriving on it, if you ask me. Unless it's the good food we're getting. Charlotte's planted a lot more vegetables since Bert's been helping and I know he's working there to pay off our debt to her, but she gives him the lion's share of the produce, unless she has guests.' Ethel nodded, knowing the guests would be women patients, desperately in need of her help, whether they could afford to pay her or not.

'Then of course she's got chickens on the allotment now, so there's fresh eggs more often than not, and he sometimes bags a rabbit or two while he's up there. You might not have noticed, but there's a couple less ducks floating on Endcliffe pond. Mind, we did have a right bad winter,' Ada giggled. 'In fact, it were that bad they lost a goose up at Mayfield around Christmas time.'

Ethel gawped at her friend. 'Ada you are shameless!'

'Aye, you might think so, but them in power are fond of preaching 'God helps them as helps themselves.' Well the government are doing bugger all to help the likes of us, especially them poor devils who gave their limbs for their country. I'm beginning to come around to my Bert's way of thinking with this union business. So long as we've a roof over our heads, enough food in our bellies and me kids are warm and dressed, then I'll support him all I can. He'll probably be going to the CDC meeting with Charlotte tonight, she likes to go, her being a socialist like, but being a woman she daren't go unaccompanied.'

'What's that when it's at home?'

'Central Dispute Committee. Bert says there's going to be some right bother if the Government try to make the miners work longer hours for less pay. It's a disgrace if you ask me, I don't know how they can ask it of 'em. Tonight's meeting is to see how other branches of the union can best offer support. If the miners do decide to come out on strike, I hope to god, our lads don't vote to come out 'an all. We've only just got turned around a strike could set us further back than we were afore.'

'Aye well, I'll not deny we just about managed on Daniels wage when he was drawing a full week, but things are right tight now he's down to three days. A general strike's going to hit us hard and it'll see a few off to the workhouse, no doubt about it.'

Ethel drank her tea in quiet contemplation and then setting her cup down in its saucer, she said, 'Bert spends a lot of time in Charlotte's company, aren't you worried there's summat going on between 'em?'

'No. They've just got union stuff in common, that and a strong belief in better standards for folks like us. Let's face it Ethel, my Bert might be a handsome devil, even with his one wonky eye, but she's way above his station. Even if she were the type to fancy a bit o' rough.'

Chuckling, Ethel got to her feet. 'I've left me washing soaking and I've all the beds to change yet, so I'd best be on me way. Maybe I'll call in tomorrow. Bye Daisy love, and you an' all, Sophie.' She turned and saw baby Charlie giving her a dimpled smile. 'And goodbye to you too, young man. You're going to break a few hearts an' all when you grow up, you cheeky Charlie.'

Chapter Fifteen - Sheffield April 1926

Mabel's hand trembled slightly rattling the cup in its saucer as she set it down. She picked up Sydney's letter which had arrived with the first post and read it again, this time trying to read between the lines. He'd written to say his revue was coming to the Empire Theatre the following week. A fact she already knew since every billboard across the city held a poster advertising it. His words of love and devotion oozed so syrupy sweet from the pages, it was a wonder the ink wasn't dripping.

When she'd finished reading it, she neatly folded the letter following the original creases, and put it in the top drawer of the dresser. Once, she would have re-read such a letter a dozen times and slept with it under her pillow. Now she didn't believe a word of it to be true. She knew he cared for her well enough, but to her way of thinking, actions spoke louder than words and Sydney's actions were notoriously dubious. What had really shocked her though, was her own lack of enthusiasm for their reunion. Usually, after one of their rare separations, her heart would have thumped into overdrive fuelling her body with adrenaline sending her into a flight of preparation. She hadn't seen him for weeks and she suddenly realised how peaceful she'd felt during that time. No, it was more than simply peaceful, she'd felt genuinely happy. She was alarmed to discover that seeing him again filled her with dread. Turning away from the dresser, she carried her breakfast things into the kitchen to wash. She had a whole week to worry about Sydney's arrival, today she had more important things to address.

Bert was busy mopping the factory floor when she arrived. She could see that the wooden benches had already been scrubbed white and left to dry in readiness for the workforce to begin chopping and peeling. He'd taken to coming to the factory straight off night shift for an hour or two, especially when it was his last shift of the week.

'Morning Bert, that looks grand.'

'I'm just finishing up before I leave to get me head down for a few hours. I'm due at the allotment later. I've set the boilers going so they'll be ready for the lasses to start the first batch of piccalilli.'

'You know Bert, you've long since repaid me for Ada's medical expenses. You must be tired. You're effectively holding down three part-time jobs.'

'Aye well, I'm glad to have any job at all and I'm grateful of the perks. I feel lucky I'm not walking in a miner's boots, poor beggars. There's a CDC meeting tonight to see how we can stand united. I hope they don't vote to come out in support. After all me spouting about joining a union I'll have to come out with 'em. But God knows how I'll face my Ada with that news. Any road I'd best let you get on. You've not come in this early for the good of your health.' He touched his forelock by way of excusing himself before he rinsed out the mop and emptied the bucket.

In the office, Mabel lit the gas under the kettle and bent to light the gas fire. The room felt chilled and slightly damp, even in the height of summer.

The heavy leather-bound ledger was open on the desk, exactly as she'd left it the day before.

Taking a sheaf of blank invoices from the drawer, she typed up customer's orders while she waited for the kettle to boil.

Sales were good, the radius of buyers was increasing. Encouraged by growing orders from neighbouring towns and villages, she had approached Fergus her father-in-law to act as salesman in Liverpool. As she'd suspected, his larger than life personality had fitted the role perfectly and he had ventured out of Liverpool and into Lancashire. Then in a stroke of genius he'd caught the ferry to the Isle of Man and called on boarding houses and hotels as well as grocers and café's, precuring regular orders prior to the summer season. Buoyed up by his achievement, he'd tried his hand in Blackpool with equal success.

The kettle was steaming its head off when Gladys walked through the door and she automatically set about making the tea before removing her hat and coat. 'Are those invoices ready?' she said, leaning over the desk. 'I'll take them down to the factory while the tea's mashing.'

They worked steadily through the day. Mabel spending much of her time on the telephone taking orders from existing customers and following up enquiries. Gladys spent her time creating new invoices, filing, and helping stick labels on the jars. Then at four o'clock, she said, 'Would you like a cup of tea, Mrs Baxter? Before I go off to my stenographer's course.'

'Yes please, Gladys, and I'll bet you could do with one to go with your sandwich. Wouldn't you prefer to eat it here in comfort?'

'I would that, if you don't mind. Rushing me food gives me indigestions something chronic.' She went off to make the tea and returned carrying a tray loaded with cups of tea, her sandwich and a plate of biscuits. 'I'm ever so grateful to you Mrs Baxter, for sending me on the stenographer's course and for giving me a whole day off as well as an evening to attend. I'd never have learned anything on just the one evening.

'You're very welcome Glady. Anyway, we're a co-operative and it benefits us all. Progress is the only way forward, so my father used to say.'

When the tea break was over Gladys collected the cups and plates and washed them at the sink in the little kitchen. 'I'd best be off then, or the class will be progressing without me.' Taking her hat and coat down from the hook behind the door, she said, 'See you tomorrow Mrs Baxter, have a nice evening.'

Gladys had been gone well over an hour when Ted knocked on the door and walked into the office, cap in hand. 'Begging your pardon, Mrs Baxter, only I was wondering what time you were planning on leaving. I was hoping to lock up about now.'

'Any chance of another half an hour, Ted?' She was surprised to see his expression fall, he wasn't usually in a hurry to leave. As a widower, he lived alone and hated it. Not being one for frequenting public houses, he complained of his evenings being lonely at times.

'Do you have somewhere to be? Ted.'

'Aye, well I've a mind to attend the CDC meeting. I believe there's a general strike coming whether we like it or not. We need to be prepared Mrs Baxter we don't know how it's going to affect our business. I was going to wait and bring it up at our weekly meeting, but as we're speaking about it now, I think I should make me feelings clear. I'm going to support the miners if they come out on strike and I think you'd be wise to close the factory in support. There's no telling what an angry mob will do to a business still in operation. We could find ourselves with a lot of repairs when it's all over.'

'What time does the meeting start? Would you mind if I came with you? I'd like to get a better understanding of what it's all about.'

A look of relief lit up his face. 'It would be my pleasure, Mrs Baxter. It starts at seven thirty, but I dare say you'll want to grab a bite to eat first.'

'I think I shall go to the Lyon's tea rooms to eat. Would you care to join me? How about we put it down to business expenses?' she said, handing him some coins from the cash tin in the desk drawer.

The meeting was well attended. All the chairs were taken, and the crowd stood three deep, shoulder to shoulder, around the perimeter of the room. Mabel and Ted found a spot over to the left near the front, commanding a good view of the platform and the room. They had been handed a copy each of the Sheffield Forum, the newspaper which the Central Dispute Committee were using to get their message across. They were both asked if they could distribute copies around the city. Ted looked to Mabel. He signed up for the task immediately she nodded her approval.

A hush came over the room as the speaker got to his feet.

'Red Friday was the day the Government offered a subsidy to the mining industry. It was a day we all welcomed,' he paused for a ripple of response. 'But it was a false promise. Yesterday, the Government revoked their offer. Yesterday, the Government's Samuel Commission recommended that in order for the industry to remain profitable, the miners should work longer hours and have their wages reduced!'

The subdued gathering erupted, men leaped to their feet shaking their fists and stamping their boots. Audible above the fracas were cries of 'The bastards. Unbelievable. Wicked buggers. Bloody management won't be taking a cut, you can bet on that.'

Mabel felt a moment of panic and she scanned the room for an escape route. She noticed representatives of the St. John's Ambulance Brigade standing on the opposite side and recognised one of the women. She had worked with her as a VAD at a military hospital during the war. As though she sensed Mabel's eyes on her, Constance turned and waved in recognition, indicating as best she could that she would meet her afterwards. Mabel felt comforted just knowing that Constance was in the room and remembered she had always had that effect on people.

Ted placed a reassuring hand at Mabel's elbow. 'Don't worry, the crowd'll settle down in a minute or two.' He had no sooner spoken than the main speaker banged a wooden mallet on the table. 'Order! Order!' he cried,

'Nothing will be solved by shouting about it. We'd do better getting us heads together and working out the best way to support us fellow union members.'

Miners from Grimesthorpe and the surrounding collieries, who had come into the city for the meeting, began chanting and soon the crowd were up on their feet again joining in.

'Not a penny off the pay

Not a second on the day'

The speaker banged the mallet frantically and gradually the excitement left the crowd. 'The miners have until the first of May to accept the new terms or there will be a lock out. The time has come when actions speak louder than words. Let us have a show of hands please, to prove our solidarity. All those in favour of a national strike in support of the miners, say Aye.' Every hand shot up, including Mabel's, although she did wonder how many people had been intimidated into it and whether those who had, would strike. She suspected they would be bullied into it anyway, within their place of work.

Being furthest from the exit, Ted and Mabel waited until most of the room had emptied. It was then that she spotted Bert. He was talking animatedly with an attractive, well-to do woman. At that moment the woman stumbled, and Bert caught her in his arms. The look that passed between them as he righted her, turned Mabel's blood cold. It wasn't the look she had grown used to seeing in Sydney's eyes when he had a new conquest in sight. She couldn't find words honourable enough to describe the emotion emanating from this pair. Whatever it was, theirs was no casual acquaintance and her heart constricted as she thought of all that Ada had recently gone through, her continued loyalty throughout great hardship and her sweet little family all holding Bert high on a pedestal. Whatever the reason for his association with this woman, Mabel fervently hoped it wouldn't have repercussions on his family.

Constance was waiting outside when Mabel and Ted stepped onto the pavement. 'Lovely to see you after all this time,' she said, holding out her hand. 'And what a lucky coincidence. I have something for you.' She looked anxiously up at Ted, then she turned to Mabel, 'Do you think you could spare me a moment or two in private?'

'Of course. Ted, thank you for escorting me to the meeting, I can make my own way home, there are plenty of people about so I'm sure I shall be perfectly safe.'

'Right you are then, Mrs Baxter. I'll see you in the morning.' Doffing his cap, he turned about and walked off in the direction of the tram stop.

'What's all the secrecy about?'

'Look, I don't like hanging around on the street. Headquarters isn't far. They don't shut until ten. We can get a cup of tea and a biscuit there while we chat in comfort.'

Constance allowed Mabel to take a sip of tea before she opened her satchel and produced a letter. 'I heard you were married. I thought you might want to read this in private.'

Mabel's face drained of colour as she registered the foreign stamp and the handwriting. 'It's addressed to the military hospital where we worked during the war. How did you come by it?'

'Pure coincidence. A member of our brigade was due to go on a training course at the hospital, but she was taken ill, so I was sent in her place. Matron still works at the hospital and she recognised me. She asked if I was in touch with you. I'm afraid I lied. But I reckoned I was your best bet, I felt certain I would come across someone who could get in contact with you sooner or later. Aren't you going to open it?'

'It's given me quite a turn. It's been a long time. If you don't mind, I'd prefer to read it in private.'

'I was afraid you'd say that. Oh, well, if it's anything exciting, like he's offering you the job of a lifetime in the South of France and you can take a friend, count me in.'

Mabel looked at the post mark. 'This was sent six months ago.'

'That's right. But I've only had it a couple of weeks. Seems like fate that I should bump into you. It's taken two coincidences to get that letter to you. I hope we can keep in touch now we've met up again.' She looked at her watch. 'Just time for another cuppa, we can drink it while we catch up on the last seven years.'

The house was in darkness and the hall felt cold as Mabel let herself in. She was glad she'd banked up the kitchen stove before she'd left that morning. It would mean she could have a bath as well as a warm drink. She took some hot ashes up to her bedroom and dropped them into the hearth to set the kindling going before she undressed.

Receiving a letter from Pierre, after all this time, had shaken her beyond belief.

She thought of Sydney. When she had met him, she had been vulnerable, still mourning the death of her parents and brother. She had been easy prey for Sydney's particular style of seductive charm. She wondered now whether she would have been so quick to marry him, if she hadn't also been feeling raw from recently ending her love affair with Pierre?

    She couldn't bring herself to open the letter tonight. But she would sleep with it beneath her pillow, for although she was bewitched by Sydney's charm, she had been forever captivated by Pierre's love. She was never the least bit in doubt that Pierre had loved her. Their misfortune had been timing. Born into an aristocratic family his fate had been sealed soon after his birth. Friends of his parents, an equally prestigious family, had been blessed with a daughter and the two families had contrived to bring about a union through their children.

    Mabel had first met him while working as a VAD in France. He was already married and an eminent surgeon with whom she should only have had the briefest of contact. Rules change when the carnage of war is raging. Her duties had evolved way beyond those of a regular VAD. Working alongside him amidst the constant stream of men delivered to their tent in a bloody mess of tangled limbs, mud and lice; love had flourished. Not the love born of dizzying physical attraction. Their love was deep rooted, the stuff of soulmates. Yet their affair was never consummated. Pierre, knowing a future together was hopeless, had gently explained that divorce was out of the question, not only on moral grounds but on religious ones as well. He and his wife were Catholic.

Mabel had accepted that he was too well bred to be anything other than a gentleman. He had not stolen her innocence to keep for himself. Had that been the case, they both knew she would never have wanted to make a future for herself with another man.

Mabel tossed and turned in the big double bed as the memories came flooding back. His letter had opened old wounds. She couldn't think why he would be contacting her seven years after their last goodbye. She didn't want to open the letter because she was afraid it might contain terrible news. Perhaps telling her he had an incurable illness. She had just about come to terms with the fact she would probably never see him again and she didn't know if she could come to terms with knowing that for certain.

The first of May dawned. The miners had not accepted the Government's terms and a general strike seemed inevitable. The people of Sheffield's response appeared to be mixed. Mabel received a leaflet from the Organisation for Maintenance of Supplies containing information about what services their volunteers were endeavouring to keep open. She threw it in the bin. The Pickle Co-operative had already made the joint decision to support the strike. She only hoped it wouldn't last very long.

It wasn't until she was passing a bill board advertising Sidney's revue, that she realised the impact it would have on the show if all public transport was out of action. Perhaps she wouldn't have to see him after all. He might cancel whichever bookings coincided with the strike and move onto the next one when the trains were running again. She knew it would only be delaying the inevitable though, and knowing Sydney, he would probably coerce someone into transporting the whole show, scenery and all, for less than the cost of the rail fare.

Chapter Sixteen – Sheffield 1926

Sydney's revue arrived in a cavalcade of removal vans and charabancs creating a flourish of publicity. He announced to the newspaper reporters that in addition to the usual afternoon and evening performances, he intended to put on morning matinees to support the miner's strike fund and a Sunday evening's performance free of charge for the sole entertainment of local miners and their families.

He'd been kept busy with the get-in and band call but had previously sent word to Mabel that a box would be reserved for her on opening night and she was to invite Bert and Ada, together with Ethel and Daniel. She wondered whether Sydney was breaking some law putting on a variety show in a public theatre on a Sunday. Perhaps it was allowed because no money was changing hands. Although, knowing Sydney, he'd get away with it in any case.

Mabel thought Ada looked beautiful. She was wearing one of Annie's dresses, it fitted like a glove, and Ada's sister, who had volunteered to babysit, had styled her hair. Bert obviously thought she looked beautiful too, judging by the way he was fussing over her. Mabel wondered anew what his relationship was with the other woman.

The curtain went up on the opening number and even with Lotti's peroxide curls, Mable recognised her immediately as being one of the dancers from the ship. So that was who had kept Sydney amused and away from her, she thought, and waited for the fist of jealousy to punch her abdomen. The experience was surprisingly pain-free.

She analysed her feelings. Was this to do with Pierre's letter? She didn't think so, after all she'd been dreading the reunion with Sydney well before the letter arrived. She leaned forward in her seat peering over the edge of the box to study the back of his head. His black hair was so shiny with pomade it reflected the beam streaming from the lighting box. She had spoken with him only briefly before going to her seat. He'd taken her into his arms and kissed her softly. His lips had all at once reminded her of a marshmallow. The memory of it caused a giggle to escape and she quickly shrank back into the dark recess of the box. She didn't imagine that Lotti's charms would keep him away from her bed tonight after all this time apart. Idly she scanned the chorus line looking for a new face, one likely to have become Lotti's competition, hoping that such a one might keep him away. Her eyes focused on the soubrette, tall and slender with a shock of auburn hair curling unfashionably long beneath a turban. She was more the type to hold his attraction. Although on reflection she looked sophisticated, too self- assured. Sydney had probably been unable to fathom her. She was sure he would have tried. Then she spotted a young brunette with a large bosom and skinny little legs, dancing third from the right. The girl was exactly his type. When the dance ended Mabel looked forward to the next routine so she could continue her game of spot the harlot. Although that title was probably harsh. Sydney's conquests were usually innocents. With that thought in mind, she concentrated hard on the young brunette during the next routine. This proved to be tricky as it was a Can-Can. It was difficult keeping focus as the dancers performed cartwheels and handstands scissoring their legs and clicking their heels into walk overs travelling across the stage. Mabel remembered the first time she had seen the Can-Can performed. She had found it exhilarating and wished she could have been up there with the dancers twirling and tumbling. She asked Sydney why the dance carried the reputation of being risqué, for although the dancers lifted their skirts to flash their garters and knickers, the knickers were so voluminous and frilly they were less revealing than other costumes.

'Because,' he had replied, taking delight in shocking her, 'the original Can-Can dancers didn't wear knickers!'

Mabel concentrated on the young brunette cavorting around the stage. Her large bosom was disproportionate to her skinny legs and the costume seemed to be straining under the battle to retain her modesty. Mabel took out her opera glasses, a relic from the days when she had visited the grand opera houses with her parents. She trained the glasses on the girl. It looked as though an amateur attempt had been made to let a piece into the bodice of her costume. When the dance troupe held their final position, Mabel trained the glasses on the girl's face. There was a slight puffiness around her cheeks and jaw. Mabel's hands dropped to her lap. She studied the back of Sydney's head. Dear God, she thought, please don't let this be Sydney's problem.

Had she thought to avoid him until she was asleep in bed, Mabel was disappointed. He was waiting for her as she descended the stairs from the box. With practiced ease, he managed to separate her from the others without causing offence and whisk her off to a club she didn't know existed. She wondered, not for the first time, how he managed to find these exclusive clubs in every town, let alone gain entry. Then as she was being helped off with her coat, she noticed Sydney slip a large roll of bank notes into her pocket, presumably to be retrieved by someone else.

The usual bottle of champagne was waiting on ice at their table. 'I took the liberty of ordering dinner,' he said, leading her to the edge of the dance floor and gathering her into his arms. He had given her a corsage of gardenias and their strong scent suddenly made her feel rather light headed and nauseous.

'You are looking beautiful my darling, although you have lost a little weight. You are not working too hard, are you?'

'No, it's because I'm not eating the rich meals served on the cruise ship, that's all.'

'I have missed you so much,' he said, nestling his cheek against her hair and inhaling her perfume. His lips caressed her ear travelling to her neck, and despite her best intention she could feel her senses weakening. He dropped his arm from her waist and brought her gloved hand to his lips caressing the tips of her fingers. 'The waiter is hovering by our table he must be ready to serve our first course.'

She had drunk too much champagne. She wondered whether she had intentionally let that happen knowing what was to come? She felt a semi-loathing for her treacherous senses; she was not yet immune to Sydney's charm after all.

Brandy had been served and after lighting his cigar Sydney leaned back in his chair and leisurely announced, almost to the room in general, that the last time they were together they had been unsuccessful in their attempt at creating a new life. Lowering his voice, he reached for her hand across the table. 'Perhaps the next few days will prove to be more fruitful.'

She stiffened as an image of the young brunette crowded her mind. 'I don't think now would be an ideal time to begin a family. You're still travelling with the revue, and I'm just beginning to see a return on the outlay at the factory.'

'It is never a good time if you plan for these things to happen. Should love not be spontaneous? And a child should always be made from love.'

How long she had waited to hear him say such words, ached for it, prayed for it. Now he'd uttered them she was repulsed. What had changed? What was wrong with her? She excused herself and headed for the ladies' cloakroom.

Her cheeks were burning and she splashed cold water over her face. Sydney's words were still ringing in her ears. 'A child should always be made from love.' Did she love Sydney? She had thought she did. But the letter from Pierre had resurrected feelings she had chosen to bury. Now she felt compelled to compare the love she had felt for him against what she felt for Sydney.

She looked squarely at her reflection and her inner voice bubbled to the surface. You've grown up, that's what's happened. You've realised that there's no comparison between Sydney and the worth of a man like Pierre.

I can't have Pierre and I'm married to Sydney.

She tried to quell her inner voice, but now it had surfaced it was relentless. The only thing that was wrong with your life before you met Sydney, was Annie.

Mabel listened, and knew it was true. Although she'd been heartbroken at the death of her parents and her brother, if she hadn't had to live with Billy's widow and forced to take a back seat at the factory, she would have been content to take her time in finding a suitable husband. She thought back to the early days of her marriage. It had been a magical time, Sydney had swept her off her feet. They had sailed away on cruise ships into the wide blue yonder.

'It could still be magical now,' she told her reflection, banishing her inner voice. 'All I have to do is surrender to his charm.' Images of the loving moments they'd shared in their cabin flooded her mind and a shiver rippled through her body as her senses gave strength to her argument.

Her inner voice was stronger. Do you want to share him with the chorus of each revue? Have you thought what will happen if your suspicions are correct about the young brunette?

She splashed more water onto her face and took a towel from a clean pile beside the sink. Tonight, and for the following week, Sydney would be living in her home. She would be a wife to him in every sense, but they would not create a new life. She had already taken measures to prevent it. After that, he would be gone.

The ever-popular revue took Sheffield by storm. The fact that Sydney had put on additional performances to support the miners had made him greatly popular with the masses, if not the pit owners, or the management of local businesses, who were worried his action would further incite their workers into joining the miners in an all-out general strike.

The additional performances were also proving unpopular with Lotti. 'I don't reckon much to these morning matinees,' she sighed, melting a block of eye black over a candle and applying it a lash at a time. The process was painstakingly slow. 'I hope Syd doesn't catch on to the idea. I say Violet, you do look rather green around the gills. Out late on the gin, were you?'

Violet fled from the room to be violently sick in the ladies toilet. She was splashing cold water over her face at one of the sinks when Gracie walked in.

After using the facilities, Gracie joined her at the sinks to wash her hands. 'Would you like me to fasten your costume?' she asked, putting down the hand towel. 'Breath in, you'll have to cut back on your visits to Davy's coffee house, Violet, their cakes are expanding your waistline.'

'I think you might be right,' Violet gave her a tight little smile.

Gracie stood in the corridor and watched her walk back to the dressing room. She knew cakes weren't Violet's problem. She wondered whether the girl herself had realised it yet.

Sydney emerged from the band room as Gracie walked by. 'Our paths have not crossed of late. I have missed you.'

'Perhaps it's because you walk a more crooked path than me,' she replied, brushing past him.

After the show, Sydney waited in the tobacconist's doorway near the theatre hoping to catch a moment alone with Gracie. She was usually one of the last to leave and while he waited, he mulled over recent events. It had been most fortunate that the cruise contract had been up for renewal just as he'd found himself between a rock and a hard place. The New York gangsters holding the monopoly on Rum running in and out of the city had got wind that someone was muscling in on their lucrative business and at the same time the customs men and police had intensified their manpower attempting to crack down on imports of illegal alcohol. He'd thought he'd got away clean and hadn't anticipated the gangster bosses sending someone all the way across the Atlantic to threaten him. Sydney realised in that moment that they'd probably ordered his assassination once his supplier in England had been located.

He lit up a cigarette and inhaled deeply. It was a good job the Manchester club Manager was experienced in the ways of villains. He'd heard back that the gangster's body had been returned and dumped in New York's harbour. Taking a drag on the cigarette he exhaled with a sigh of relief, he was convinced he'd acted swiftly enough in changing his supply route and covering any trail leading back to himself. No one else would come after him.

He turned his thoughts to Mabel, when he'd arrived in Sheffield, she'd worried him, she had appeared aloof and distant. It had taken patience and skill to win back her affection. Now convinced that she was once again besotted with him, he'd felt confident in allowing himself a few late nights.

Lotti had forgiven him for excluding her from his club. She'd been excited by the furtive liaisons in the theatre after it had closed. He had tipped the night watchman a hefty bribe to turn a blind eye to his nocturnal activities and the bottles of champagne and picnic hamper secreted in the band room in readiness.

Then he thought of the little brunette. Hells bells, it was so long since he'd spoken to her, he'd forgotten her name. Violet, that was it. Ever since that one night she'd spent in his bed, she had proved to be more elusive than Gracie. His charm must be slipping. Perhaps it was just as well. Delores would be on the Isle of Man. His revue at the Gaiety Theatre followed her show in. She had arranged to stay on with him for the first month of his revue's run. If Mabel decided to join him as well, and she was quite likely to, since that was where they'd met, then he would be juggling the three women. Despite his already complicated web of deceit, he could not resist another attempt at enticing Gracie.

He stamped out his cigarette and stepped onto the pavement as she walked by. 'I will not detain you,' he said. 'I wanted you to have this.' He put his hand in his jacket pocket and pulled out a marcasite wrist watch. It dangled between his forefinger and thumb, flashing where the gas light reflected off it.

'This once belonged to my godmother, I loved her very much. It was among the few items she bequeathed. It is very precious to me. Now I would like you to have it.'

Illuminated under the light, her face portrayed a medley of emotions. Shock?... Certainly. When her features softened, he felt tentative strands of his web reaching out and taking hold. It was the first time he'd seen a soft light in her emerald eyes, but it was merely a glimpse before they became green ice. His stomach lurched when he realised that he'd mistaken her look of compassion, for pity.

'I thank you for your offer,' she said. 'It's a most generous gift. However, I must decline. Something of such great sentiment should always be reserved for one's wife.' She raised her arm and a taxi appeared as though plucked from the air. The driver jumped out and opened the door, blocking Sydney. Then the door slammed shut. She stared at him with sombre eyes as the taxi pulled away from the kerb.

Chapter Seventeen - The Isle of Man 1926

Mabel had refused to accompany Sydney to the Isle of Man. She'd made the excuse that it was a bad time to leave the factory during the middle of a strike. He had said he couldn't see the problem. 'Is it not the perfect time to declare a holiday?' he'd protested. His protestations were false. He'd been relieved to have one less female to contend with. Delores could be insanely jealous and because of her predatory attitude she was the one woman who had riled Mabel more than any other. There was no telling where it would have all ended had she discovered Delores was on the Isle of Man.

Now, on the ferry across, Lotti clung to him like a limpet. It occurred to him that she'd been distant of late. She seemed to relish their secretive meetings but had happily scooted off to her own room afterwards. A fact which puzzled him, she usually sulked like a petulant child when she couldn't spend the night in his bed.

'Where is Gracie? I haven't seen her aboard the ferry,' he said, shrugging off Lotti's grasp.

'That's because she's not. She's catching a later one, she had some family business to attend to.'

His spine prickled, he had a sixth sense when it came to business. He suddenly knew for certain she was auditioning. She was free to leave his revue at any time. She'd talked the booking agent into giving her a get-out clause in her contract. He'd been working on the cruise ship at the time, and with Delores moving on, he'd urgently needed a replacement soubrette for when the revue opened in Liverpool shortly after the ship docked. He'd agreed to her terms, confident that the lure of his famous revue would be enough to hold her. It had never entered his head that she might consider leaving before the end of the tour.

'What's up, Syd? You've gone a bit pale. You're not going to puke on me, are you?'

'I'm going on deck for a smoke.'

Lotti shrugged as she watched him stagger out, then she turned up the collar of her coat and snuggled down in her seat to let the motion of the ferry lull her. She hadn't got much sleep during the night. A smile tugged the corner of her mouth as she reflected why.

Delores was waiting for him in a taxi outside the Isle of Man ferry terminal. He smiled knowing that she would have kept the taxi waiting in readiness to whisk him away to her hotel room. Six months was the longest they'd been apart since their affair began three years earlier. Sophistication was her attraction. That and a caustic personality which he found amusing. Intrigue came from her enthusiasm for the experimental, late at night in hotel rooms.

'You took your time,' she said, lighting two cigarettes and passing him one. She had loosened her coat enough to reveal a gown cut too low to be classed as a respectable day dress. The taxi drove off along cobbled streets causing her protruding breasts to wobble and her legs to part ever so slightly, giving Sydney the odd glimpse of garter. He reached out to stroke the milky flesh of her inner thigh, and she sighed exhaling little puffs of cigarette smoke. He lifted her hand to kiss the tips of her fingers, turning it over to plant a kiss in the palm.

Then shifting places to sit beside her, he folded her hand in his and placed it in her lap. Dewy-eyed she reached up to draw him into a kiss, oblivious of whether the driver noticed or cared.

The taxi drew alongside the kerb and Sydney jumped out to pay the driver, giving him a generous tip. Then he turned to help Delores step out. 'You had better fasten your coat Delores, before we walk across the foyer, you are revealing your garters.' Sydney whispered, after seeing the driver's cheeky wink as he doffed his cap before driving off.

Her room turned out to be a suite, and he wondered whether she had acquired such luxury to impress him. He knew how much she got in her pay packet. She could not afford such luxury on a regular basis.

'How were things in Sheffield?' she asked, handing him a glass of whisky.

'Depressing. The soot blackened city is all the darker for being landlocked. At least in Liverpool the water seems to freshen the air. Of course, the strike hasn't helped in adding to the gloom.' He paused to sip the whisky. 'Fortunately, Mabel lives across the city from the main factories. There are a few smaller ones close by, but the toxic fumes do not seem so prevalent. Although the occasional smell of hops from the brewery can make one feel quite nauseous.'

Bored by small talk Delores sat down beside him at the foot of the bed and ran her hand up his inner thigh to still his chatter. She could feel him tensing, but her hand journeyed upwards to slip between the buttons of his shirt and glide in exploratory circles over his smooth skin.

She nuzzled his ear, before tracing a wet trail across his cheek in search of his mouth as she worked loose his shirt and tie, then she shimmied out of her dress to stand naked before him, but for her silk stockings. He groaned as she straddled his lap wrapping her arms around his neck, crushing her breasts against his chest as she wriggled closer. Her mouth smothered his groans before blazing a trail of kisses down his torso to work free his belt and linger there, her kisses driving him almost to the brink. He cried out when her kisses deserted him to trail down his thigh and over his calf until the remainder of his clothes lay discarded on the floor. Then she retraced her path, breasts grating against the hairs on his legs. She rose up, back arched and his mouth captured a nipple, enflamed and hardened into the semblance of a small raspberry. She slipped from his grasp sliding high up his body her thigh brushing his cheek and it was almost his undoing. He flipped her over, completing their union, locking into her rhythm until she cried out. Only then did he drive on to a glittering release.

Sydney lay on his back smoking a cigarette, his other arm draped around Delores. 'I have missed you,' he said, kissing the top of her head, 'and I have a surprise.'

'I've missed you too. You, incorrigible man.' She propped herself up on her elbow and reached for his cigarette. 'What sort of surprise?'

'Do you want the job of soubrette in my revue for the rest of the tour?' he said, taking another cigarette from the packet beside the bed. 'I have heard a rumour that Gracie is auditioning elsewhere. I do not want to be left without a good soubrette. I'm going to push her before she jumps. You are my first choice.'

'What about her contract?'

'She talked the booking agent into giving her a get-out clause.'

Sydney realised in that moment that he'd be glad to see the back of Gracie, she disturbed him in a way he couldn't fathom. She had become an obsession.

Delores was only too delighted to show her appreciation. Cigarette smoke caught in his throat as she slipped beneath the sheets.

Room service delivered a bottle of champagne, a selection of cold meats, salmon and French cheeses.

These pickles are delicious,' Delores said, offering him a bite of cheese and pickle on a biscuit.

'They taste remarkably like the pickles Mabel makes at her factory,' he laughed. 'I must tell her when I speak to her.' He glanced at his watch. 'I promised to telephone when I arrived. I must go down to the telephone booth in the foyer.'

'What's wrong with sending a telegram?'

'Nothing. Except Mabel now has a telephone installed at home as well as in the factory and so I must make use of it.'

Before speaking to Mabel, Sydney first asked the telephone operator to make a person to person call to the manager of the private club he frequented in Sheffield. He held the line and listened as the operator spoke to several people before establishing the contact. 'I have Mr Sydney Baxter on the line. Please hold Sir, while I try to connect you.'

Sydney heard crackling and a click before a man's voice said, 'Hello, are you there?'

'I trust my driver was efficient,' Sydney asked.

'Like clockwork, he set off at the estimated time and arrived yesterday.'

'Thank you for your assistance in this matter.'

'My pleasure. I look forward to being of assistance next time,' the manager said, and disconnected the call. Sydney was relieved to learn the consignment of alcohol had reached its new destination safely. He waited for the telephone operator to come back on the line and then asked to be put through to the hotel where Lotti and the cast were staying.

'Where the hell did you get to?' Lotti spoke sulkily into the phone after the porter had finally located her.

'My darling, I told you. Don't you remember? Relatives of Mabel own a hotel on the island. I knew they would be waiting for me to take me to their hotel when we disembarked. I could not be seen leaving the ferry with you on my arm. I am going to miss you this week.'

'What do you mean, miss me? Can't we make the same arrangement as last week.'

'I'm afraid not. The theatre manager also has connections with Mabel's family. They may get to hear if I bribe the night watchman. Do not worry my beautiful girl, I will think of something. Remember to give me your best smile in the tap number tomorrow night. I will be watching.'

The telephone operator came back on the line and he gave her Mabel's number. It took quite a time to connect the trunk call to the local operator and then Mabel took an age to come to the phone. He was about to hang up when she answered. 'I was in the garden taking washing from the line. I couldn't hear the telephone ringing until I neared the house.'

'It's good to hear your voice my darling. I am missing you already. Are you sure you cannot come over here to be with me, if only for a few days? I am here for the season. There is time for the strike to have ended by then.'

'I will consider it. It all depends on getting the factory up and running. If we can't, then everything that we've worked for will be lost.'

'Please say you will try, my darling.'

'You have my word, but no guarantee.'

'Do you know, it's the strangest thing. I had pickles with lunch which tasted exactly like your brand.'

'They probably were.'

'How can that be, how did they get here?'

'Your father.'

'My father? 'What has he to do with your pickles?'

Mabel sighed. 'Syd do you ever read any of the letters I send you?'

'Darling it is not my fault they go astray at the theatre,' he lied.

'Your father is working as a salesman for the Pickle Co-operative. He's done very well selling to the hotels and boarding houses on the mainland and on the Isle of Man.'

'But why have neither of you told me about this before now?'

'We have, in our letters... Syd I've got to go, it's started raining and I have sheets on the line.'

It wasn't until after the call was disconnected that he remembered it was Sunday. He doubted very much that Mabel would have been hanging washing out on the Sabbath.

Delores was just getting out of the bath when he returned to the room. She sensed the beginning of one of his rages, she was not as afraid of them as most. 'Who's rattled your cage, lover boy?' she asked, rubbing her hair vigorously as she walked out of the bathroom.

'Do you know how Mabel's pickles got onto that tray?' he pointed an accusing finger at the remains of their lunch.

'Is this a test, or can you give me a clue?' She knew her flippancy would rile him, but she couldn't change her personality to pussy foot around his childish behaviour.

'My father!'

'Your father. What?'

'My father is working as a salesman for my wife and neither of them thought to tell me.'

'Perhaps if you read their letters once in a while, instead of throwing them in the bin, you may have been forewarned. Anyway, although I can't say I like your wife very much and not only for obvious reasons, I take my hat off to her for the quality of her pickles and for her initiative in employing your father. If he's anything like you, he could charm anyone into buying anything. Why are you angry anyway?'

'They have been secretive, doing things behind my back.'

'That's rich,' she chortled, 'coming from a man whose whole life is one big secret. A man who's currently complaining to his mistress, about how deceitful his wife has been, over a jar of pickles.'

He turned about and stormed from the room slamming the door behind him. Delores did not concern herself - she'd seen it all before.

Sydney went in search of Lotti. He would tell her he'd invented some excuse about an all-night get-in to escape the relatives he'd so conveniently acquired to escape her in the first place. When he arrived at the hotel, he discovered Lotti was out, so he ordered a scotch from the bar while he waited. Surveying the room in search of a familiar face, his eyes settled on Violet, the young brunette from the chorus. She was curled up in her usual spot, a big chair by the bay window.

'Hello, we really will have to stop meeting like this,' he said, coming to stand beside her. 'Can I buy you a drink?' He waited to hear her usual cheery 'I should say so' but she snapped her head around looking at him like a startled rabbit caught in a headlight.

'What would you like to drink?' he repeated, holding aloft his whisky glass.'

'A ginger ale would be nice, thank you.'

'Are you sure you don't want a whisky in that?'

'Perfectly sure, thank you.'

He ordered her drink and another for himself then sat in the chair opposite. He placed his glass down on the small table between them and lit a cigarette leaning back in his chair and leisurely crossing his legs. 'I hope your roommate did not lock you out while I was living at home.' He raised his eyebrows enquiringly, viewing her through a haze of smoke.

'No, I made sure we went up at the same time.'

The waiter arrived with their drinks and Sydney paid him, before continuing the conversation. For some reason, it was becoming hard work. He remembered Violet as bubbly, chatting ten to the dozen.

'Forgive me, Violet, but are you feeling quite well? You don't seem to be your usual self.' To his astonishment fat tears welled up and trickled down her cheeks.

'Oh, Mr Sydney, I don't know what to do, really I don't. I need to tell you something and I don't know how.'

'Usually the best way is to come straight out with it, get it over with.' The advice was something he personally had never adhered to, but it was the first thing that came to mind.

'Not here, we can't talk here. You never know who might be listening. Can we go for a walk or something?'

He'd noticed a park opposite on his way in. There was a band stand with chairs set out. 'It is a nice evening for a stroll, and I think there is to be a concert in the park later. Shall we go?' He stood up offering his arm.

As it turned out, the concert had been in the afternoon and a sudden shower scattered the stragglers. Sydney and Violet made a dash for one of the covered shelters. 'Now, you must take a deep breath and tell me how I can help you.'

'Mr Sydney, haven't you noticed anything different about me?'

He studied her. 'No, I'm afraid not. You still have your glorious chestnut curls and you are as beautiful as ever. What is it that I should have noticed?'

'Well these for a start,' she said, grasping a breast in each hand and hoisting them up. 'They were half this size when I started working for you.' She took hold of his hands and pressed them against her breasts. 'Feel 'em, like a pair of rocks they are. Given you a clue, have I, Mr Sydney?' Seeing his clueless expression, she said, 'Stand up and put your arms around me waist.' She turned her back to him. 'What do you feel now?'

'Very severe corsets,' he laughed, nuzzling her neck and returning his hands to the most magnificent pair of breasts he'd had the good fortune to fondle in a long time.

'Why do you think someone my age needs to wear corsets like that?'

'It's the fashion, or so I'm led to believe.'

She sat down heavily on the bench covering her face with her hands. When she looked up there were tears in her eyes. 'Mr Sydney, can you remember the last time we was together and what happened between us?'

'I should say so,' he mimicked, attempting to cheer her up, but his humour only succeeded in bringing on fresh tears.

'I can't give you any more hints. Don't you understand. I'm trying to tell you I'm pregnant.'

He was non-plussed for a moment, absurdly wondering when he'd have time to audition her replacement.

She took his blank expression to mean he'd missed her point again. Five months pregnant to be precise. How's your maths Mr. Sydney? Ringing any bells yet, am I?'

He stared at her in disbelief as his mind registered her meaning and he sank down beside her. Holding her gaze he reached out, his palm reverently spanning her belly. 'My darling girl, this is the best news you could have given me. Of course, it will not be possible for me to leave Mabel, but I can support you and the child, find you somewhere beautiful to live. I will have a hand in his upbringing, we will almost be a real family.

'Are you mad? I'm eighteen years old, I don't want to be saddled with a kid. I only told you about it so's you'd help me get rid of it.'

'What are you saying? You cannot do such a thing. I will not help you get rid of my child.'

'Yes, well, it's not your body that's got to part with it, is it? I bet you wouldn't be so eager if it was. How will I ever become famous after me body's grown fat and ugly.'

'Listen to me, Violet. You are young, your body will recover. I can help you to become a star. I have contacts. I can open doors for you. If you do this for me and bring this child into the world, I promise as soon as it's born, I will make you into a star.'

She studied him for a moment. 'What are you going to do with it when you've got it? Who's going to look after it?'

'That will not be your problem. Leave everything to me. I will arrange somewhere comfortable for you to stay until the baby is born.'

They walked back to the hotel in silence. As she was about to step through the door, he caught her arm. 'You can stay with the revue for as long as you think fit. Does anyone else know of your condition?'

'You're the only one I've told.'

He nodded lifting his fedora in farewell. She watched him go, thinking that although she hadn't told anyone, she'd bet a week's wages that the rest of the cast weren't as bloody ignorant as him.

Chapter Eighteen – Sheffield 1926

The Pickle Co-operative had ceased its manufacturing of piccalilli when the strike began. The smell of it cooking, would have alerted everyone in the vicinity to the fact that inside the factory the workers were still active, busy pickling everything they had in stock, to prevent it from perishing.

'That's the last jar filled, Mrs Baxter, thanks to you and Gladys helping out.'

'Many hands make light work, Beattie. We couldn't afford to let our produce go rotten.'

'When do you think the strike will end Mrs. Baxter?' Gladys asked.

'I wouldn't like to guess, it's the fourth of May today, so that's only three days since the government's ultimatum. In the morning paper, it said there were one and half million of Britain's workforce out.

'Trouble is,' Iris said, 'the country might not be as disrupted as the strikers thought, what with that Organisation for Maintenance of Supplies taking over the running of public services. They've even recruited special constables and I won't deny I wasn't grateful to see a tram coming along me route this morning.'

'They're only volunteers,' Beattie pointed out. 'I expect it depends on how long they can keep it up. Any road, I'd best get this lot stacked and give the preparation areas a good scrub. Ted and Bert will be back from their strike duties any minute now.'

'Yes, and you and I had better make a start in the office, Gladys,' Mabel said, rolling down her sleeves.

By the time Bert and Ted returned to the factory they were ready for a sit down and a cuppa.

'Come and take the weight off your feet,' Beattie fussed around Ted. 'You look fair done in. Kettle's just boiled. Have you had anything to eat?'

'No. Like a daft beggar, I went and left me snap where I'd made it, on me table.'

'Good job I've made plenty then, There's your tea. Help yourself to a sandwich, you 'an all Bert. How did your morning go then? Did you get rid of all your newspapers?'

'Aye, we did, and I can tell you the families were right glad of the food parcels. It knocked us back a bit seeing the state of some of 'em.'

'I'd welcomed a united workforce in bringing about the strike,' Bert said, 'but I'll admit I'm right shocked to see at first-hand them families more desperate than me own. I didn't think it were possible. Do you know, there were little lads playing football with a rusty tin can on them cobbled streets with nowt on their feet? They were wearing jumpers with more holes than wool, and trousers too tight or else over-sized and held up with a bit of mucky string. Either way, they were that frayed they were nearly in ribbons.' He gulped his tea, trying to compose himself. 'And them little lasses, Ted. Not much older than me own. Little skinny arms and legs. Did you see what they were wearing? One of 'em had on a little thin shift dress, looked like a bit of old sheeting. It was fastened at her neck, but the back was gaping wide open. She must have been frozen cos it looked like she'd nowt underneath it. And sitting on a cold stone step 'an all. Did you see her

Ted? She were in that group huddled around the front step playing with a couple of peg dolls. Any more tea going Beattie? Make it strong with plenty of sugar, if there is any.'

Beattie looked at him in surprise. She'd never known him take sugar in his tea. She exchanged a worried look with Ted.

'Aye, well,' Bert said, taking the mug of tea from Beattie, 'it's families like them that fuel the fire in me belly to bring about a reform. We've got to raise their standard of living somehow. I only hope such families don't see the inside of the workhouse afore they see a rise in their income.

When the general strike ended after ten days Mabel felt great relief. She was happy to assist Ted and Bert in their continued support of the miners, but she couldn't help being pleased that the strike hadn't destroyed everything she and the others had strived to build up during the past few months.

Her thoughts turned to Sydney she was feeling guilty for cutting short their telephone conversation. She wondered not for the first time, what kind of hypnosis he possessed to ensnare people in his web? For although her senses had succumbed while she was with him, now that she was out of his radius, she had little desire for contact.

Business was in full production now that the strike had ended. It seemed to have made little difference, her contacts still ordered a constant stream of supplies. Their brand of pickles was becoming well known in households across the city and beyond.

She'd been working steadily through the orders for the greater part of the morning when the third step from the top creaked announcing someone's arrival. Ah good, she thought, Gladys is back from sticking on labels. Time for a cup of tea. She stood up to light the gas under the kettle, smiling as the door opened expecting to see Gladys, but it was Pierre who walked into the room.

'I was about to make tea,' she said lamely, since nothing else would come to mind. Then her knees gave way and she sat down heavily on her chair and burst into tears.

'It looks like I shall be making the tea,' he said, striding across the room. 'Let's see if I can remember how. I have servants to do this sort of thing these days, you know. My tea is specially imported. I became addicted to the stuff working on the British front line. Though I recommend it is much better served in china cups rather than tin and without the lingering essence of petrol.'

She laughed then, and he handed her his handkerchief. 'That's better. I had hoped you would be pleased to see me.'

'I was. I am. It was the shock. What are you doing here?'

'Taking a chance. You have not read my letter, or you would not ask. Have you even received it?'

'Constance Newton managed to get it to me. Do you remember her? She's St. John's Ambulance, now.'

'Then why have you not read it?'

'I was afraid. I haven't heard from you in seven years. I could only imagine why you would be writing to me. I was afraid that you must be terminally ill and only had months to live. I don't think I could have borne it. You aren't ill, are you?'

'No. I am fit and well, thank you. On top of the world as you English say. Here's your tea, strong with a little milk and no sugar, yes?'

'Yes,' she smiled, taking the cup and saucer from him. 'Pierre, what are you doing here?'

'Taking you out to lunch. My car is parked downstairs and I have a picnic hamper in the back filled with delicious things. The weather is fine, and the sun is shining from a blue sky. What better time to take a stroll in your City's beautiful Botanical Gardens? We can eat our lunch seated on a blanket beneath the shade of a tree.'

Looking up at him, she knew she hadn't felt such joy since the last time they were together. Whatever this day brought she would treasure it along with the other trove of memories stored in her heart. 'I'll have to speak to Gladys and the others before I leave,' she said. 'Shall I meet you at the car?'

Pierre parked near the entrance off Ecclesall Road and they strolled hand in hand up through the gardens until they found a suitable place to picnic. He'd provided quite a feast and she realised he must have brought much of the produce over from France. Pate and a variety of French cheeses, with early grapes and strawberries.

'Pierre why are you're here?'

'Are you happy Mabel?'

She paused a fraction too long. He knew her too well. 'That's what I'm doing here.'

'Where does Claudette think you are?'

208

The shadow of a frown glanced his brow. He took a sip of champagne from the tall fluted glass in his hand and set it down on top of the picnic basket. 'Claudette died of influenza.'

'What! During the epidemic, but that was years ago. Why has it taken you until now to find me?'

'Mabel, I have a son. He was months old at the height of the epidemic. I had to try and keep him safe. I was terrified for his life after I had been unable to save his mother. When the danger was past, I made enquiries. I discovered you had married. I had no wish to interfere and perhaps cause you unhappiness.'

'And now? What has changed your mind?'

'Let us say I have been keeping an eye on you. Your husband's notoriety has blazed a trail across the globe for so many reasons… Then one day, after reading an article about him, I knew I had to write to you and find out for myself if you were truly happy. At first, I didn't have your address, only an idea of where you used to live in Sheffield. I thought the Military hospital might still hold your personal records and would be able to forward my letter to you. When, after several months I'd heard nothing from you, I hired a private investigator. He has been able to piece together your life. His reports have made startling reading. Mabel, do you realise the man you have married is a serial adulterer? In fact, I would go so far as to say he must be mentally deranged. Not only that, he moves in the same circles as some very dangerous villains.'

She knew everything he was saying was true, but it had shocked her to hear the facts spoken aloud. She looked down at the picnic rug, her cheeks burning with humiliation.'

'If nothing else, I live in fear for your safety and your health,' he said, covering her hand with his own.

'It has crossed my mind,' she whispered, 'but I have consoled myself with the fact that he usually targets innocents.'

'Mabel would you like to come to France? I wish to show you my home, my chateau. I did not only lose my wife to influenza but my parents also. I have made many changes in the intervening years. I think you will like my home. It is very beautiful. The grounds are magnificent. There are woods to explore with streams meandering through, as well as the grape vines and vineyard. So many times, during the war, we have talked of my home, my little part of France.' He reached over to move a stray curl from in front of her eye and tuck it behind her ear. 'Now you can come and see for yourself whether I have exaggerated its beauty.'

'Pierre, I told Sydney I was too busy building up the factory to join him on tour. How can I explain suddenly going off to France?

'Can your factory run well enough without you?'
'For a while, yes. I'm sure it can.'
'Does your husband not lie to you, repeatedly?'
'Yes, I suppose he does.'
'Then why do you consider his feelings?'
'Because he's my husband.'
'Do you love him?'
'I did once.'
'Do you love me?'

She was taken aback by the unexpected question. She took her time gathering her thoughts, studying his face. She saw the love in his eyes and the hint of fear put there by uncertainty. Finally, she gave her answer. 'I loved you then, I love you now and I will always love you, that will never change. But I'm married, nothing is simple.'

'Have we not wasted enough precious time considering other people? We have been given this chance, an opportunity to spend the rest of our lives together.'

He reached for her hand and pressed his lips into the palm. The tender gesture brought tears to her eyes.

'Mabel, I want to marry you,' he said, stroking the tears from her cheeks, 'but I will not rush you. Come first to my beautiful chateau for a holiday. We will take each day as we find it, getting to know one another again.' He tipped her chin with his finger and kissed her ever so briefly, setting her lips tingling and yearning for more. With him beside her, everything seemed so simple, as though she could fly to the moon, if she wished. She had no idea how she could overcome the obstacles ahead, but somehow Pierre always made the impossible seem a reality. She looked around, they were alone, shrouded by the weeping willow. She slipped her arms around his neck and drew him down into a kiss. His lips felt how she had known they would, firm yet sensitive, responsive to her tentative kisses as she traced the contours of his mouth, exploring, tasting, hungry to savour the long-forbidden fruit, intoxicated by the familiar scent of his cologne. With a groan his impatient mouth captured her lips, demanding, eager to claim the soft inner recesses. He wrapped his arms around her crushing her to him igniting the flickering flame of passion.

    'There they are! What did I tell you? See for yourself.'
    Mabel was the first to break away, she spun around to see a matronly woman accompanied by a uniformed park-keeper bearing down on them.
    'Now then, Sir,' the park-keeper said. 'There'll be none of them carryings on in 'ere. I'd be obliged if you'd pack up your things and clear off.
    'Bonjour, Monsieur et Madame. Excusez-moi, ce qui semble être le problème?
    'What's he talking about?' the woman turned to the park-keeper.
    'Search me. All I could make out was problem.' He glared at Pierre. 'The problem is,' he shouted exaggerating his words. 'The problem is, you can't be carrying on and kissing in a public place like this!'
    'Mon Dieu! désolé. C'est ma faute.'
    'What's that your saying?' the park-keeper pushed back his hat and scratched his head.
    'My apologies, Monsieur, I have not seen my wife for some considerable time.'
    'That's as maybe, Sir, but it's no excuse for carrying on in 'ere. And if I may make so bold, the pair of you would be best off at home. Now I'll give you time to pack your picnic things away, but I'll be back to check you've gone.'

'Only to be expected of them foreign types,' the women sniffed looking back as she made her way to the gates.

'Shame on you Pierre Durieux,' Mabel laughed, 'for confusing that poor man by speaking in French.'

'Well he deserved it. Pompous ass. Isn't that what you English say? Come,' he held out his hand to help her up. 'I will take you home. What time would you like me to collect you for dinner?'

'How do you know I will be joining you for dinner?'

'Because, mon amour, you have told me that you love me.'

Bert was not pleased that the strike had ended and his temper hadn't cooled during the walk from the bottom of the Moor to the top of Endcliffe Park. He was still steaming as he walked up the path to Charlotte's allotment. He banged loudly on the gate and waited for her to let him in.

He pushed past her, waving the newspaper in the air. 'Have you read this yet? Have you seen the headline? The TUC have called off the bloody strike. That's because them other traitor unions who didn't want to strike have taken the TUC to court. The bloody judge has declared the strike illegal. It says here, some firms are taking legal advice. The unions are going to be sued. They can't do that. Can they?'

'They'll probably have a good try. They're wanting to claim back loss of earnings caused by the strike. They stand a good chance with the judge deciding the strike was illegal. But, if you'd paused to read the Forum while you were delivering it, you'd have seen that the miners are not giving way. They're staying out on strike and Sheffield has pledged to support them as best it can. So, my friend, you should have saved your energy for fund raising instead of getting yourself all in a lather marching up here.'

His legs suddenly felt weak. She'd taken the wind out of his sails and he sat down heavily on an upturned orange box.

'Here take this, I've just made it. Don't burn your fingers, that tin holds the heat.'

He looked at her retreating figure. She, more than most, should know he'd held a few tin mugs in his time. She returned with a bottle of whisky and poured a liberal measure into the tea. 'Drink that, it'll put a better perspective on things.' Then she produced a note pad and pencil from the pocket of her gardening apron. 'Now first things first – a list – nothing like a good list to prepare for battle. Let's get our heads together and see how best we can help the strikers.' She smiled, and Bert's eyes crinkled at the corners as he returned her smile. 'By heck lass, you know how to turn a bloke around.'

Mabel bathed and dressed, with care. Taking a last-minute appraisal of her appearance in the hall mirror, her heart thudded in her chest anticipating what the evening may bring. She had been an innocent young woman, and Pierre, an eminent and married surgeon when they had last been together. After six years married to Sydney, she was far from innocent, and Pierre was widowed. Now they were back together she was more than a little anxious about how far the tables of their circumstances had turned. She jumped when the door knocker rapped. Expecting to see Pierre, she was startled to see a telegram delivery boy on the doorstep.

'Telegram for Mrs Baxter,' he said, doffing his cap.

'Yes, I'm Mrs Baxter.'

'Right you are, sign here please,' he brought out a pencil from behind his ear. Mabel tipped him from a bowl of loose change she kept on the coat stand and closed the door. She had never recovered from her fear of telegrams since the war, although common sense told her they were bearers of glad tidings as well as bad. She walked through to the kitchen and sat at the table using a knife to slit the envelope neatly. Her heart skipped a beat as she read the contents. Whatever news she'd imagined the telegram held, she hadn't imagined this.

The restaurant was Mabel's favourite. It was one she had frequented with her parents. She was pleased Pierre had asked her where she wanted to go, unlike Sydney, who automatically assumed his choice was agreeable. The maître d' welcomed her warmly and she felt quite emotional that he'd remembered her after such a long time. Although she supposed she shouldn't have been so surprised considering the vast amount of money her father must have spent there during his lifetime.

Pierre chose from the wine menu as that was his area of expertise, and since it was conversation and not food that was the priority of their evening together, they quickly ordered soup followed by roast beef.

'Have you given any further thought to coming to France for a holiday?'

Mabel took a long sip of the red wine, it was warming, fortifying even. 'I received a telegram just before you arrived. It was from Sydney, he's catching the milk train on Sunday morning to Sheffield, he must be sailing on the last ferry from the Isle of Man to Liverpool. I imagine it will be a short visit, he will probably stay one night, if that. I can't think what is so urgent that he must see me in person. He never leaves the revue during a run.'

'I will not be here. I'm returning to France tomorrow. I didn't know what welcome I would receive, so I have booked rooms at my club for two nights only.'

'You're still a member of the club?'

'But of course, I was a regular there when I worked at the military hospital in Sheffield. I pay my membership. Why should they care where I live now? His eyes held her captivated. 'I miss those days, when I lived here in Sheffield, Mabel. I miss you,' he reached for her hand.

Some instinct made her retract it. 'I have missed you too.'

'I have missed talking to you,' he said, 'and the feeling of contentment just being near you brings. I enjoyed working with you, despite the horror all around, especially your courage in the blackest of hours. We made a good team then, you and I, working by instinct as much as knowledge. You took on responsibilities far beyond the duties of a regular VAD. I imagined you would take up nursing when the war ended. You had a gift for lifting the fear from those men, those boys, who were brought to us. Even the ones with no hope.'

Still capturing her gaze he was quiet for several moments, then his eyes sparkled, crinkling up at the corners. 'I miss your wayward curls,' he laughed, 'springing every which way, no matter how often you smoothed them under your nurses cap. It is strange, is it not, that it is the smallest detail one remembers about the person one has loved and lost?'

The food was excellent, as good as she remembered. They decided to forgo dessert in favour of coffee and liqueur. It was then, that Mabel noticed the maître d' talking to a woman sitting at the table across from them. She was alone, which was unusual in this establishment. Mabel realised where she had seen her before. She'd been with Bert at the CDC meeting.

After speaking with the maître d', the woman rose and walked towards the exit, she paused as she reached their table. 'Good evening. 'Mrs Baxter, isn't it? I'm Charlotte Gregory. I believe we have mutual friends in Ada and Bert Brown. My evening has been curtailed, the maître d' has just given me the message that my dinner companion has been taken ill.'

Mabel was surprised that the women recognised her, and realised Bert must have pointed her out at the CDC meeting. She thought quickly, here was a chance to get to know something of the woman who kept Bert so enthralled. 'Yes, that's right,' she said. 'Ada and I have been friends for many years. This is Pierre Durieux we worked together in both Sheffield and France during the war. He's visiting Sheffield briefly.'

'Enchanted to meet you Mademoiselle,' Pierre rose to his feet, reached for her hand and kissed it.

'Madame,' Charlotte corrected him.

'It seems a shame to leave, won't you join us?' Mabel said. 'We're happy to sip coffee and replenish our liqueurs if you're hungry and would like something to eat.'

'To be perfectly honest, I'm not feeling at all hungry. It was to be a business meeting of sorts.'

'Of course, you're a surgeon. I remember now,' Mabel feigned a slip of memory.

'Then Madame, we have something in common. Please do stay and join us,' Pierre pulled out a chair for her. When the waiter had brought fresh coffee and liqueurs, Pierre said, 'There are many more women training to become surgeons since the war, but unfortunately, few openings for them.'

'Even during the war, it was difficult to get a placement until the need for surgeons became desperate. At first, I worked in military hospitals in England and later I managed to get transferred to France. But since the war ended,' she shrugged her shoulders, 'as you say Monsieur Durieux, it is difficult to be accepted into a profession dominated by men. Therefore, I presently run a small private practice from my home. How about you, which is your field of expertise?'

'Like you, I was a surgeon serving the British Army on the front line. Even though I was mostly performing surgery on the body during that time, the effects of trauma to the brain fascinated me as well as the brain's capacity to recover, given the correct stimulation after a length of recuperation. Since the end of the war, I have specialised in the study of the human brain, both as a surgeon and therapist. Like you, I run a clinic from my home and I have built a hospital also, in the nearby town.'

'I hadn't realised you were married Mrs Gregory,' Mabel said, thinking this was a new slant on her assumption of Charlotte and Bert's affair.

'I'm widowed, Mrs Baxter.'

'Forgive me, I didn't know.'

'My husband, is, was, also a surgeon. His unit was on the front line during the last days of the war. They were caught up in the intense fighting and apparently most of their unit ended up on the German side. After everything had settled, only a handful of his medical team were picked up. They were able to give some sort of account as to what had happened. Edwin was posted missing presumed dead.'

Charlotte pushed back her chair. 'I'm sorry to have intruded on your evening. The subject of my circumstances tends to put a damper on the jolliest of occasions. Thank you for your hospitality, I will leave you to enjoy the rest of your evening.'

They watched her retreating figure and Pierre said, 'I doubt they will ever find his body. So many missing soldiers, so many unmarked graves.'

Mabel could read him well, even after all this time apart. There was something he was mulling over. She knew better than to ask. He divulged his thoughts only when they were relevant to share.

Chapter Nineteen

The morning after Pierre's visit, Mabel was up and dressed early, waiting in the living room when she heard Sydney's key scrape in the lock. It had been her intention to foil his plan of finding her in bed and seducing her into agreeing to whatever it was he wanted. She saw surprise register in his eyes. He covered it well.

'Mabel, my darling, how I have missed you.' He gathered her into his arms, but she turned her cheek to accept his kiss and wriggled free. 'The kettle's boiled, I'll make tea. You must be exhausted.'

He slipped his arms around her waist nuzzling the back of her neck as she poured water into the tea pot. 'Sydney, you're going to scald the pair of us if you're not careful. She turned suddenly, swinging the kettle purposely in front of her and he jumped out of the way.

'There's bacon and sausages in the oven. You must be hungry after your long journey.'

'Only for you,' he said, reaching out for her again. Her heart thudded in her chest. The room seemed to have shrunk. She couldn't bear to be in his proximity. Her instinct was to become over bright. She kissed his cheek and playfully pushed him away. 'Sit down at the table, breakfast will be ready in a moment. The Sunday papers are on the dresser.' She hurried through to the kitchen and busied herself, scrambling eggs and slicing the loaf. Her mind whirring. By the time she set a plate of food before him, she had formed a plan. 'You need to catch up on some sleep and I, unfortunately have promised to take an elderly neighbour to church. Her daughter is unwell and as I didn't know you were coming, I volunteered. By the time you've rested, I'll be back. Perhaps we can go for a stroll through the park before lunch and then you can tell me what you're doing here.'

'I'm your husband, why must I have a reason to come and see you?'

'I'll see you later,' she said, reaching for her hat and coat.

Out on the street, she kicked up her heels and ran. She realised she was heading towards the church. Perhaps that was as good a place as any to sit and contemplate which direction her life should take. The service had started when she slipped into a pew at the back. Several marriage banns were called, the Vicar followed on by preaching about the sanctity of marriage. Mabel shifted in her seat as he droned on about forsaking all others and for better or worse. Unable to listen to the man's drivel, warning the congregation against a life he'd never experienced, she slipped out of the door and headed to the pavilion in the park. She ordered a tray of tea and took it outside to listen to the band playing. It was a beautiful late spring morning. The park was full of families and couples strolling in the sunshine.

'Was the service not to your liking?' Sydney sat down beside her.

Words sprang to her rescue without thinking. Perhaps more of Sydney had rubbed off on her than she realised. 'My neighbour has caught whatever it was her daughter had. She was too unwell to go to church after all.

I came here so I wouldn't wake you. Did you manage to get any sleep?'

'No, I wanted you beside me.'

'Sydney,' she paused, searching for the right words. 'I find it difficult switching my affection on and off. It's difficult for me to be apart from you for so long and suddenly fall into your arms on demand upon your return.' It was a lie of course. It was the first time she had admitted to herself that she had fallen out of love with him. She hadn't seen Pierre for seven years, but after leaving the restaurant last night, had he taken her into his arms she would have been utterly powerless to resist. Ever the gentleman, he hadn't. Instead he'd kissed her fingertips, his eyes smouldering with passion. 'Come to my Chateaux Mabel,' he'd said, but his meaning was clear. A shiver ran along her spine at the memory.

Focusing her thoughts on the present, she realised Sydney had spoken. 'I'm sorry,' she said, 'Do you mind if we walk. My nerves feel a little on edge today. I didn't sleep well.'

They walked along the Monkey Rack, remarkably void of courting couples, and on around the lake. 'Would you like to hire a boat?'

'Not today, I prefer to walk.' She could think of nothing worse than being in the confines of a rowing boat with him. Then the thought of tipping him over the side and ruining his pristine image with mud and pond weed popped into her head, and she had to stifle a giggle.

'Mabel,' he reached for her hand and tucked it under his arm, 'do you have any news for me?'

'News for you? What sort of news?' For a wild moment she wondered if he'd somehow heard of Pierre's visit.

'I was hoping for news of a child, Mabel. We have been married for many years. I have no wish to offend you my darling, but do you think it might be that you cannot conceive? Come and sit over here for a moment.' He guided her towards a bench. When they were both seated, he took hold of her hands. 'Sweetheart, I have an idea that I wish to share with you. I have been thinking recently that if we cannot have a child of our own, perhaps we could consider adopting one?'

For a moment she was too surprised to respond, she sat blinking up at him in the bright sunshine. Then she said, 'For most of our marriage you have dismissed my longing to have a child. Why have you suddenly decided that you want a child to the point of adopting one?'

'Not any child, there is some urgency because an opportunity has arisen for the perfect child to be adopted by us.'

A horrifying thought flooded her mind. She had to get away from him, she hurried off in the direction of home, but in two long strides he'd caught up, she maintained her pace. 'And this child,' she asked, 'is it a boy or a girl?'

'The child has not yet been born, that is the beauty of it. We can have the child from birth. It will be as if it is our own.'

'No, it will not be our child, Sydney. But it will be yours, won't it? Yours and the young brunette's, third from the right in the chorus.'

If she had slapped his face, she could not have caused more of a sting. She had totally floored him. For once the master of deceit was unveiled.

They had reached the foot of the stone steps leading up to the house. 'You are not welcome in my home, Sydney. I've put up with your cheating lying adulterous ways for six long years. I thought it was because I loved you. The moment I read the letter from the solicitor, informing me of Annie's death, I realised it was because I'd had nowhere else to go. Now I have. Good-bye Sydney.' She turned and fled up the steps and along the passage between the houses. He thundered after her, his feet echoing in the confined space. She managed to slam the gate and bolt it before he could push against it. She fumbled trying to get the keys into the lock of the back door. He hammered on the high gate with his fists making her jump and she dropped the keys. They slithered towards the drain, but she managed to stamp on them before they dropped out of reach.

'Mabel, you cannot mean this, you are exaggerating things my darling. Let me in, we need to talk.' He was hefting his shoulder against the gate, she could see the screws in the bolt giving way.

At last she got the key in the lock, she let herself in and secured the kitchen door behind her. She knew he was too proud to make an exhibition of himself. He would soon leave her alone, for now.

Chapter Twenty – Late spring The Isle of Man 1926

The Sydney Baxter Revue had done much to draw the crowds into the Gaiety Theatre in Douglas on the Isle of Man. Tourism had dropped when the war began and had been slow to pick up after it ended. Now the crowds were back and flocking to see the revue and the theatre had been fully booked every night since the revue had opened the previous month.

The ever-popular Can-Can finished to thunderous applause. When the play-off music began, the dancers leapt up, and shaking their frilly petticoats, ran whooping and screaming into the wings. Violet stayed down in the splits as though rooted to the spot. Sydney instructed the orchestra to keep playing until she moved, but eventually the stage manager closed the front tabs.

'What have you done, torn a hamstring?' Lotti said, rushing on stage with two other dancers to help her up. They gasped when they saw that Violet was sitting in a pool of blood.

The stage manager came striding out of the wings to see what she was playing at. 'Can't you sort yourself out better than that? You dozy mare,' he shouted when he saw the mess. 'If you're not on stage for the next number you'll have your wages docked.' Two stage crew hastily ran across with a bucket and began mopping. 'Be quick about it,' he snarled, heading back into the wings.

The two dancers' helped Lotti get Violet into the toilet, then they dashed back to the dressing room to change for their next number. 'Has anyone got anything to lend Violet to pad herself up with?' Lotti asked.

'She can have this,' Phoebe the lead dancer said. 'I'll take it. I'm already changed.'

'You'd better take these as well,' Gracie handed her a pile of newspapers. The two women exchanged a knowing look.

Screams reached Sydney in the orchestra pit. He couldn't think what was amiss, but he kept the orchestra playing nonstop attempting to muffle the sound from the audience until the front tabs opened again and he could play the intro for the next act. When Violet didn't appear on stage with the rest of the dancers, he fought to stop bile rising as he realised it must be Violet screaming. In the interval he rushed through the orchestra pit and banged on the dancers dressing room door. 'What's going on? Whose screaming?' he demanded.

Lotti opened the door. 'Bugger off Sydney. This is nothing to do with you.' She slammed the door shut again.

A piercing scream alerted him to the Ladies toilet. 'Violet, is that you? Shall I call an ambulance.'

'No, you ruddy well won't!' she panted. 'They'll put me away when they find out I'm pregnant and not married. Shove off and leave me to it. No, wait, get Lotti, will you?'

Sydney banged on the dressing room door again shouting for Lotti to go to Violet.

'What does she think I can do for her?' she answered.

'What about that young man?' Phoebe said. 'You know, the one that's always leaving you flowers and chocolates at the stage door?' Isn't he training to be a doctor? Couldn't you bribe him with a night out in exchange for helping Violet?'

'It's worth a shot,' Sydney said. 'She won't go into hospital she's frightened of the authorities locking her away.'

'Well she's right,' Phoebe said. 'I've known it happen to a couple of girls when their families wouldn't vouch for them. Locked 'em up with the lunatics they did. Magistrate said they couldn't have been right in the head to get themselves in that predicament in the first place. Go and see that young bloke, I bet he'd do anything for you.' Lotti bundled Giles Hereford through the stage door and into the ladies toilet before he had chance to realise where he was going.

'I've brought someone to help you, Violet,' Lotti banged on the cubical door. 'Open up.'

Giles took one look at Violet, her face ashen, squatting over the blood splattered newspaper and incorrectly assessed the situation. 'I can't be a party to this! I'll be struck off before I'm even qualified. Who did this to you, someone with a sharp knitting needle?'

'Not ruddy likely,' Violet gasped as another contraction took hold. 'This is coming away on its own.'

'Can you stand up?' He held out his hands to help her. 'Do you mind if I examine you?' He gently pressed her distended abdomen and held her securely as another wave of pain hit. 'How far on are you?'

'About six months.'

'The foetus feels more developed than that to me.'

He turned to Lotti, 'Can you get a cloth or something to spread on the floor, so I can examine her more thoroughly?'

Lotti dashed off to the dressing room and returned just as the call boy came running through announcing five-minutes to the second half opening. She had her arms stacked with towels which each dancer had donated and nearly collided with him. She dodged out of his way and into the toilet just in time. 'Here take these,' she said, shoving the towels at Giles chest. 'I've got to go, I'll see you when I come off stage.'

Violet's contractions were coming thick and fast. In between them, Giles managed to ascertain the pregnancy was most likely full term. He looked at his watch. Are there any women in the theatre who aren't on stage right now? The shops will be closing shortly and you're going to need things for you and the baby.'

'That's the finale music. It's the end of the first house. Florrie, the wardrobe mistress might be able to nip out between shows. Performers aren't allowed out of the theatre with their stage make-up on.'

Violet was in the final throes of labour when Lotti returned. She'd had to force her way passed the other acts gathered outside the toilets. Word had got around, and someone was taking bets on whether it would be a boy or a girl.

Giles barked a list of things that Violet would need and gave Lotti the money to get them. Lotti despatched Florrie the wardrobe mistress, a motherly matron with plenty of experience.

Florrie returned with a stack of napkins and baby clothes together with fresh towels, soap and flannels as well as the other items Giles had ordered, just as the angry baby came squawking into the world, her tiny red face screwed up indignantly. Giles wrapped her in a towel and rubbed quite vigorously before tying off the cord and cutting it. He handed the baby over to Florrie who billed and cooed over her while Giles worked on Violet. 'What are you going to call your beautiful daughter?'

'Gillian. It's the closest thing to Giles I can think of,' she smiled sleepily.

'Where are you staying? Will you be able to keep the child with you there?'

'Not likely, I'd be out on my ear. She knows I'm not married.'

Then Sydney appeared in the doorway. 'Violet is a member of my revue and therefore my responsibility. She has told me of her condition and I have said I will help her. She can recuperate in my suite of rooms.' He turned to face Giles. 'Do you know of a nurse who could attend to Violet and the baby?'

'I know a qualified nurse, but she may well report Violet to the authorities. I also know an equally capable unqualified woman in desperate need of money, who will not ask questions. She's done this type of work before.'

'Good, then that is settled. Violet, I will ask the hotel to put an additional bed in your room for the nurse, and of course a cradle. Is the child well, she has arrived several weeks early?'

Giles caught a warning plea in Violet's eyes. 'She's perfectly healthy,' he said evasively.

'Please arrange for Violet and the baby to be settled into my suite with the nurse and send your bill to me at the hotel.' Sydney said.

Giles knew he wasn't entitled to payment, he wasn't yet qualified, but Sydney's arrogant attitude had annoyed him. He would send him a fee for expenses and make sure the nurse was well paid.

By the time Giles had everything arranged and had overseen Violet and the baby settled with the nurse, the second house show was finished. The performers were filtering into the hotel anxious for news and to wet the baby's head. Lotti met Giles in the doorway on his way out. 'Come back in and let me buy you a drink,' she said, linking her arm through his.

'I think I'd better get home it's been an eventful day and I'm working on the early shift tomorrow.' Lotti pressed against him whispering into his ear how she might show her gratitude for his help. He lifted her hand from his arm and dropped it. Then looking directly into her eyes, he said, 'All those times I have waited for you at the stage door, I was simply hoping to take you to dinner. Now I have learned how you people conduct yourselves, I have no wish to be a part of it. Good evening to you.'

She watched him walk away thinking how she had classed him as another stage door Johnny. Laughing at his pathetic attempts to woo her with chocolates and flowers, comparing him to Sydney and his sophisticated charm. Giles unexpected remark had struck a stinging blow. She suddenly felt cheap standing alone on the steps.

Then Delores' shrill voice reached her from the bar. 'How dare you install one of your little tarts into my suite of rooms? No, not yours Sidney, mine. Booked and paid for by me. You'd better find yourself another soubrette because I quit.'

Lotti stormed into the bar. 'So, she's the reason you've been giving me the cold shoulder. You are a lying cheating bastard. If I wasn't tied by a contract, I'd quit the show too.'

'Then it is very fortunate for your career that you cannot leave, because you are the replacement soubrette.' Sydney knew he'd played an ace, he could live without Delores, she was becoming tiresome, but he didn't want to lose Lotti. She was easier to appease and enjoy. He turned to face Delores, his lip curling slightly at her shocked expression. 'Do not let us detain you from packing your suitcase.' Then he turned his back on her and caught Lotti's arm. 'Come, we have a lot to discuss before tomorrow's first house.'

Chapter Twenty-one - Whitsuntide Sheffield 1926

The big bass drum kept the tempo for the marching feet of the Boys Brigade and the happy throng of people in the Whit Monday procession making their way along the crowded streets to the park. The silk woven tapestry banners with their tassels fluttering in the breeze, bobbed along high above their heads, guiding the way.

Dray horses, their manes and tails plaited with ribbon, proudly clip clopped along pulling flat top lorries draped with silk and flowers carrying the May Queens and their attendant maids. Each queen depicting a flower, looked splendidly regal perched on a throne crafted from velvet cushions and silver painted chairs. The May Queens were the envy of many a little girl, dressed as they were in long flowing gowns of taffeta and silk, swathed in velvet cloaks.

Whitsuntide was Ada's favourite holiday. Even better than Christmas, for at Christmas the cold weather and expense of buying presents made it an anxious time of year. But at Whit, the sun shone and the children all wore new clothes. She had fashioned her own children's outfits from Annie's cast offs, some of which hadn't been worn. They had proudly gone around the neighbourhood parading their new clothes for all to see and had collected a pocket full of coppers each for their trouble. Ada wondered how the tradition had begun for folks to give money to the little ones for showing off their new clothes.

She breathed in the heady scent of lilac, stocks and snap dragons, flowering in front gardens. Bert had decided in favour of the Whit sing in Endcliffe Park.

'After the singsong the kids can play on the swings,' he'd said, 'and I've enough put by to get 'em an ice-cream a piece.' She took a deep breath savouring the scent in the air, and the jolly ambience. A little thrill of happiness shivered through her. She felt strong and well. It had been a slow recovery after the birth of Charlie and the operations which had saved her life. Bert was a demonstrative man and she loved him dearly. It was a relief to embrace his advances without the terror of pregnancy. A smile tugged at the corner of her mouth as she relived their recent early night. She wondered if she should feel guilty to be so relieved that there would be no more babies. And immediately questioned what sort of god would want children to be born into poverty and starvation. Any lingering guilt melted away.

Trumpets pierced the morning air as drummers set up a different rhythm to the big bass, beating out quick repetitive drum rolls. It was a day to be glad she was alive.

Bert caught her smile and reached for her hand. Their three older children skipped happily alongside the young ones in the pram. 'By, you look as pretty as a picture. I'm a lucky man to have you as me wife. Is that a new hat? It suits you.'

'New to me. I found the hat in the jumble and trimmed it up meself.'

'Well you've a talent for it lass. It looks grand.'

The procession turned into the park and gathered on the main field. The congregation was too vast to provide chairs for everyone, so they stood and sang their hearts out to the familiar hymns. Ada and Bert had their own reasons to rejoice and gave private thanks to the words they sang, hoping God was in his heaven listening to their gratitude. Then the bands took up their instruments and played their way out of the park and back to their headquarters. People began to disperse and soon the only sound was that of children's happy voices and popular tunes coming from the bandstand.

'I think we could all do with a sit down for two minutes,' Ada said, eyeing the chairs set out before the bandstand, 'my legs are aching. Dad's got a surprise for you if you can sit still long enough to find out what it is.' She watched Bert walk across the grass towards the pavilion, his broad shoulders pulled back, head held high. He lifted his cap in greeting as he passed an acquaintance and the sun picked out the copper glints in his ebony hair. Her heart swelled with love and pride at the sight of him. Then she sat back in her chair listening to the music and singing softly enjoying the feel of the sun on her face.

'That's a grand voice you have there, if I may say so.'

'She looked up into blue eyes twinkling down on her. The man had a wide grin and an open honest sort of face.

'I didn't realise I was singing aloud,' she blushed.

'Softly, but beautifully. I would be honoured if you would grace us with a song,' he said, offering his hand to help her up.

It was then that Ada took in his uniform, his stance, the shape of his broad shoulders, and she realised he was the conductor for the band. She had only ever seen his back view before.

'Oh no, I couldn't,' her hands flew to her burning cheeks.

'Awe go on mam,' Georgie encouraged her, 'Dad always says you should've been on the music halls.'

The man was still holding out his hand, his head on one side enquiringly.

As though in a trance Ada found she had taken his hand and he was leading her up the steps to join the band. She gave them a choice of her repertoire and hoped she would sing the correct words. Often as not, she made them up if she didn't know the real ones. After a tentative start, during which she thought her legs might give way, her voice carried clearly across the park as she sang 'I'll see you in my dreams'. The song ended to enthusiastic applause from the sparse crowd and she was encouraged to sing 'Rosemarie' and 'Moonlight and Roses.'

By the time she'd finished, a large crowd had gathered, and she hastily negotiated another medley of songs.

Hearing her voice, Bert was stopped in his tracks. He'd already turned and started back towards the bandstand when he felt a hand tugging at his arm. He was surprised to see Charlotte, her face chalk white and clutching her stomach. 'Bert I'm so relieved to see you. I feel quite unwell. Could you help me to the bench over there?' He took her arm and guided her into the shade of a tree and she sank down onto the bench with her head between her knees, breathing deeply.

'What's up, a touch too much sun or are you badly.'

'Neither, I'll be alright in a moment. Do you have a clean handkerchief? Could you dip it in some cold water for me please and place it on the back of my neck?'

Bert did as he was asked keeping an eye on Charlotte and an ear cocked towards Ada's singing. What was Ada playing at? He wouldn't have imagined in a million years her getting up in front of a crowd. But accompanied by the band, he didn't think he'd ever heard her voice sound sweeter.

'There you are lass,' he said, placing the wet handkerchief across the back of Charlotte's neck. 'Would you like me to get you a cup of sweet tea?'

He was astonished to see her grab the handkerchief and vomit into it. 'Well you're the doctor,' he said, 'but tha' looks badly to me right enough whether you think so or not.'

'Bert, I'm not ill. I'm pregnant.'

The colour drained from his face until he looked paler than her. 'I told you. I bloody well warned you. I've only to look at Ada and she's pregnant. Now what's to do?'

'There's nothing for you to do. I have the where withal to cope.'

Bert's mouth twisted into an ugly grimace, 'You mean you can get rid of it,' he spat the words at her.

'Do you think I would destroy a blessing, destroy the life of a child I have yearned for since losing my first? This baby will be loved and cherished. I have the money to care for him and employ the staff to help me. Don't be angry Bert, you have granted me a wish.'

'I'm not a bloody Genie. We've spent a lot of time together you and me. There's bound to be talk. The only reason Ada's not jealous is because she thinks I'm too far beneath your station for you to consider me, even with me dark curls and cheeky grin.' He burst out laughing then, and to Charlotte it was as though the sky had suddenly painted a rainbow. 'It will be some time before my pregnancy shows. For now, you go and enjoy your day out with your family. I feel a little better, I'll just sit here a while longer.'

'Look, I promised to get me kids an ice-cream, let me do that first, then I'll come and walk you home. It's not far, by the time they've finished eating it, I'll be back. Are you sure you'll be alright for now, if I nip off?'

'Perfectly,' she smiled up at him thinking Ada was a very lucky woman. She didn't envy her though, Bert wasn't Edwin. She smiled hugging her husband's image in her mind's eye. During the war it had been easy to believe someone with such a powerful physique and larger than life personality was indestructible. But somehow somewhere, Edwin had been destroyed, snatched from her. The worst was not knowing. Even now, after eight long years she clung to the hope that he was alive. Every now and then, somewhere, families were still being reunited with loved ones they had believed dead. If Edwin was alive, she knew without a doubt it would be his mind stopping him from coming to her. If Edwin was alive, wherever he was, she knew he would have lost his mind.

Mabel had spent her morning sitting in the garden enjoying the sunshine, reading the newspaper and listening to the singing in the park. Walking up the path towards the house thinking of what to have for lunch, she heard the telephone ringing. Her first thought was that it was Sydney and she decided to ignore it, but the ringing persisted for so long, she felt obliged to answer it.

'There you are Mon amour, is the sun shining on you also? It is a lovely day here. How are you and when are you coming to see my beautiful chateaux?'

'Hello Pierre, yes it's a lovely day. I've been sitting in the garden listening to the Whit Monday sing. How are you?'

'Tres Bien, but I miss you and you have not answered my question. Would it make your decision to come and see my beautiful chateaux any easier if you had a travelling companion?'

'What sort of travelling companion?'

'Do you remember introducing me to a female surgeon? Madame Gregory, I believe her name is. She is a widow, yes?'

'Yes, her name's Charlotte Gregory. Her husband went missing presumed dead at the end of the war.'

'That is what I remember. Since I returned home, I have done some investigating on her behalf. In my line of work, I help many displaced men, survivors of the war who cannot recall a life before joining up. Their minds have been damaged by trauma and the horrors they have experienced. Unfortunately, there are some who may never recover, but others respond to stimulus of the senses, such as smell, music, taste and certain images. For these men I hold out more hope. A familiar person would be a very powerful stimulus. I do not want to give Madame Gregory false hope, but I think as a surgeon she would find my clinic and hospital very interesting. Meeting my patients would be good also, because no doubt, like me, she will have restored many such men to physical health. She surely cannot fail to be intrigued about my research into now repairing their minds.'

'It would be wonderful if she did find her husband, for more reasons than you know. I'll explain it to you another time. There are things I must put in place at the factory before I can come, but yes, I think your idea is an excellent one.'

She replaced the handset on its cradle, reluctant to let it go, as though by holding on to it she could keep connected to Pierre.

Over lunch she thought through everything they had discussed. She couldn't help but compare their conversation to the phone calls Sydney made, usually about how much *he* missed her, how much *he* needed her, how *he* couldn't live without her, whereas Pierre had not only invited her to France, but had also shown concern for his patients and a woman he'd only met once. A little thrill of excitement bubbled up, she would go to France with or without Charlotte.

Chapter Twenty-Two - The Loire Valley France - Summer 1926

The train journey to London, then on to Dover, seemed surreal to Mabel. She couldn't quite believe she was travelling to France to meet Pierre openly and be accepted by his friends. She hoped she would meet his son. Although she could understand that Pierre might not want to introduce her, not yet. She was also feeling a little uncomfortable around her travelling companion. Charlotte was perfectly pleasant and not one to make small talk for the sake of filling a silence, but Mabel felt a sense of being a traitor. Ada was one of her closest friends and Charlotte was possibly Bert's lover.

They had booked a berth for comfort on the ferry crossing and a hotel in Calais. The next day they caught the train to Paris where they broke their journey again, staying over-night at the Ritz, before catching the train to the Loire Valley.

Pierre was waiting on the platform as the train pulled in. 'Bonjour ma chérie,' he said, taking hold of both Mabel's hands and looking deep into her eyes. Then he removed his hat and kissed her on both cheeks. Turning to face Charlotte, he reached for her hand. 'Bonjour Madame Gregory. It is very nice to meet you again.'

'Thank you for inviting me to visit your home,' she said, allowing him to kiss her hand. He instructed a porter to take their luggage then offered an arm to each of the ladies. Together they stepped out of the station and into the brilliant French sunshine.

Their journey took them along narrow meandering lanes flanked on either side by grassy banked hedgerows. The boughs of the trees met overhead forming a shady green tunnel revealing fleeting glimpses of blue sky. After a while, the road began to climb steeply, leaving the village and patchwork of fields behind. Mabel watched the river glistening in the distance until it was lost from view as they drove into woodland. Coming out the other side, the land plateaued and there in the distance stood Pierre's chateau, its coned turrets piercing the fluffy white clouds hovering above. He had not exaggerated its beauty.

He drove his car over a bridge spanning a moat and into a square courtyard. The mellow stone walls partly covered by dark green foliage, baked in the heat. Water in a central stone fountain trickled down over three tiers into the basin, creating the ambience of a refreshing oasis. Two footmen rushed to greet them and take their luggage. Then Pierre guided them along a cool, marble floored hallway, from which a magnificent staircase rose towards an impressive stained-glass window before branching off right and left to the next level. He opened a door and welcomed them into a quintessential French drawing room where elegant chaises longues and comfortable looking sofas, interspersed with occasional tables and high-back chairs, were set around an enormous marble fireplace. Across the far side of the room a grand piano stood, its lid open, displaying its full beauty. Mabel walked over to one of the many French doors facing onto a knot garden and a back drop of the woodland which they had driven through earlier. She turned away from the view and continued her perusal inside. The room was peaceful and cool. Set in a corner against the wall was a lady's writing bureau on which stood a large lamp and a bowl of white roses. She imagined Pierre's late wife sitting there. Mabel wondered if Pierre had written his letter to her, while sitting at the bureau. She would like to imagine him sitting there writing to her after she'd returned home.

The door opened and a maid came in carrying a tea tray, followed by another bearing jugs of lemonade. They returned with dainty sandwiches and a selection of pastries. Pierre instructed the maids to open the French doors. 'Thank you. We can manage to serve ourselves.' With a bob they turned and left the room.

'This evening, we can dine on the terrace if you wish. Right now, it is perhaps a little too warm.'

Feeling hot and thirsty Mabel and Charlotte tucked into the spread gratefully. Pierre sipped his tea, settling back into one of the heavily upholstered chairs across from them. His manner was relaxed bringing a pleasant ambience into the room.

Charlotte was first to finish, she set down her napkin and settled herself comfortably into the sofa. 'I'm very interested in your work here, Mr Durieux. It was frustrating during the war to be repairing a man's body when his mind was also damaged, knowing the powers that be were only interested in getting him physically fit enough to bulk up the cannon fodder. What exactly is it that you do here?'

'My colleague Marcus Leman and I are exploring the workings of the mind with the hope of helping our patients and eventually others. There are still so many men mentally scarred by the war. The men in our hospital, I prefer to call it that, rather than a home, for I have high hopes that they will return to their own home one day, are particularly traumatised. It is very sad for them, but their condition has been invaluable research for us and will help others and future generations.'

'The survivors from my husband's unit were adamant that the rest of the unit, including Edwin, would have been killed. Although I have hoped and prayed that Edwin is still alive somewhere, I cannot dare to hope after all this time, surely?'

'One of the reasons I invited you here is because many of my patients are misplaced.' He shrugged his shoulders spreading his hands. 'I do not wish to get up your hopes, but you have no idea what happened to your husband so what have you to lose. Have you a photograph of him which I may hand around to my colleagues? There is to be a conference here in two days' time. It's not a coincidence that your visit coincides.'

'Yes, I have a photograph and I'm most grateful to you for your compassion, but I don't hold out much hope. Although I'm looking forward to learning more about your work.'

'It is my pleasure. One thing I must mention, is that if you do discover your husband, he will most probably not recognise you. He might however recognise your scent, a familiar perfume you always wore. Or your voice, a favourite song or tune. The touch of your hand. All these things seem buried deep in the psyche.'

He looked across at Mabel, her eyelids were beginning to droop. 'Forgive me, you've had a long journey and must rest before dinner.' He stood up and walked over to the fireplace where he pressed a bell in the wall. Within moments the butler appeared in the doorway.

'S'il vous plaît montrer nos invités à leurs chambres,' Pierre said, then he turned to Mabel bringing her hand to his lips. 'There will be plenty of time to talk later,' he gave her hand a squeeze before releasing it. 'Barteau will show you to your rooms now. Rest well, I will see you at dinner.'

They followed the butler up the staircase and at the top he turned to the left. Charlotte's room was near to the stairs, but Mabel was shown to a room further along the landing, passing three further doors along the way. She wondered which one was Pierre's.

Although the salon downstairs was impressive, she hadn't been prepared for the splendour of her bedroom. A large bed beneath a fabric coronet dominated the room. The counterpane and drapes were a lemon and gold embroidered brocade as were the full-length drapes hanging from two sets of French doors leading to a balcony overlooking the garden. Two further doors, white with gold trim, were set in the far wall and concealed a bathroom and a clothes closet. She discovered the lady's maid had already hung up her dresses. She opened the top drawer of a chest of drawers and discovered her underwear neatly laid out. Exhaustion suddenly overwhelmed her and she stripped down to her chemise, hung her dress in the clothes closet then lay down on the bed to rest.

A light tapping on the door woke her, a maid entered the room carrying a small tea tray. 'Excusez-moi Madame. It is time to dress for dinner. I will prepare your bath?' she asked, setting the tray down beside the bed.

'Yes, Thank you. And would you lay out my dress, please? The green chiffon.'

The maid was waiting to help her dress when she emerged from the bathroom. She also styled her hair in waves before gathering the length at the nape of her neck in a half bun and fanning it out. Mabel was thrilled. The style suited her, it was up to the minute without being cut short. The soft green dress was a cross over style, pleated across her bosom and clasped at the side of her hip. The skirt was scooped close around her calves like the petals of a tulip and an under skirt of long fringing hung to her ankles adding a touch of the bohemian. Last of all the maid fitted the matching headdress in the Egyptian style which became fashionable after the discovery of Tutankhamen. Mabel knew it was a little out of mode, but the style suited her.

On her way downstairs, she tapped on Charlotte's door. A maid answered. 'Madame is unwell, she has asked for a light super to be brought to her room.'

'May I see her?'

'She is sleeping.'

'Very well, please let me know if she needs anything.'

Pierre was waiting for her on the terrace. Glasses of champagne cocktails were set out on a silver tray, he handed one to her.

'Charlotte is unwell and staying in her room,' she said. 'We're going to be beyond tipsy by the time we've made a dent in those,' she laughed, indicating the cocktails.

'Ah, but this is Champagne made from the grapes of my vines. It is of the highest quality. Delicate, full of flavour and less intoxicating. Santé, my Mabel,' he raised his glass, 'You are here in my chateau at last. Did I exaggerate its beauty?'

'No, you certainly did not. It's truly beautiful.'

'Tomorrow, I will take you on a tour to see where the vines grow and to the vineyard. We can take a picnic and sit beside the river.'

Barteau, the butler appeared then and asked Pierre if he wished him to serve dinner. They ate at a leisurely pace, dining informally on the terrace. Torch flares were lit, and stars began to prick the darkening sky until it was ablaze with them.

A melodious tune floated out. Someone was playing the piano.

'My son's governess,' he said, noticing the questioning lift of her brow.

'Your son is here in the house?'

'No, he is away at school. His governess acts as my assistant when he is away. It is her habit to play music in the evenings.'

Mabel settled back into her chair with a satisfied sigh. She couldn't ever remember feeling so happy and content.'

'You cannot know how much it means to me to have you here,' Pierre said. 'You surely must have realised why I put in for a transfer to an English military hospital so late in the war. It was simply to be near you for as long as possible. When I left you at the end of the war it was as though my heart had been torn from my body. During the journey back to France, I was determined to speak to Claudette and explain how I felt about you, and then explain it to my parents. Make them understand how miserable they had made Claudette, as well as me, with their plotting and scheming. But when I arrived home, Claudette was visibly pregnant. Our son was conceived during my last leave before I followed you to England.'

She reached up to touch his cheek, using her thumb to smooth away his frown. He turned his head and pressed his lips into her palm, and then suddenly she was in his arms. His lips moving over her mouth, slowly, sensually exploring, seemingly drinking in the scent of her as he traced the curve of her throat down to the swell of her breasts. He released her to look deep into her eyes, his own glittering with desire. Taking her hand he helped her up.

In a daze she followed him, climbing the stairs and along the corridor. He opened the door nearest to her room, holding it wide for her to enter. The large bed was covered in white and silver brocade. Matching drapes, suspended from a black fringed central coronet, were tied back with black tassels either side of an ornate headboard. Many lamps cast a soft glow.

Unsure what to do, she walked over to the window. There was a new moon hovering above the horizon.

'It is supposed to be unlucky to see a new moon through glass,' Pierre said, guiding her through the French doors.' She stood on the balcony with her hands resting on the stone balustrade, he stood behind wrapping his arms around her and resting his chin on her head. 'You may make a wish on a new moon, mon amour. If your wish could come true, what is it that you would wish for?'

'I would wish for you.'

'Then your wish has been granted, for you already have me.' He nuzzled her neck, releasing the pins from her hair, delighting in the heavy chestnut curls cascading down. He brushed them to one side and his lips traced the smooth curve of her shoulder nudging the strap of her dress until it slid down her arm. She turned within the circle of his arms and his hand slipped inside her chemise cupping her breast, his thumb caressing her nipple. She gasped as his mouth captured the tight bud.

He lifted his head gazing into her eyes, brushing back her hair from her brow before capturing her mouth, bruising her lips. Then he released her, breaking the kiss long enough to draw her back inside the room. He nudged the remaining strap from her shoulder and the dress slid to the floor, leaving her standing in her silk chemise, surround by a sea of green chiffon.

She reached up to release the cravat at his throat, her hands travelling down his shirt, flicking open the buttons. He shrugged the shirt from his shoulders and the sight of him sent a hot bolt of desire surging through her to pool somewhere at her core. His shoulders, sun kissed and toned from time spent toiling in the vineyards alongside his men, were broad and solid. A dusting of dark hair covered his chest and a darker central line ran down his torso to disappear tantalizingly beneath his waistband. Her fingers fumbled with the fastening and his breath hissed through his teeth as her knuckles brushed his swollen flesh.
The clasp gave way as her kisses blazed a trail across his skin. His fingers combed her hair, clutching strands of curls as he drew ragged breaths fighting for control, his

excitement heightened by years of longing. He reached down and lifted her up drawing her over to the bed. They lay together arms and legs entwined enthralled by touch, fascinated by the feel of skin. Slowly he removed her chemise, his eyes following its trail, his lips retracing its path until she cried out pulling him to her breasts begging for fulfilment. Their union was everything she had known it would be, an act of pure love.

The lark had begun his call and a tinge of grey was appearing on the horizon as they drifted into an exhausted sleep locked together in a tangle of limbs, cocooned in their love.

They ate breakfast on the terrace. Fruit, cheeses, jams and croissants. Charlotte nibbled on grapes and toasted brioche. She managed a few sips of orange juice but declined tea or coffee. Pierre studied her surreptitiously. 'Do you feel sufficiently recovered to join us on a tour of the vineyard and a picnic by the river?'

'No. I feel in need of a day resting. Would you mind awfully if I stayed behind here?'

'Of course not,' Pierre couldn't keep the grin from his face. 'My household is at your disposal, please feel free to request whatever it is you need to be comfortable.' Charlotte sat on the terrace looking beyond the garden and down into the valley. The river shimmered in the distance snaking a path through the countryside. She hadn't failed to notice the bloom of happiness on both Pierre and Mabel's faces this morning. The furtive glances, the secret smiles. She would not have spoiled their day by tagging along even if she had been feeling well. A worried frown creased her brow. She didn't recall feeling this sickly with her last pregnancy. Soon she would be showing. This was the urgency which drove her to seek out Edwin. If indeed he was still alive, he would be the one to rescue her from shame. He would not judge her, not ask questions. They had both agreed that they had witnessed too much suffering of the kind that destroys souls, to stand in judgement of anyone. If he had truly lost his mind, what then? She would bring him home of course. She would care for him in her clinic, pay for the best professionals, and even then, he would be the one saving her. Who would blame a man for needing the comfort of his wife after so long apart. Even a man who had lost his mind.

She was startled by Barteau appearing at her right elbow. Clearing his throat, he said, 'Excusez-moi Madame. Monsieur Leman is here and asking for permission to join you while he waits for Monsieur Durieux to return.'

'But of course.'

A tall, broad shouldered figure strode across the terrace with his hand outstretched. As she'd suspected, she found herself looking up into a pair of familiar blue eyes twinkling mischievously as ever.

'Hello Marcus,' she said, taking delight in catching him off guard.

He faltered in his stride his hand dropping loosely by his side. 'Charlotte! What the ruddy hell are you doing here.'

'Looking for Edwin. How about you?'

'Working with Durieux. Why are you looking for Edwin Gregory?'

'Because my dear Marcus, it may surprise you to discover that despite your best endeavours, you didn't know everything that was going on in camp. Edwin is my husband. We kept it quiet, because I'd never have found work as a surgeon, anywhere, not even on the front line as desperate as things were, if they'd discovered I was a married woman. I kept my maiden name as my professional name.'

'Well I'll be blowed. No wonder you gave me the brush off after Edwin arrived. I can see now why he watched me like a hawk. It always puzzled me what his game was. Has Durieux told you about our work? Is that why you're here, hoping to locate Edwin? I would have said there's a pretty fair chance except I've worked with nearly every patient in the Durieux clinic and similar ones dotted across the country. I hate to dash your hopes old girl, but I think the chances of me not recognising him are pretty slim.'

The butler returned carrying refreshment, she was glad he hadn't brought tea, her stomach churned at the thought. She poured herself a glass of lemonade and Marcus stole a slice of lemon for his 'gin and it'.

So, tell me, what have you been up to since the end of the war? Still in practice?'

'Via the back door. Yes.'

'How so?'

'I'm registered with hospitals in Sheffield and the surrounding area. They only send for me when they're desperate. I also run a private practice from my home.' She didn't tell him about her voluntary work. She didn't know how well she could trust him.

They reminisced for the best part of an hour before Marcus spotted Pierre's car meandering along the road from the valley. 'The wanderers are returning,' he said. 'Do you have plans for tomorrow?'

'Pierre is supposed to be showing me his hospital, why?'

'Perhaps you would allow me to escort you around the place, introduce you to one or two of the chaps. They're devils for a pretty face some of them. You ask the nurses. Mind you, those nurses can give as good as they get. We try to keep the atmosphere light you know, for those chaps on the right road. The poor devils who haven't found their way back yet, tend to like it quiet, or else listen to a favourite musical piece.'

'Marcus! You're early.' Pierre strode across the terrace to shake his hand. 'I see you have introduced yourself to Madame Gregory,' he said, slapping him on the back.

'Actually. Charlotte and I are old acquaintances.' He winked at her surreptitiously.

Charlotte clamped her lips to prevent a giggle. She wondered what Pierre would think if he knew just how well she and his old friend had become acquainted in the camp before Edwin had been posted there. 'If you will excuse me, I must go up and change for dinner,' she said, glad to escape and rest for a while. Seeing Marcus again had affected her more than she would have thought.

Dinner that night was a jovial affair. Marcus held court as usual, regaling them with amusing anecdotes. He'd filled out in the intervening years, it suited him. She wasn't surprised she had fallen for him, working alongside him under the pressures of war with no idea whether Edwin was alive or dead. But he had been alive, then. When he'd been posted to the unit where she was working, she'd quickly ended her affair with Marcus, unable to explain why. He'd taken it remarkably well. As had Edwin, who could always read her like a book.

She was the first to break up the dinner party. The early stages of her pregnancy quickly drained her energy. Both men stood as she made to leave. Marcus kissed her on both cheeks, whispering, 'Until tomorrow.' The heat of his breath brushed her ear sending shivers along her spine. She looked up, wide eyed, she hadn't expected to feel anything for him after all this time. For a moment, his twinkling eyes locked with hers, then with a slight bow he returned to his seat.

The day was hot, though it was barely ten o'clock. Charlotte chose to wear a wide brimmed straw cloche hat and a long-sleeved silk dress to keep cool and protect her skin.

The hospital was closer than she'd expected. Originally a large chateau, it was located at the head of a long, wide driveway. There were several groups of men about. Some kicking a ball back and forth on the grass, while others appeared to be tending the beautiful flowering shrubs. Over to the left of the driveway, a game of boules was in progress and in the distance a game of cricket.

The impressive front door opened into a square hall and Charlotte looked up the beautifully crafted wooden staircase to a stained-glass window. Its colours, enhanced by sunlight, cast rainbows on the highly polished wood.

Marcus opened a door to the right. 'This is our craft therapy room.' She walked past him into a large room facing the garden. Natural light flooded in from a bay window. Sitting at a large central table, men were busy weaving baskets. She was surprised to see several more men grouped around smaller tables working on embroidery and tapestries. She moved amongst them chatting easily, curious to know what they were making. Some were horribly disfigured. Many amputees. Most struggling in one way or another to overcome their disability and complete their task. Only a few had the blank hollow look she remembered from her days as a surgeon on the front line.

'A spot of tea now, I think,' Marcus said, opening the door for her. He was astounded when she ran from the room with a handkerchief clamped to her mouth.

He found her outside sitting on a bench. 'What's wrong? It's unlike you to have a queasy stomach.'

She looked up into his face. 'I'm pregnant.'

He sat down beside her. 'I see. And the father?'

'Not someone you would know, and Marcus, you don't see. How could you?'

'Then tell me.'

She looked down at the handkerchief in her hand, twisting it round her fingers as she spoke. 'Towards the end of the war, I lost a child at birth. I didn't tell anyone I was pregnant. How could I? I wasn't supposed to be married. Edwin's unit had been moved on by then. The pregnancy didn't show beneath those voluminous surgeon's smocks, so I carried on working, far too long. You were there, you know what it was like, the never-ending stream of casualties. How could I turn my back on them? Eventually I collapsed from exhaustion and was carted off to the nearest civilian hospital. On the way, I went into labour. It progressed very quickly, but I couldn't make the staff understand. They thought my screams were hysteria. By the time they realised, it was too late. The baby was dead, and I had damaged myself irreparably, or so they told me. I thought I could never conceive another child. To be carrying this baby is a miracle, a gift I'm cherishing.'

'And the child's father? What does he have to say?'

'I told you so.'

'I beg your pardon.'

Charlotte laughed. 'Bert's a grand man. The salt of the earth, as they say. He's married with five children. He warned me that he only so much as looks at his wife to get her pregnant. I told him I couldn't have children. He's probably worried out of his wits right now.'

'How on earth did you get involved with a man like that?'

'Like what?' she stuck out her chin defensively.

'Married with five children for a start,'

'I met him while working on my allotment, he helps me with the heavy digging. I feel unable to commit to a relationship without closure on Edwin. Bert's an attractive man, and unattainable. He's very much in love with his wife. He made that plain from the start. And then we have a shared interest in politics. He's a union man. You already know mine and Edwin's beliefs.'

Marcus sat still for a very long time watching his patients go about their numerous activities in the hospital grounds. Then without turning to look at her, he said, 'You know we could do with a good surgeon here. You've seen the horrific facial scars on some of those men. Their minds are almost healed, but they lack the courage to leave this place. Plastic surgery has come on in leaps and bounds since the war.' He turned to face her. 'You're going to need an income to support that child. Would you consider coming to work for us?'

'Income is not an issue I have private means. But I would like to remain in practice and I'm tired of competing for a place in a profession biased towards men. So yes, I will take you up on your offer, but only on an ad hoc basis. I don't want to work full time I want to be with my child. Can you help me find suitable premises to rent close to the hospital?'

'It will be my pleasure, and in the meantime, we will continue our search for Edwin. Now are you sufficiently recovered to try a spot of lunch?'

On the last night of their visit, both women took extra care over their appearance. Charlotte was beginning to emerge from the drowsy sickly first trimester of her pregnancy and her eyes and hair shone brightly in the light of the candelabra. After dinner, they played cards, Whist and Gin Rummy. Then they danced. When Marcus held her close, Charlotte was alarmed by the wave of emotion rippling through her. She was in no doubt that he'd felt it too. They slipped quietly away, leaving Pierre and Mabel locked in a world of their own. Outside her room he stooped to kiss her, igniting feelings for him she thought were long buried. For a moment she surrendered to his kiss. Then she pressed the palms of her hands on his chest and gently pushed him away. He gazed at her curiously, his eyes heavy with desire.

'Marcus, don't, not now.' She drew a shuddering breath to steady her emotions. 'Marcus, I think I have always been just a little in love with you, from the first time I saw you striding across the camp, your face like thunder because our fresh supplies had been blown up enroute.' She smiled then, her heat cooling. 'Perhaps I shall always be in love with you, but the time is not right for us just now, for so many reasons.'

'Time is a precious commodity, but for you, I will wait.' He stooped to kiss her mouth then turned abruptly and walked away.

Mabel lay with her head cushioned on Pierre's shoulder, marvelling again at the contrast between this man and her husband. She snuggled deeper into Pierre's side, relishing the memory of how much he'd shown he cared with each caress.

Sensing her stir beside him, he turned to plant a kiss on her forehead. 'I will miss you chérie, don't stay away too long. We have already spent too many years apart.' He stroked her face looking deep into her eyes. 'Have you given further thought to the situation of your marriage?'

She lifted her chin to look at him. 'Plenty of thought, but I haven't yet reached a decision.'

'When you wish to proceed, you simply have to say. I have enough evidence against the man for you to divorce him many times over, but no real photographic evidence. You do know what I mean by that, don't you? How intimate such evidence must be?'

Satisfied that she understood, he planted another kiss at the centre of her forehead. 'And now chérie, it is time for us to get on with our day. I have neglected my work for quite long enough. Is it not great news that Charlotte will be joining our hospital?'

He climbed out of bed and put on his robe. 'My chauffeur will drive you to the station,' he said, reaching for her hand and drawing her from the bed to fold her tightly in his arms. 'Au revoir, mon amour,' he whispered kissing her lips. 'I will leave you now, to bathe and dress. I cannot stand drawn out goodbyes, and neither can you.' He strode across the room, at the door he paused and turned. 'Phone me when you arrive home, yes?'

Chapter Twenty-Three - Sheffield 1926

Mabel let herself into the empty house. She was bone weary. She couldn't understand why the journey had taken so much out of her. Someone had lit a fire in the hearth and damped it down. She picked up the poker and stirred it into life, feeling utterly grateful to whoever it was. She set the kettle on to boil and went upstairs to her room to change out of her travelling clothes. Sure enough, a fire was smouldering there too. Ethel must have been, or perhaps she'd given a key to Bert.

    She was sipping a welcome cup of tea when the telephone rang. It was Gladys. 'Hello Mrs Baxter, did you have a nice trip? I've processed those orders you sent us from France, they should be arriving about now... Mrs Baxter, there's something else I'm telephoning you about. Mr Baxter was here. We told him you was away on a business trip, but he wasn't best pleased. Caused ever such a fuss he did.'

    Mabel felt a wave of nausea hit and she clutched the hall table. 'When was this Gladys?'

    'Monday, he said he'd come back again at the weekend. So that's three days from now. I know it's none of my business, Mrs Baxter, but will you be alright? I mean, he was in ever such a temper. Ted's offered to stay with you, if you'd like him to.'

    Unexpected tears sprang to Mabel's eyes at the thought of meek mannered Ted taking on Sydney in a rage. 'Thank you for letting me know, Gladys. Tell Ted, I thank him for his offer, but I know how to handle the situation.'

    The second she'd disconnected the call, she lifted the aspidistras plant by its leaves and was violently sick in its pot. She sat on the stairs the pot between her knees with her head hanging over it. The bitter taste of tannin from the tea was at the forefront of her senses. Perhaps it was because she'd drunk so much coffee in France. When she thought about it, Charlotte hadn't drunk a single cup of tea for the whole of the time there. And she'd been feeling very tired. She was just beginning to buck up, by the time they were leaving. Maybe they'd both contracted some infection during their journey abroad. She thought back over the dates trying to piece everything together. It was then that she realised she had forgotten one very important date. She caught sight of her wan face in the hall mirror and realisation dawned. She lifted the telephone handset again and rang the operator.

Pierre answered the phone himself on the third ring, 'Mabel, mon amour, you are home safe, yes?'

'Yes, but it no longer feels like home. Pierre, the time is right. Do you understand?'

'Leave it to me, everything is already in place awaiting your word.'

'Pierre, I will be safer in France. Sydney's been here terrifying the factory workers. I need to sort things out at the factory and with the bank before I leave. There are a few other things I need to put in place as well. Can you give me, say, thirty-six hours before you set any wheels in motion? I don't want to get caught in the backlash of Sydney's temper.'

'Take care chérie, tread wisely. You know the man better than I, but from my understanding of the human mind and my observations of him, there is some slight imbalance there.'

'Pierre, there is something else I must tell you. I have brought home an unexpected souvenir.'

She heard his deep chuckle rumble down the telephone wire. 'Ma chérie, I believe I guessed before you. All the more reason for you to take great care. Do you want me to come over to England and escort you back to France?'

She was about to say no, that she could manage, that his patients needed him, but she suddenly felt very weepy. 'There is nothing I would like more. Thank you.'

'Then mon amour, I shall be with you the day after tomorrow. Do you have anywhere else you can stay until then? Perhaps move into a hotel?'

'So long as I'm gone by the weekend, I will feel safe enough here until you come. Pierre… I love you.'

Mabel arrived at the factory within the hour. The co-operative workers were packing up for the day when she called them together. 'Thank you for taking over the running of the factory while I've been away. I'm so very sorry you had to deal with my husband's behaviour. My marriage hasn't always been a bed of roses. That of course, is my problem, not yours. My future, however, is your problem, because it concerns the running of the factory. Thank you for offering to look out for me, Ted,' she smiled warmly at him. 'It won't be necessary for you to act as bodyguard because I intend going back to France.' She registered their surprise but ploughed on. 'If we set up a system whereby the factory can function without me being on the premises, are you happy to take over the running of it? The clerical side will fall heavily onto your shoulders,

Gladys. I can come over twice yearly to help with the accounts and at other times in between, if necessary. I'm only a telephone call away, should you need me. Please don't divulge that number to my husband. I doubt he will be back once I've put my plans into action, but if he does come, don't hesitate to phone the police.

    Foremost in my plans, I would like to offer Bert a full-time position working here. In fact, I think he's capable of being the manager. I will take a pay cut to accommodate his wages. What do you think?'

    Ted was the first to speak. 'I think employing Bert's a champion idea. He can turn his hand to anything round here and I won't deny that it'll be nice to have another bloke about the place, what with having all these females to contend with.' He winked at Beatti. 'And while we're laying our cards on the table, I've some news of me own. Beatti has agreed to be me wife. We're getting married in September.'

    'That's marvellous news,' Mabel said, genuinely thrilled, she knew how lonely he'd been since his wife passed away. 'I will certainly try to get back for that. I think it's time to take another nip from our whisky reserve,' she said, and everyone trooped up to the office where Mabel retrieved her bottle from the secret compartment in her father's old desk. 'Here's to Ted and Beatti and the new co-operative format. The room was filled with cries of hip, hip, hooray and congratulations, then just as swiftly, the laughter and chatter faded as everyone made their way back down to the factory floor, leaving Mabel and Gladys to sort through the clerical work.

It was late by the time Mabel and Gladys had finished. Mabel left Ted to lock up and made her way directly to Bert and Ada's house.

Ada was putting the children to bed and Mabel was pleased to have a quiet word with Bert on his own. 'The other co-operative members are looking forward to you joining them full-time at the factory,' she said, 'What are your thoughts?

'Well I can't deny I'm right glad of your offer, Mabel,' he said. 'It's been like sitting on a tinder box at work not knowing whether or not the boss might hand over me cards at any moment. I've enjoyed tinkering about at your factory. It'll be good to work there proper and be back in full-time employment. You're offering me more money than I was earning when I was on full-time shifts in the works, are you sure you're not overstretching yourself?'

'It's all been sorted officially, Bert. Don't worry. Ah, here's Ada, there's something else I wanted to speak to you both about.'

'Do you mind if I get a cuppa on the go first?' Ada said. 'That lot have worn me out.'

When everyone was settled with a cup of tea, and Mabel with a sandwich, Ada sat down to listen to what she had to say.

'What I'm about to tell you is very personal and I want you to keep it to yourselves. You can tell Ethel, but that's as far as I'd like it to go.' Mabel said, surreptitiously moving her cup of tea to one side and taking a deep breath trying to settle her stomach. 'I've discovered that Sydney has got one of the chorus girls pregnant, not only that, he came to ask me if I would agree to adopting the child as our own.'

Ada gasped and tutted, but Bert remained silent. The colour had slipped from his face. Mabel eyed him suspiciously as she continued. 'I've had enough of Sydney's philandering ways. I've reached the decision to divorce him. A kind friend, an ex-colleague as a matter of fact, is helping me to gather the evidence and set the wheels in motion. I'm afraid though, of a backlash. Sydney has a violent temper. He's never really been aggressive towards me, but this may tip him over the edge. I'm going back to France, at least until everything settles down. That's one of the reasons I've offered you a permanent job, Bert.'

Ada turned her head sharply to look at him.

'Aye it's true.' he said, squeezing her hand. 'I'm back in full-time employment.'

'My other problem is the matter of my house. I have a stiff mortgage outstanding because Annie took out a loan against it. I need to rent it out and I wondered if you would like it for the same rent as you pay here?'

'Oh Mabel, do you mean it?' Ada said, and burst into tears. 'I've always dreamed of living in one of them big houses overlooking the park.' She dabbed her eyes with the corner of her apron and delved into her pocket for a handkerchief to blow her nose. Then she hiccupped, loudly.

'Steady on lass.' Bert said, rubbing her back. 'Anyone would think you were moving into Buckingham Palace.'

'Well it's as good as, to me, living up at Endcliffe. Oh, Mabel, are you sure? Do you really mean it?' she asked again. 'We don't pay a lot of rent down here you know. But it's as much as we can afford.'

Chapter Twenty-four - The Isle of Man 1926

Sydney was not happy. His web was becoming unravelled. Delores had gone. Mabel was off gallivanting somewhere and he was left holding the baby. If the stupid girl hadn't got herself pregnant in the first place, he would never have considered wanting a child. He'd only told Mabel he wanted one to keep her sweet after the episode with Delores. He'd known Delores was trouble from the start, he was relieved she'd gone. Only his pride was dented that she'd left so readily. It was his pride that had stopped him chasing after Gracie. He should have tried to locate her when she first left. Perhaps he should get his agent to offer her a new contract for more money. Lotti had filled the role of soubrette better than he'd supposed, but she didn't have Gracie's star quality.

He paced up and down the corridor outside his suite of rooms drawing heavily on a cigarette and wondering what he was going to do. He'd promised to take the baby and make Violet into a star. He'd miscalculated Mabel's desire for motherhood, believing her need was so strong, that any baby would satisfy her.

'What are you doing?' Lotti appeared at his side.

'Finishing my cigarette, before I go in to see Violet and the baby.'

'Well you'd better be quick, she's packing.'

'Packing? Where is she going?'

'I don't know. Ask her yourself. Something about getting married to the baby's father.' She waved her hand dismissively and walked away.

'Getting married to... but I'm the... Lotti, wait.' He caught up with her. 'Do you know where I can get hold of Gracie?'

Lotti looked him up and down. 'Still got it bad ain't yah. You're wasting your time you know. You're not her type. I am. She's got a magnetic charm that one. She even turned my head for a while. But guess what? I prefer a drop of the hard stuff,' and she grabbed a handful of his crotch making him wince. 'You're definitely more my type. Get my drift, big boy?' Then she released him and strode off along the corridor without a backward glance.

He let himself into the suite. Suitcases and clothes were scattered over the bed. 'What's going on, Violet?'

'Oh, hello, Mr Sydney. I'm glad you caught me. I wanted to thank you for all your help. You'll be relieved to know I'll be out of your hair any minute now. My fiancé's coming to get us.'

'Your fiancé?'

'Yes, the baby's father. I've to thank Delores for tracking him down. The Navy was no help to me, see, when I tried to get a message to him. I thought he was ignoring me letters on account of me being pregnant. But it turns out some jobsworth Lieutenant was withholding his post for not shining his shoes good enough. Anyway, Delores knows some Admiral or other who she said owed her a favour. Well, when my Ron found out, he was here like a shot waving a special marriage licence under me nose. He's got compassionate leave or something and we're getting married this afternoon, at three o'clock.'

'You told me I was the father of your child.'

Violet stopped packing and sat down on the edge of the bed. 'I'm right sorry I tricked you, Mr Sydney, but I was desperate. I didn't know what else to do. How was I to know you'd want to keep the baby? I had only wanted you to help me get rid of it. Still, it's turned out fine in the end, hasn't it, Mr Sydney?' She jumped to her feet and continuing her packing. Sydney supposed it had, but looking down at the sleeping infant, he couldn't quite fill the aching void in the pit of his stomach.

Lotti was posing for a photograph outside the stage door when Sydney arrived at the theatre. She followed him in while the photographer took shots of the chorus girls in various poses.

'Who's he?' Sydney growled.

'Some reporter from a local paper doing a write up on the theatre. He says he'll give the revue a good plug.'

The orchestra struck up as the house lights dimmed and soon the music began to work its magic on Sydney's soul. All his troubles melted away as he concentrated on conducting. He had to admit that Lotti had stepped up to the mark as soubrette. He was pleased he'd been able to give her the opportunity to rise above the chorus and allow her star quality to shine. Although she'd never be in Gracie's league.

Later that night, when he and the rest of the cast returned to the hotel after the show, Sydney was surprised to see the same photographer propping up the bar. He appeared to have been there for some considerable time judging by the backward slant of his hat and the angle of his tie.

What an idiot, Sydney thought, as he approached the bar.

'Ah, the impresario himself,' the man slurred his words. 'Allow me to buy you a drink.'

Never one to miss an opportunity, Sydney ordered a double scotch and a round of drinks for the cast. The man seemed unfazed and even offered to carry the drinks over to the table. Sydney didn't see him slip something into his scotch.

'Come on folks how about a group shot for the round of drinks I just bought.' The powerful flash filled the room with light. Dazzled by the brightness Lotti turned her face towards Sydney's shoulder, she looked up just as another flash went off.

'That's all folks, much obliged.'

Shortly afterwards, another tray of drinks arrived, compliments of the photographer. He was nowhere to be seen.

Sydney couldn't wait to get Lotti upstairs to the suite. He'd never experienced a sensation like it. His head was light and woozy but the burning desire he felt was all consuming. It felt as though white-hot steel had invaded his loins and was demanding release. Lotti was only too pleased to oblige, she would have torn open his waistband there and then in the lift, had he not restrained her. He fumbled with the keys in the lock, dropping them to the carpet twice, before Lotti took them from him and opened the door. The minute he stepped over the threshold her mouth captured his. She pulled off his tie, tore open his shirt and slipped her dress from her shoulders leaving a trail of discarded clothes as they made their way to the bedroom. They fell in a tangled heap across the bed devouring each other. She pushed Sydney onto his back and straddled him just as flashlight illuminated the room. She ducked down to one side leaving Sydney's face exposed to the camera as another flash went off. Growling like a wounded bear Sydney leaped from the bed. Dragging on his trousers he set off in hot pursuit of the photographer. He ran along the corridor just as the lift was descending. He set off running down the stairs to the floor below trying to intercept the lift. He was wasting his time. The photographer was sitting on the fire escape removing film from the camera, just in case he should encounter Sydney. He didn't think he would. It was a pleasant moonlit night but he'd no intention of climbing down the fire escape. He had a good view of the corridor he'd simply wait until Sydney returned to the suite then take the lift like a civilised person.

  The girl had played her part well. Everyone has a price for betrayal, he thought, but none were so easily bribed as the cheated lover. His diligence to the job had paid off, he'd made another discovery while shadowing Sydney Baxter. One which his contact at Scotland Yard would pay well for, after he'd seen the evidence. The top brass at the yard had recently become friendly with the cops across the pond and the New York police didn't take kindly to smuggling, especially since prohibition. Sydney had contacts scattered across the British Isles all delivering crates of alcohol to his contacts at Liverpool docks. From there the contraband was loaded onto the cruise ships bound for New York. The photographer smiled, all the photographic evidence he needed was hanging in his dark room.

From the safety of the fire escape, he saw Sydney return and slam the door to the suite behind him. Then, still smiling smugly, the photographer made his way indoors to the lift. Sydney Baxter had better look out, he was a doomed man whichever way he turned.

Lotti set her suitcase down on the station platform. She knew Sydney would be furious when he discovered she'd left the revue, but she doubted he'd sue for breach of contract. He wouldn't waste money trying to locate her. Hopefully he would never find out the part she'd played in his divorce. She looked up anxiously at the station clock, the train was late and she was short for time. She had a boat to catch. Gracie had arranged for her to work her passage to New York singing in the piano bar. She had also arranged an audition for a new Broadway musical. Gracie was playing the lead.

'Sydney might think he's a big shot,' Gracie had written in a letter to her from New York. 'But he's small fry in the big world.'

Lotti hadn't lied when she'd told Sydney she preferred what he had to offer, but she wasn't fussy, she could turn her charms to whoever was most useful. Right now, Gracie was promising her a chance on Broadway.

She felt the platform tremble beneath her feet and moments later the train rumbled into the station. She climbed aboard in a cloud of steam. The guard slammed the door behind her and blew his whistle. Then the train chugged clear of the station gradually picking up speed propelling her into a new adventure.

Printed in Poland
by Amazon Fulfillment
Poland Sp. z o.o., Wrocław